THE MUSIC OF SWORDS

John de Búrca

The Music of Swords

First Published 2023 by PerchedCrowPress
An imprint of Philip Hughes Publishing

Source illustrations by Shutterstock. FXQuadro, Swetapol, Kiselev Andrey Valerevich, Kitoumi, Sicegame, Ecleposs 3D, Luis Louro, Warpaint

PCP

For Rebecca and my mum, Mary.

Contents

PREAMBLE

THE CAST

The following are the main characters you will encounter:

Eimear – *eemur* – A girl. Half human and half gruagach

Bégha – *baya* – Gruagach father of Eimear

Nin – Human mother of Eimear

Mirdhí – *myr-ee* – Duillechán - wise woman

Barragh – *bara* – Duillechán guide

Crea – Smallsky denizen – watcher of the Fandside portal

Arthmael – Twarv

Hógar – *Hoe-gar* – Gruagach brother of Bégha

Aébhal – *Ay-val* – Fathach first son of the Fand and the Fane and heir to the title of the Fand

Cromm – Sídhe second son of the Fand and the Fane

Doireann – *Dur-enn* – The Fand

Ferragh – *Ferra* – The Fane

Caen – Lost son of the Fand and the Fane

Serrisa – Twarv leader

Seasún – *sha soon* - Human carpenter

A NOTE ON DRAÍOCHT

Draíocht - *dree-ocht* * Powerful magic originating from the draoí, draíocht is drawn towards creatures and things that are gifted, making those gifts more potent. It imbues that which is worthy with gifts. It is not interested in the mundane. It is attracted to the fantastical, to beauty, to talent and to those things, places and beings that are wondrous. A skilled wielder can manipulate draíocht to their needs.

For other terms used throughout, go to our glossary at:

https://philhughespublishing.com/glossary/

THE DRAOÍ

The draoí—occupants of The Otherworld—are ephemeral beings who are the source of all magic, or draíocht. They are a powerful race, who control much of the worlds in which the other races live.

THE MUSIC OF SWORDS

CHILD

***

An rud a chíonn an leanbh is é a níonn an leanbh.

What the child sees, the child does.

***

BÉGHA MADE NO sound as he ran, his cloven hooves hardly touching the forest floor. The din of the chasing hound pack was all the more alarming as it drew nearer.

There was no escape to the Fae realm for him. He could not leave them behind. No escape here either. He would just have to keep leading the pursuers away from Nin. His mind flitted to the birthing. Would she still be on the move, or had the time come? Would it be over? Had the child been born? Though he would never know or meet the child in this life, he would protect it as best he could. With any luck, all the pursuers had followed his trail.

Tiring badly as he came to the rockface, he cursed himself for only attending to his pursuit and not enough to the path ahead. To his left, a thicket sprang from the rockface making the way impassable. To his right, a curving hillock. Over the rise, the treeline ended. The red sky above bled into the treetops, making dark promises. He had led himself into a trap, which ensnared him. By their sounds, the chasing pack were nearly upon him.

His mind raced. Surely, he was far enough away. He looked at the blood covering his shaking hands. Closing his eyes, Bégha took a deep breath and sang the song he would so often sing to Nin's bump. She had always said the song was too sad, but Bégha had hoped to one day explain the words and how a sad song can carry the happiest message. The sound of the dogs grew louder.

He loved Nin so. The bump too, whatever it was. Tears streamed down his face. He should never have come to this place. In an effort to find a safe corner, a quiet corner, into which they could bring this child of two worlds, he had led them to hatred, pain and now this.

Bégha wished he could have changed it all. He would never see the child's face. Never hold it close, as he longed to.

"It's here," came the cry just before the arrow pierced his back. He fell, sobbing loudly.

Another arrow hit his furred thigh, and another thudded quietly into his body. He screamed. Screamed his frustration; his regret; his pain. The hounds surrounded him and started to attack. His screams grew louder.

As the flesh peeled away from his leg, he wondered whether his child would be a girl or a boy.

***

Nin gritted her teeth and pushed once again. It was taking too long. There was a mess of blood on the forest trail, where she had tried to keep moving away from them until the last possible moment. Her baby had decided to come what seemed like a long time ago. Her mind was awash as she tried to catch her breath between pushes.

"Come out, little one," she wept. "Please."

Nin no longer felt the pain, as if something inside of her was broken. She was failing; catching her breath was a constant struggle.

Our baby will die.

Putting all other thoughts aside, she pushed. She dug her nails into the cold earth and pushed hard. The effort produced a forced cry. The sound that came from within her was a sound she had never heard herself make. It was a fitting noise for this wild place.

Again. She pushed. One of the fingernails broke away.

She bared her teeth. Her dry mouth caused her lips to remain hitched. *I am so thirsty.*

Again. She pushed. Stinging sweat dribbled into her eyes.

Searing hot pain lanced between her legs, and the feral sound came again.

Again. She pushed. A hissing gasp escaped her cracking lips.

Increasingly aware of the dark puddle growing around her, she averted her gaze through the treetops to the crimson sky.

How had this happened? All they had wanted was peace and quiet and now she lay dying on the woodland floor, birthing a baby that would die in or beside her. She scanned the small clearing—such a place. Wild animals might devour her child here.

Again. She pushed. And the baby started to come.

"Come on, little thing," she gasped, hearing the hope in her own voice for the first time in many days.

"Yes, little thing. Come on," said a voice entirely devoid of hope.

Nin screamed. Lliam had found her. His three sons were with him, armed and grinning.

"You have left a bloody trail, you filthy bitch," Lliam said. "But you reap what you sow. Or, in this case, we will."

Nin just screamed. There was nothing she could say. The baby kept coming, although she wished to the Gods it would not.

"Shut her up, Da," said the son with the bucked teeth.

"Now, now, Torann. Let's examine what we have. A baby born from a witch and a Fae creature. That will surely be of value to the Fae; indeed, they might pay gold for it."

"Are you mad?" another said, with a shock of red hair. "The Gods won't be happy. Let's burn them both before it crawls out of her wound and infects us all."

And as they debated, a noise arose in the distance: a pack of hounds savaging something and screaming from their likely prey.

"It seems like they found the Fae creature, at least. The Gods will be happy that we have ruined this unnatural union. Surely, they might allow us some spoils."

Nin heard the sounds and tried to say something. All she could manage was a primal groan from deep inside.

Lliam moved towards her; lip hitched in disgust.

"It's almost out anyway."

Nin watched in horror as they stared down at her splayed legs. She saw them staring, in disgust, at her baby being born. A wave of fear washed over her; rage followed after.

She saw the one with the bucked teeth looking at her, grinning, those yellow rotting teeth. She spoke a curse onto them that the Draoí themselves must have heard. Her hatred and fury drew more draíocht unto her than Bégha had ever managed to coax. Such was the hate that the earth around her nails grew black.

The one with the bucked teeth dropped his spear. His hands moved to his face, a groan escaping between them. The teeth grew longer and broader; all of them competing for an increasingly small amount of space. His jaw crackled as the teeth and bones broke into shards.

The lanky brother beside him watched in horror as the bones in his arms started to lengthen. The skin stretched and cracked, then peeled apart in places, exposing the flesh underneath.

Lliam howled, as his ribs started to break out of his torso, growing rapidly and intertwining before him as if he was locking his fingers to pray to his Gods. His spine erupted from his back and cloak, and he fell to

15

knees, which were breaking away from his crackling legs.

The noise of their howling was deafening. Nin screamed her hatred until her lungs burned. Bones pierced through flesh as the men died in terror. The men's bones grew tall towards the treetops and dug deep into the soil.

As the baby came into the world, her little eyes, though sticky from blood, were open and she listened. She listened and she understood.

In her first moments, she heard the agonised screams of four men dying. She heard the rage-filled screams of her mother dying too. As the screams in the small clearing stopped, the distant screams of her father being eaten alive by hounds replaced them.

***

"Eimear," Samhla called from the door of her main hut. "Finish with the cattle quickly. You must go to the village for me. My last needle broke."

Eimear nodded, head bowed.

She was well used to working quickly in the cold with her calloused, ten-year-old hands. Finishing the last cow, Eimear left the brimming wooden bucket beside the well.

Her worn leather slippers were filth covered, so she went to the long grass to clean them off as best she could. Knocking on the hide door-covering to signal her readiness, Eimear then walked back to the outer hut to start filling the cart with enough turf to trade. That Samhla did not allow her inside the hut, no longer bothered her. Donkey seemed to realise what was happening and moved towards the front of the cart by himself. Eimear nodded solemnly to her only friend.

"Eimear," Samhla said from just behind her. "Don't be gone long. Get whatever needles you can and bring them quickly. If you're not back in time, I will beat you and give your food to the animals." The disdain in her voice was clear, as she turned on her heel and went back to the warm hut.

Eimear went to hitch Donkey when she noticed how she had skinned her hand while carting the turf. A large flap of skin at the base of her thumb was white and exposed. She bit it off and spat it onto the ground. The blood came shortly after and started to run across her palm. She continued working, occasionally wiping the blood on her filthy clothes. When Donkey was hitched, they took off walking on the muddy, rutted path towards the village.

***

By the time she arrived, drizzle-soaked hair fell into her eyes, and she was shivering a little. She passed a villager in a thick, hooded cloak. Envy made her hunch her shoulders.

The village was as sodden and unpleasant as the journey had been, with few villagers visible. Usually, many would be out at this time of the day. The trickling sounds of the nearby stream added to the damp feeling.

Stone huts and roundhouses dotted the misty landscape. Thin wisps of smoke rose towards the sullen sky. A wolf howled somewhere in the distance.

The remnants of the ringfort gave the small place its familiar scent of rotting wood. She went towards the hut of Seasún. It was always warm in there, and the wood smelled of comfort. Eimear relished the thought of standing in for a while.

Wiping her already wet hands on some nearby sodden grass, she cleaned them as best she could, taking care to rub off the dried blood. She scratched behind Donkey's ear and touched her forehead off his. He waited there as she navigated through the wooden constructions outside Seasún's thatched wooden hut. Broken carts for repair, batches of shaped studs for building, latches for doors, handles for tools, and longbows in the making—some wrapped in hide for protection from the elements.

Seasún told Eimear how he had been experimenting with painting a mixture of pressed yew and haw oils to see if it would protect the wood from the wet. Though he hadn't had much success, he was obviously very impressed by his cleverness.

He was one of the only people who spoke to her kindly, even knowing she would not speak back. The people in the village had no idea that she could talk; she did speak at one stage in her young life, but not for some time. She no longer wanted to.

Eimear knocked on the wooden door.

"What?" came the response.

She knocked again.

"What, I said?" came the gruff voice, followed by, "Oh, Eimear, is that you love? Come in."

As she lifted the latch and pushed in, her face softened to the closest she had to a smile.

"What does that old bat want today, Eimear? Other than a good kick up the hole?" Seasún asked.

Eimear pointed towards the beautifully crafted needles for knitting.

"Ah. Needles, she needs?" he said with a smile as he took four and handed them to her.

Of all the grown-ups she had encountered, Seasún was the kindest. He had thick shaggy blonde hair and piercing green and brown eyes that lit up when he spoke. A missing tooth always made his smile seem a bit crooked.

The inside of the hut was like a smaller version of the outside. Seasún had organised all manner of wooden tools, implements, and oddities on shelves and tables, or rattling from overhanging strings.

"Did I ever tell you about needles and where they came from, Eimear?" he said.

Eimear shook her head. She had hoped he would be in the mood for a story. Moving towards the firepit, she sat down on the floor. Eimear had seen other children sitting on their parent's laps for stories and wondered what it would be like.

"It was back in the old days. People had nothing to wear, only hide and skins. They were simple folk but honest and kind-hearted. Not like some you might meet today," he scowled.

"The sheep back then, you see, ruled the lands with an iron fist. Or hooves, if you get me. That's where the term 'hooves of iron' comes from. They were very nasty creatures and would bite your bum if you so much as laid eyes on them. There lived a man in those times with a strange idea. His name was Woolly O' Knit."

Eimear rolled her eyes.

"He then said to the people: 'We must make the sheep work for us and not we working for them. We should take their clothes and make clothes for ourselves. But we will need tools to fashion such clothes. I will need to consult,' he said, 'with my great Fae friend, Needle Mac Pointy.'"

He was trying, as always, to make her smile. One day she would.

"'I will travel to the blue Fae tree near the Three Wells of Wonder.' Actually, I don't know if you knew this Eimear, but that's where the expression: well, well, well came from. The Three Wells of Wonder. A marvellous place with lots of water to drink, but that occasionally smells faintly of malodourous cheese." He stopped to glance at her, one eyebrow raised. If Eimear had ever laughed, it would have been now.

He patted his sawdust-covered apron. "Now. Where was I? Well. I was here, I know, but in the story. Oh yes. The blue Fae tree... 'I will travel,' he said, 'to the blue Fae tree and speak there to...'"

"Seasún," roared a voice from outside the hut.

The woodworker's face went pale.

"Hide, Eimear," he whispered, pointing at a pile of shaped boards. He lifted a section of them and shoved her into the small nook. He covered her over as the door burst open. She peeked through a gap.

"You rat, Seasún!" said the man. He was tall and hairy and fat. He carried an old sword in one hand and a battered-looking brown scabbard in the other.

"You rat. She was mine, and you desecrated her. She loves me, not you. She told me so."

"Hold on, Dónal. Just wait until I explain," Seasún said, arms raised.

"No, rat. I will not hold on." Dónal took the sword and ran it through Seasún's body. Seasún screamed, and Eimear's heart leapt. As always, the pain-wracked scream made her feel a wave of excitement amidst the horror of watching what was happening.

Seasún turned to where she hid, eyes open wide with panic.

The attacker followed his gaze and seemed to look directly at her. She wasn't sure if he saw her, but she stood, pushing the boards away.

The attacker and the dying man looked at her and then at each other.

Dónal seemed shocked out of his rage and immediately sheathed the bloody sword.

"Little girl. Where did you come from? Who are you? Seasún, who is she?"

Seasún was dead.

Dónal stuck his head out the door.

"Get back to your huts," he roared at whoever was outside. "Get back, or I'll come out to you after. Little girl," he said. "Tell me your name."

Eimear just watched. She was not afraid. She felt only the need inside her.

"Little girl. You're safe. Just tell me who you are. You're not his, anyway. Who are you?"

He knelt and beckoned her over. She noted his hand dart back to check the sword's position. He was breathing heavily, his chest heaving.

She looked at Seasún. His eyes stared at her in death. A puddle of blood formed around him, creeping across his proudly levelled and sanded wooden floor. The sight of the blood made her feel nauseous, as always, but the memory of the man's dying screams made her close her eyes, savouring the sound.

Eimear stood and ambled towards the fat man. She held a knitting needle in each hand. As she walked, she watched him slowly reach for the sword, as if by moving slowly, he might not alert her to the plain fact that he was doing so. He was still kneeling.

Everything was slow. *This man means to kill me.*

Rushing forward, Eimear stabbed him in the eye with one needle, and in the neck with the other. He screamed, and she gasped. She pulled the needle from his neck and stabbed his other eye. *He cannot see.* She pushed the lump of the man over and kicked the door shut.

A large set of shelves, brimming with various wooden items, stood next to the doorway. Eimear emptied the shelves and threw the things at the man, finding he made a wonderfully, distressed noise as each one struck. She threw each curious trinket as hard as she could.

As she threw, she heard the villagers gathering outside the hut. Looking for something to stop them entering, she thought of the shelves. It took Eimear several heaves to push the robust wooden frame onto its side in front of the door. It would serve. She looked at him lying under the pile of wooden tools and ornaments, before pushing some of them away. As she did, he lashed out with his arm, knocking her down.

Eimear narrowed her eyes. Breathlessly, she searched for the sword. Her hand had felt empty without it, though she had never held one. Spotting it where it lay near the pile of wood, she rolled over and took it up. Examining the battered old blade and handle, she could see it had not been well cared for.

Neither have I, sword.

Eimear hefted the sword before slashing down at the man's arm. It sliced his skin and muscle through to the bone, and he screamed again. His screams filled her heart with joy, and she hummed her song to make the music.

The sound of villagers attempting to force the door open grew louder, more frantic, but the shelves continued to serve their purpose.

"Girl, please," he cried.

Eimear tutted because those listening would know she had a part to play. Between that and the noises of the door, she knew it was over. Still humming, she cut across his exposed thigh, and he howled. Eimear drank in the sound as best she could. It made her whole being tingle. She wanted to stop and listen as she hummed the sad song she had always known. Screams alone were a gift; the sad song mixed among them was sweeter than life.

She was interrupted by the commotion outside. Moving around to the firepit, she kicked the burning turf around.

A layer of sawdust ignited, causing the fire to leap into life around the hut floor.

Reaching for the scabbard to save it from the hungry flames, she slid the blade inside. She took a leather strap from the floor, tied it around the top of the scabbard. Flinging it over her shoulder, she made ready to leave. Eimear noticed Seasún's food bag hanging from a low hook. She took it and searched for his cloak. Taking that too, she screamed herself. Her scream only ever sounded hollow, but it was probably wise to make it seem like she was in danger. If the villagers outside the door felt she was responsible for killing a man, there would be problems.

The sounds of the villagers forcing the door open stopped momentarily as those outside heard the high-pitched scream. Smoke clouded the room but was escaping from the small oilcloth-covered windows.

The villagers intensified their efforts to open the door, finally bashing their way in to find a room of nightmares. Dónal had lost his mind in anguish and was writhing around, his clothing starting to burn. Seasún's body was alight.

Eimear darted past them as they stared, enjoying the ripping scream that one of the womenfolk released as she surveyed the scene. It would take them time to realise that it was Eimear who had been at work.

Eimear saw that Donkey was watching her escape. Nodding towards the creature once, she ran away as she had so many times in the past.

DUILLECHÁN

***

*Is fearr beagán den ghaol ná
mórán den charthanas.*

A little relationship is better than
a lot of charity.

***

A SMALL CREATURE, chewing a hazelnut, sat on a stone and watched the child walk through the dreary surroundings. The creature scratched at her eyes, always itchy in this part of the woods. Shifting gingerly, she freed the matted grey hair from under her and ran a hand through it. It was time to cut it if it was down to her bony old arse again.

She had hoped that the child might have found a home this time. Yet, once again, Eimear turned to chaos. Mirdhí was sad to see that the child had also found a weapon, a sword, which did not bode well.

"A new plan is needed, methinks," she said to herself. "This way is not working."

She wondered if she should go back to tell the others. They would be disappointed again, but there would be no shock. She shook her head as she rubbed her eyes. Or was it time to approach the girl herself? That would give her quite a land.

As her eyes cleared, Mirdhí scanned the trees for the girl. She had been there a moment ago. *That child,* Mirdhí thought, *must have some bit of duillechán.*

A flicker of movement to her right caused her to turn, and she almost leapt from her skin when she found the child standing a stone's throw from her, watching her solemnly. It had been a hundred years since a human had laid eyes on her, and never had one come so close. She was too old to escape from this child. Too tired. A chill passed through her.

"Hello, Eimear," she said.

The child's brow furrowed. She was filthy. All manner of dirt covered her tattered clothes, caking her. Living in a shed next door to the pigs meant the child was starting to become one of them. Her dark brown eyes were sad.

"You're wondering now, what kind of creature I may be and how I might know your name?" Mirdhí said.

The child nodded slowly, clearly not threatened by Mirdhí. In the child's sad eyes, Mirdhí must look like an old woman who was shorter than herself, indeed one of the most wrinkled women that the child would have laid eyes upon.

"Eimear. I know you can talk when you want to. Now is probably as good a time as any, would you not think? And stand up tall, *girlín*, when I speak to you."

The child's head tilted a little. Her hand moved to the scabbarded sword hung over her shoulder, and panic started to creep through Mirdhí's small frame.

"The music. Isn't that what you call it? You want me to make it for you."

The child nodded.

"And now that you have that," she pointed a gnarled finger towards the sword, "you feel such a thing will be easier?"

Another nod.

"Fine. Away you go so, and there'll be no helping you after. I'll scream, and you can sing and let the animals of the wood find the whole thing odd." Mirdhí put her hand to her side when she saw it shaking noticeably. "Or you might calm yourself down, talk to me, and learn a bit about who you are and where you came from."

There was no movement from the child as she appeared to be mulling it over.

"Eimear. The sword will help you make music, yes. But you will be hunted and killed within a short time as your parents were. Your real parents."

Eimear's hand drifted from the sword, and she took a step forward. A studious gaze moved slowly around the shadow-darkened forest glade, the ancient trees, and Mirdhí seated among them.

Eimear's gaze drifted back to Mirdhí, and there they stayed, looking at each other.

"I will tell you, but you must ask," Mirdhí said.

"Who are you?" came the child's quiet voice.

"I am Mirdhí. I watch over you," she said, palms upturned.

"Why?"

"I was among the Fae who first found you."

"Fae?"

"You have heard stories of us, I am sure. Have you not?"

"Yes."

"Well, I am one of them. My people and I found you just as you were born. We put you with your own kind when you were strong enough, but you have always found it … difficult to settle down. You have a thirst for something you have been unable to quench."

"Why did you take me?"

"Because you are beautiful. And you have *draíocht* around you from your parents."

The child's eyes narrowed.

"My parents?"

"Hunters killed them. Killed them because of what they were, not what they did. You have Fae blood in you and are very unusual to my people and your own. Your father was a gruagach—a guardian of the longshores. Your mother was a human *cailleach*, a young witch of some renown. Both bathed in *draíocht*. He left his life there behind to be with her. And you."

"Why?"

"Love, Eimear."

"Love?"

Mirdhí's wrinkled old hands rubbed her glassy eyes. "Though you may not have felt it, your parents loved you so. And there are those of us here who love you too."

"Yet, you left me with people who had no love."

"It's true. We could not care for you when you were so small." She smacked her thighs and wriggled from the rock to stand. "Eimear. It is becoming wildly apparent that our care may be exactly what you need. More so since you decided to pick that up." She nodded towards the sword belt hanging over the child's shoulder.

"And, you found me, which is a thing of itself. That's sign enough for me. I must speak with my people on this side. You will come with me. Unless you have anywhere else you would prefer to be?" she asked, raising an eyebrow.

Eimear shook her head slowly. "I have nowhere. Nothing."

"Well. That is not wholly true. You have folk who care about you. You just haven't met them yet."

The child stood staring at Mirdhí for a moment. Mirdhí felt a sudden urge to leave. She could smell the pungent moss from the forest floor around her.

"Oh," said Eimear. She looked around her; either way, back the way she had travelled, then back to Mirdhí, her little hand moving slowly towards the hilt of the old sword.

"Is that what you have decided so?" Mirdhí said, a heavy sigh escaping from her.

"I do not know," spoke the child, unblinking.

She is still contemplating, thought Mirdhí. *If I use a géis to command her, I will never know if she can control her urges.*

"Do you believe me that I am the only one who can give you answers to some of your questions?"

Eimear's features creased. "I do."

"Do you know that you are not in danger from me?"

The child's eyes rolled a little. "I do."

"You have never controlled your future, Eimear. They have led you by the nose from one place to another. I offer you a chance to be free of that world. But you must swear to me to never raise the sword at me or my folk."

"Oh," Eimear's hand moved neither closer to nor further from the hilt.

"To make a change, you must first want the change to happen. Besides," added Mirdhí. "I'm someone who can offer you a warm place, with hot food, and no danger. Doesn't that sound like a treat? Yes? No?"

It was Eimear's turn to sigh. Her hand dropped.

"Swear it, Eimear."

The child's deep brown eyes closed for a moment.

"Eimear, you must learn to trust. It is the start of a new way. Trust is the key to a door you have created. Swear it."

"I swear it."

Mirdhí released a breath she had not realised she was holding.

"I will help you in whatever way I can, child. Trust in that too."

The two stood silently with other for several moments. Mirdhí wondered what the girl was thinking, but the sad brown eyes hinted at nothing.

"Come. Come along. There are those on the other side who have also been eager to hear tell of your progress. We must consult them."

"Them?"

"She. The Fand. Not for now, though. Come with me."

"What are you?"

"I am a duillechán."
"I thought so."
"You did?"
"Seasún told me stories about you."
"Well. Aren't you lucky indeed? Follow me, child."

CHILD

***

Is túisce deoch ná scéal.

A drink comes before a story.

***

EIMEAR'S HEAD BEGAN to feel strange as they walked.
Then it swam. She didn't feel dizzy, but it was what
dizzy felt like. The trees started to grow around them as
they went. No. Eimear already knew trees grew, but the
trees grew larger around her quickly. And then she
realised that it was she who was getting smaller. She
felt the duillechán keep an eye on her with sidelong
glances. More than one such glance alighted on the
sword.

Eimear wanted to hear the sound the man had made
again. She longed for it dearly. Walking beside this
creature was all she could do for now, however. The
world felt changed, quickened, out of control. Eimear

32

had many questions for Mirdhí, but she was sick from the sound of her own voice and was happy to revert to silence.

She blinked as her eyes stopped making sense to her. The tree in front of them, looming and vast, had faded from view as if shrouded by fog. Mirdhí continued to walk, and Eimear stayed with her.

They walked for a long time. When Eimear's eyes adjusted again, they were in a clearing with several tiny, pointed huts. The trees were back to normal size, but they were lush and green as if it was the height of spring. The duillecháns built their huts with small stones layered expertly, arching up towards the wooden poles protruding from the top, and tanned hides belted around the structures. The huts were neat and well-tended. Eimear could see smoke coming from several of them through openings at the top. A noisy herd of goats was going about their business in a stone-walled meadow nearby. There were tools on a cart, showing signs of recent toil, and rows in the soil nearby where leafy plants were growing. It was beautiful.

"Hai," Mirdhí called.

Six small creatures, duillecháns, appeared from various points and, one by one, gasped at the sight of Eimear. Eimear found the creatures strange to observe. They were like tiny people, like humans. They all had humped backs and kind faces, but there was more. Something that she could not see exactly. Something about them. In the air around them, perhaps. Eimear thought she could have sensed their presence even with her eyes closed. She had not felt this before.

Not one of them moved. They were looking at her in a strange way. Mirdhí spoke quietly.

"Take your hand off the sword, Eimear. You are scaring them."

Eimear noticed her hand was on the sword's hilt, though she didn't remember reaching for it. She did not remove it.

"Where am I?" she asked.

"You are where we live. We call it Crúach."

"Is this the Fae world?"

"No," Mirdhí said. "More like a Fae place in your world. We have little pockets where we can live in peace as long as we remain undiscovered. As a matter of fact, many Fae settlements don't often get names because Fae folk end up moving more often than folk here. Strange, when you think of it. Take your hand off the sword and leave it down."

Eimear found it hard to think. She saw Seasún's eyes in her mind and heard him scream.

Those screams.

"Eimear," Mirdhí said, whose voice had changed. Eimear listened. "Lay down the sword."

Mirdhí's voice was so strong and clear. It made Eimear want to help her. To make her happy. She immediately put down the sword and looked back up to see if Mirdhí was more pleased. Mirdhí was watching her with wrinkled lips pursed.

One of the other creatures took the sword and disappeared with it. Something changed. Eimear suddenly felt different about Mirdhí's voice, as if something had stopped.

"What was that?" Eimear asked. "What did you do?"

"I used a *géis* on you. A word of command."

"Why?"

"You know why, that's a clever girl. Come and sit with us."

"How did you do it?"

"Draíocht. Do you know about draíocht, Eimear?"

"I want my sword."

"Your sword now, is it?"

"Yes."

Mirdhí moved closer to Eimear. "You are a kind-hearted soul, of good nature and spirit. The sword is not for you. I will show you. Come. Sit with us."

The others sat around in a circle at the centre of the clearing. They were all short—not even up to Eimear's shoulder—wearing similar garments of yellow woollen trousers and dyed green woollen longshirts, leather waistcoats and brown, boiled leather shoes.

Eimear noticed it was warm here. As if in summer. She went to join them. The one who had taken the sword was back. He had a jagged scar from his brow to his chin that creased his face.

"I will tell you everyone's name though you may not remember them easily. To your left are Pédhar and Brónag. Beside me are Tildhe and Ísa. Those two are Sabh and Barragh."

Barragh, the one with the scarred face, spoke first; his voice as ruined as his mouth.

"You may find this strange, Eimear," he whispered, "but we have watched over you these years. We had wondered if we would ever meet you. Now, Mirdhí has brought you to us."

Eimear felt irritation ripple through her. "You watched over me? When Samhla left me blooded and hungry? Or before Samhla, when Seac took me in to care for me and tried to put his hands up my dress? Or when the boys from the village near the lake would take turns kicking at my legs until I could not walk?"

One of the females spoke. "I am Brónag, Eimear. We watched you as closely as we could, but interfering was difficult."

"Ah," Eimear said. She did not understand.

Mirdhí's eyes brimmed full of intensity.

"Tell me what happened to Seac, Eimear?"

"He got drunk and killed himself with a dagger."

"Was he often drunk, Eimear?" asked one of the others. The tallest one of them, Pédhar.

Eimear thought for a moment. She had never seen Seac take a drink. "No."

"Or had you seen the dagger before?" Pédhar asked.

"No." In hindsight, she had never considered the strange knife and its sudden appearance.

"And the woman who happened to pass by Seac's house the next day and take you in as her own. The one we thought seemed kindly enough. Did you not think that strange?"

"I was young."

"You were. Did you know that two boys from the village by the lake both got the pox?"

"No."

Pédhar nodded slowly. "It was excruciating for them. They suffered with it for many months. We did what we could for you, Eimear."

Eimear went quiet. It all made her head spin. They were looking at her fondly. She felt a warmth from them.

"I do not know what to do," she said.

"Nor do we, child," said Mirdhí. "That is what we must discuss. Would you like to stay with us, or would you prefer to rest? You must be hungry as a bear."

"I do not care," Eimear said.

Brónag stood.

"Come with me, Eimear. Let's get you settled, and the rest of them can talk about you." She moved off towards one of the huts. Eimear followed.

As they entered the neat little home, Eimear was nearly overwhelmed by the strange smells. Over the firepit, there bubbled a busy black pot. Steam raced up towards the smoke hole as if eager to explore. There were benches around the edge of the hut with various vials, pots, jugs and jars, each seemingly more unusually coloured than the last. Strange bits and pieces hung from above: ornaments, tools and trinkets. An array of hides littered the floor. It was a fascinating place.

Eimear watched Brónag. She seemed a deal younger than the rest, though still ancient. Brónag wore a light shawl, even though Eimear thought she might stew in it.

"The world has been hard for you, little one," she said.

Eimear nodded absently. She had spotted a beautiful ceramic ornament and was curious. On it was a tan-coloured and ferocious animal that she did not recognise.

"Have you pangs?"

Eimear nodded again.

"Stew and black bread when you have pangs. That's what's called for. Sit," she bade.

When Eimear was sitting, Brónag passed her some food in small bowls and a mug of tepid water. Eimear was ravenous and gobbled it down. She sighed contentedly.

"Hunger is a good sauce," said the Duillechán.

"You'll need new clothes and to scrub yourself clean. Follow me."

"I need to make water," Eimear said. She felt her head get hot. She did not want Brónag to be offended.

"Yes. All that…" She paused. "This might sound strange to you, Eimear, as we have never met. But I have wanted to look after you since the second I laid eyes on you. And now, my little sweetgrass, now that I have the chance, I am going to mind you until your head might fall off."

Eimear felt her face softening to match her contentment.

***

As her eyes opened, Eimear tried to remember where she was. She felt warm. Comfortable. She couldn't remember when she last woke up feeling such things. Her eyes adjusted slowly, and she remembered lying down on a hide rug in Brónag's hut. Sitting up, she wiped the sleep from her face.

Mirdhí was sitting by the firepit, stirring the pot.

"I hope you slept well, Eimear. You have a fine snore, like a heifer. It gave us a good giggle."

Eimear nodded and stretched a little.

"Before I tell you about our meeting, I need you to explain something to me. Someone raised a concern that I… we, need to understand." Mirdhí pretended to be disinterested, but Eimear knew she was uneasy about this conversation.

"When you stood with your hand on the sword. What were you thinking about doing?"

Eimear decided that she would answer but she had to consider it. What had she been thinking about doing? *Making them all scream.*

"I was afraid."

Mirdhí added some leaves into the pot; lips pursed in thought for a moment.

"No. No, child, you were not. I can understand that you do not trust us. Except for that old donkey you befriended, I think you have never trusted anyone. I suppose it would not be right for me to ask you to trust me, but I will ask you to trust yourself. Trust your feelings about us. Think about what I have asked you. You can answer later if you decide."

She took the wooden spoon and blew on it, trying a taste.

"Have some more of the stew. You are scrawny and underfed. Let's make you into a little round *putóg*."

Eimear did very little for the day. She had never had a day like it. She relaxed by the stream with Brónag and bathed in the unseasonal warmth of an exuberant sun. She should have been able to enjoy it, to feel carefree and even childlike for the first time in memory. But every time she closed her eyes, she thought of the screaming, and wanted to hear it again. She hummed the sad tune as she watched Ísa make a basket. The tune seemed to stave off the strange urges that were growing in her.

***

Days passed and turned to weeks. Eimear felt more relaxed than she ever had before. She found a little pond that she swam in with whomever of the Duillecháns were around. She helped tend to the goats and the plants, making sure to keep the two apart. Eimear learned about hunting and fishing, foraging and mushroom picking, healing and tracking. The duillecháns spoiled her with treats and gifts. When Sabh handed her the orphaned kid, Eimear started to feel like this might be her home. The tiny goat needed constant attention. When the others asked her to name him, Eimear decided on Little Goat. After a bit of over and back, the duillecháns couldn't convince her otherwise. Little Goat it was.

The strange day that changed the world for Eimear once again came when Pédhar, Sabh and Barragh left early. Tildhe gathered up his gear for fishing and left too.

Ísa was jovial company as she made bread. She had sleepy blue eyes and a razor-sharp wit. Eimear sat against a bench, feeding Little Goat and humming her song. Eimear knew that Ísa heard her hum and that she stopped kneading to listen. Strangely comfortable in her role as the kid's protector, Eimear continued to hum for a while.

"That was a lovely sad tune," said Ísa, returning to her work. "I hear you hum it often. Where did you hear that?"

"I never heard it except from myself." Eimear wasn't sure that made sense.

"To make music of such beauty is a rare gift, Eimear." Ísa's wrinkled face twitched as she worked.

Eimear felt kindness from her in every word. Every action, however mundane.

"That is what I want to do. To make music." Her eyes lost focus for a moment, and she remembered again. A keen urge stung at her.

When she shook herself free of it, Eimear found Ísa's face had twisted into a grimace.

"I see. Yet I feel that a bone flute might not be the instrument you had in mind."

Mirdhí and Brónag came to sit cross-legged with them.

"Can I stay here forever?" Eimear asked, tracing a finger across Little Goat's knobbly head.

"Would you like to?" Brónag said, openly excited.

"I think maybe, yes." *If I tell them, they might help me.* Eimear searched her mind for a way to explain to them.

"There is something wrong with me."

"Oh?" Mirdhí said. Eimear found her voice calming.

"I don't feel much. Not anything strongly. Except one thing."

"What is that, child?" Mirdhí asked.

"It is … strange. I want to hear people … suffering."

There was silence for several moments.

"We all suffer when Tildhe tells us tall tales about his fishing exploits," said Ísa. "Is that what you mean? That you want us to experience uncomfortable situations?"

"No." Eimear felt weary as she spoke. "I want to listen to you all scream, to cry … to be in pain and despair."

"Despair. Isn't that a great word for a small child to know?" Ísa muttered, the grimace back.

Brónag tutted. "You poor girl. You were born into the world amidst those same sounds. You have lived a life, until now, that has been miserable and joyless. It's understandable that you feel anger at the people around you."

"I do not feel anger," Eimear said. "I feel this as you might feel hunger pangs. But more. A lot more. I don't know if I want anything else except the sounds I am talking about. I felt the sword could help me when I had it. I still want to have it. It is mine, after all."

The three duillecháns looked anxious. Eimear could feel their discomfort and did not enjoy it.

"I told you," she murmured to them. "There is something wrong with me."

"For all that ails folk, there are cures," Mirdhí said. "We need to get a cure for you. There are Fae who have great knowledge of healing draíocht. We can invite them to come here. You are among family now, Eimear. You've settled in here and have become a part of the place. We all love you dearly and will help you. We have all waited for your smile to appear. We are not going to give up."

"They will not need to come here," Pédhar said from behind them. He was flanked on each side by Sabh and Barragh. "We spoke to Crea. The Fand commands us to bring Eimear to her palace."

Eimear's tummy fluttered, and she felt sick.

The duillecháns bowed their heads as one, replacing their kindly faces with frowns and tight lips.

Brónag appeared to be the most worried. "Come child. We must get you fat and then prepare you for your travels."

***

Over the coming days, the duillecháns prepared Eimear as best as they could manage. They were the happiest days that Eimear had ever had and the saddest. As her new friends cared for and minded her, they spoke to her about the strange world she would be visiting, even though much of it was nonsense to Eimear. All she could think of was that she had found her home, and now she had to leave it.

Travel into the Fae realm was only possible through one of three portal dolmens. Eimear had understood portal dolmens to be grave sites, but Brónag had talked about things in the Fae world that were like a strange distant cousin of what Eimear knew.

They told her the journey to the Fand would be both beautiful and treacherous. They warned Eimear about agents of the Fane. He vehemently opposed mixing humans and Fae, wanting the destruction of such offspring. Brónag searched Eimear's face. Eimear merely nodded. She was not afraid.

When Eimear asked who would be going with her, Brónag smiled sadly.

"We all want to go with you, child. Now that you are here, we wish for nothing else but to be with you. It may not be possible, however. We must make the right decision, not the decision we wish to make."

Eimear did not quite understand Brónag.

"What is draíocht?" she asked.

"Ah," Brónag said, pausing for a moment. "What are you good at, Eimear?"

"Milking cattle," Eimear shrugged.

"I see. Well, if you were so good at milking cattle that it got the Gods' attention, they might enhance your

43

skills with draíocht. Make you an even more special milker. It doesn't seem to happen often in this world, but the Fae realm is closer to their influence. Draíocht intertwines everything we do there."

"The Gods?" asked Eimear quietly.

"Well. Not the Gods. The draoí, who are like Gods. In a way."

"A more special milker…" Eimear trailed off.

"I think I did not explain that very well, Eimear."

"The draoí did not enhance your explaining skills, Brónag," Eimear said, feeling very confused.

The duillechán howled laughter until tears streamed down her face.

"Oh. Child. Is it any wonder that we all love you so?"

Eimear felt a sting. *Sadness.*

"I wish you could have shown me before this," she said. "I never knew."

The laughter stopped abruptly, and Brónag gazed at her.

"We will just have to make up for time lost with extra care."

***

More days passed, during which her new friends, her family, claimed it was so they could prepare her for the journey and make some last-minute decisions. Eimear watched them around her and knew they did not want her to leave. Brónag's suggestion that she would receive extra care was not an exaggeration: they spoiled her rotten.

Eimear found herself puzzled by the strange turn of events which led her here and then threatened to lead her away again. She did not want to leave. She was starting to forget about the screams. The sun warmed her face, and the breeze curled her clean hair. She had not shivered once. It was as though she was starting to learn how to live in a different world with a whole new plethora of feelings to match. Leaving seemed like a bad idea. Eimear felt she should tell them, but the duillecháns had made their decision.

The duillecháns gathered after their evening meal, which had been warming and wholesome. They asked Eimear not to bring Little Goat, suggesting a more serious meeting. All seven sat with Eimear and were largely silent until Mirdhí spoke.

"Eimear. We have a question to ask you before we can make a final decision as to who will go with you. You must answer honestly whether you trust in us or not."

Eimear nodded.

I want them to know me. I want to know them.

"Is it your intention to bring the sword with you?"

"Yes."

"Why?"

"I … need it with me," Eimear said, shrugging.

"What is it you want? The sword or the sounds."

"I do not know."

"What if we hide the sword from you?"

"If I must leave here, I will. I do not want to. I know I want to stay and live this life. To help you all and to raise Little Goat. If I leave? I will find a different sword if I do not have that one. I will need one if I go away from here."

45

Mirdhí's face crumbled a little, and Eimear thought she might cry. The old duillechán nodded, and Barragh brought out the sword, putting it in Eimear's lap.

"Remember this place," Mirdhí said, her voice straining. "Come back here someday. Someday soon. If we did not have to heed her command, we would hide you away with us." She shifted uncomfortably. "Yet, we cannot. And so, you will leave us, but not alone. Eimear. You have pangs that you cannot fully control, and they will make you a danger to those around you until such time as you learn to control yourself better."

Eimear looked at the sword in her lap and then back to Mirdhí. This time, she felt her own face crumble a little. Mirdhí continued.

"We would be in danger. You might cut any of us to hear the sound you seek. It is not your fault, beautiful child. Not at all. But it is true. However, you cannot go alone. And so, Barragh will accompany you."

The scarred, worn, duillechán stood near her, one eyebrow raised as if waiting for her reaction. He opened his gnarled hands for her, his scarred face twisting into an ugly smile.

"Barragh's voice is old. He can only whisper. So, no matter what you feel tempted to do with him, he will not be able to make the sounds you seek. He might be able to keep you on the right path too, and with blessings from the gods, bring you back to us here." She smoothed her long shirt. "That's if you want to come back to us at all."

"I do."

"Then you must try not to cut Barragh into pieces," Ísa said, smirking.

There was wry laughter from everyone except Barragh, who was gnawing on his cracked lip. She shrugged, and the others laughed once more. Eimear thought that she could one day love the sound of Brónag's cackle more than any music.

***

They each bade her farewell in their way and each in a way that made Eimear want to leave less and less.

She heard words coming from her mouth that she knew to be true. "I will miss you all. I wish that I had come here first."

"We wish that you had too, Eimear. We made mistakes," Pédhar said quietly, his bottom lip quivering.

Eimear went to spend some time with Little Goat. He was fat from milk and dozing happily. She hummed the song for him and let him sleep. They would raise him now, probably better than she could. An ache in her chest made a tear dance down her face.

"Goodbye, Little Goat."

As she paused to inhale the now familiar scents of this safe place, the sun-bathed warmth faded for a moment.

She turned, and Barragh led her away from the clearing.

"How do I come back?"

"With me," he whispered.

"What if you come back before me? Or if I get lost?"

"If you get lost, we will find you. It might take a little while, but we will. Now. We will leave here in a moment. Hold on."

As they walked, Eimear's eyes lost focus once again. The world warped. They kept walking until she stepped back into the familiar cold, dampness she was used to at this time of year.

"We're back." A shiver hardly waited for her to finish speaking.

"See here," Barragh whispered. "There is the top of the hill that would remind you of a bald man's head, with one small straight ear and one big crookedy one. There are the tallest trees in this valley. Search for this rock. It is shaped like a giant tooth."

Barragh produced a small smooth pebble that had a line of colour running through it.

"Walk yourself over to that rock and take the pebble between your finger and thumb. Rub it three times one way, three times the other and then wriggle a bit. Then call one of our names as loud as you can and wait."

Eimear, who had been listening intently, realised she was being made fun of.

"Barragh," she said, shaking her head. "So, I only have to call you?"

"When you're in this place, my loveen, you will only ever need call once. We'll wait for you to come back no matter what happens." His attempt at a warm-hearted smile was a dreadful mess.

Eimear reached out and gently touched his scarred forehead.

"You have all been so kind to me."

"We all love you, child. You are a very special little pishkin."

"I am ... wrong."

"Eimear, there are plenty of shaggin' things wrong about the worlds. Best focus on those right when we can. Are you ready?"

"To go to a portal dolmen?"

"Yes. Well. We'll travel to a portal dolmen in the land of the Fae. On this side, we don't need them. Watch."

Barragh's curled fingers started to perform a strange dance. They moved in all directions with no apparent pattern.

"Watch what?"

"I like to think of it as draíocht tickling."

"Why are you tickling draíocht, Barragh?

"Well, apart from the fact that it could probably do with a laugh, it also allows me to do this."

Beside him, a black space appeared. Eimear took an instinctive step back.

The black oval shape reminded her of the chunk of skin she had taken off her thumb as she had stacked turf onto the cart. The black shape looked as if it had cut a way under the world. She could not see into it or past it, making her uncomfortable. It was like the middle part of someone's eye.

"Is that not a thing to behold," Barragh whispered. His fingers reached out a little and moved apart. The shape of the black oval grew to a size that they would fit through.

"Eimear. Don't be afraid. We are going to a portal dolmen that is safe and protected by people who will not harm you. Just remember, try not to look up straight away. Just stay looking in front of you. There'll be enough in that to start."

"I am not afraid," Eimear said.

49

Barragh nodded slowly, raised his eyebrows, shrugged a quick shrug, and disappeared into the black oval shape.

Eimear found it hard to follow. She did not want to leave. Her thoughts strayed back to Crúach: her friends, her family, the little animal who depended on her. Heavy breaths jolted her chest. *I need to go back.* She had to tell Barragh. Nothing good would come from her going into the black place.

Go, urged the sword.

Eimear was stunned. *I did not know that you spoke.* There was no response from the old blade.

Can you do it again? Can you hear me? You can talk to me more if you want.

Barragh's ugly face appeared through the black.

"Not scared, is it? Come along, Eimear. You're safe with me."

The single word spoken by her sword echoed in her mind.

Go, it said. I must go. I must do what needs to be done.

She took a breath, walked into the black, and … stepped out into a huge alien valley, vast and colourful beyond words—more than vast. Eimear looked up and immediately wanted to run back through the black. There was no sky above her. Instead, she could see distant valleys, mountains, rivers, and deserts, of greens and more greens, of browns and yellows, of greys and even areas of snowy white. The world curled upwards and around. She was inside a ball. There were areas of a million different colours and areas with none. A thick black line passed through it all like a giant finger had carved out a rift, dividing the world in two.

Or creating two worlds?

Looking at the jet-black rift made Eimear queasy, so she avoided looking directly at it.

Huge sections of pale nothing covered areas of both sides of the black line. Smaller, misshapen pale areas dotted the strange land.

A ball of light was in the centre of the space above her. Akin to the sun, except she could stare at it without her eyes hurting; a tired sun that tried to mimic the one she knew but failed. Between the yellow ball and the ground was a rocky island; atop it a dolmen of enormous boulders. She held out her hand but felt no warmth from the yellow ball.

Her chest began to pound. No sky. Just a world laid bare before her.

"Eimear, you goose. Didn't I say not to look up?" He took her hand. "Just take a few breaths. There is no sky here, just the land above us. Somewhere over there is where we will be going. Think of what a bird would see soaring in the distant sky. That is what you see. All around you. Meadows and forests, mountains and lakes. You might struggle to find our cities and towns, our settlements and whatnot. They are built into the world around them instead of piled on top of it. They are there, though, I'm not coddin' you."

It was difficult to even listen to him as he pointed to places that she could not see.

"There," he pointed at the sections of pale nothing. "Our two oceans. Very different places but similar to the oceans of your world I reckon. No salt in ours. You can see that the lakes appear similar."

What a bird would see? She shuddered and squinted into the furthest distance to try and make out details,

51

but there was only a blur of faded colours. The trees around her were familiar shapes and sizes. There was brush and undergrowth, birds chirping from the treetops and a slight wind moving the branches they sat on.

She was only half aware of Barragh waving his two arms as if to signal to someone. She followed his gaze but saw only distant snow-capped mountains over the tops of the small colourful trees to her right.

A thought struck her. "When is there night-time?" she asked.

"We have darker times, where work stops, and we sleep. Midsun does not always stay so bright. We do not have night, as you know. It can take some getting used to, even for me, when I come back here. Some suggest that's why those rare visitors cannot help but be spoiled. Me? I think it's the Draoí..." Barragh's face twisted, and reddened and he stopped whispering. He threw a crooked gaze at her. "I will take care of you, Eimear. My world won't spoil you. I promise it."

Eimear did not know what to say. This world was not like where she had come from, but she had never felt at home there until Crúach. Perhaps, if she allowed it, her home could be here.

"She will be coming: the winged one. Stand up and let her see you close when she comes," he whispered, straightening himself to his tallest.

Still looking towards the mountain range, he added, "I am very proud to be here with you," out of the side of his mouth. "Proud of you, girl."

Eimear followed his gaze. In the distance, she saw a speck, it grew into a dot and the dot became a shape. The shape, like a bird, had wings and flew towards them. As it grew closer, Eimear noticed the bow and bright-coloured armour; she noticed the long flowing hair of ebony and the almost human face. The flying woman landed before them. It—she—was incredibly tall with a face that could have been human were it not for her eyes. Eimear remembered similar eyes from when she lived in a barn with an owl. Jet-black orbs, with orange rims, that were enormous on her beautiful pale face, with its thin lips and a button nose. The ornate bow she held was as tall as the woman herself, and the arrows in her shouldered quiver were taller than Eimear.

"Barragh's return at last," hailed the flying woman. "And what do we have here?"

Her wings transfixed Eimear, gossamer thin, the shifting colours of a rainbow; they folded behind the woman to almost nothing.

"The introduction of a rare thing entirely," Barragh whispered, as he bowed his head. "The sum of two worlds."

The flying woman's piercing gaze came to rest upon Eimear.

"You are one of very few of your kind to come here. It is a momentous thing. I would not have thought it possible that draíocht could so utterly bathe one born on your world. Who are you, child?"

"I am Eimear."

"I am Crea smallsky denizen."

"There is no sky here."

"There is, so to speak. We just have less of it than you."

"What do you do here?"

"I watch this portal." She nodded towards where Eimear and Barragh had come from. The black shape had gone. There were huge rocks, set like the portal dolmens she knew, but they were far larger and had intricate carvings from base to tip. The rocks matched the structure on the floating island far above her.

Barragh addressed the flying woman. "The Fand is happy for us to continue?"

"She is that. The Fand has asked that you proceed with as little fanfare as possible. Should the Fane discover what transpires, he will be deeply dismayed. We may feel his wrath. They had agreed, Barragh, that this would not happen again."

"I understand, Crea," Barragh whispered. "We'll be but a gentle gust on the path. His agents will never know and that I can promise you."

"The court of the Fand is no longer secure. That side may already know of the plan to bring the child to her. The Fand must have a motive, unclear to me. The child may be the harbinger of great unrest."

"Can you help us on our path?"

"I will watch over you from my perch while you travel. Be wary of hoodoons, Barragh. The creatures are getting bolder and range far from their normal hunting grounds. Strange things are happening. Remember too, should you enter a Settlement, I will not be able to see you easily. Be careful who you trust."

The huge eyes regarded the sword belt resting on Eimear's shoulder.

"You are prepared for battle, child?"

"I do not know battle. I cannot prepare for what I do not know."

"You are wise ..." Crea stopped mid-sentence as she looked behind Barragh and Eimear.

They turned and gasped in unison. Out of the squat, colourful trees came an enormous, cloaked figure. Much taller than any human could stand. Eimear knew that it must a fathach—a Giant.

The cowl covered the face in shadow, but Eimear thought she could see a red tinge of colour trying to escape the dark. Crea spoke behind them.

"Aébhal, you should not have come across the crease uninvited. Does the Fand know you are on this side? The Fane?"

The cloaked fathach did not speak but walked around them; the thuds of his footfalls were rhythmic against the sound of his long steady breaths.

The three stood stiff. Eimear felt fear from Crea and Barragh.

"What are your intentions?" Crea asked.

"What have you done, duillechán?" asked a deep, honeyed voice.

"You heard my questions, Aébhal, and should answer," Crea said, taking a step forward.

"I heard you, servant. Now be silent. Or do you intend to draw your bow on me?"

The question had a hard edge, though the voice remained honeyed. Barragh pushed in front of Eimear.

"You well know that I will not use my bow lightly. If I draw it on you, it will not be to threaten. I will not ask you the question again."

Her words caused the giant to pause.

"No, Crea. She is not aware of my presence on this side."

There was a strange silence. Eimear could feel the shock from Crea, the fear from Barragh and a wave of hatred from the hooded giant.

"What are you doing, Aébhal? How could you be so brazen? How did you know about this? You will cause the end of the peace, maybe even of the arrangement."

"I only came to see for myself what was happening here. Hard as it is to believe it is happening at all. Crea, let us say I was drawn here. I assure you I will go before the Fand, so no harm done, eh?" He smiled a terrible smile then; though she could not see it, she could feel it. Eimear could hear her heartbeat in her ears.

"I think the Fand has made a terrible blunder bringing you here, child. A terrible blunder indeed. Any breaking of the peace will surely see her as the cause. What is your name?"

"Don't speak to him," Barragh whispered, grating voice urgent. "Not a sound to him."

Eimear's hand rested on the hilt of the old sword. Not speaking was easy for her.

"So brave," said the giant, "for one so young." He began to move forward once again.

Crea spoke softly.

"I ask you to leave us and go to the court of the Fand. Now."

The giant stopped again as if considering.

"This abomination has already defiled our beautiful soil." There was a movement of the cowl towards Eimear and then back to Crea. Eimear was relieved that it had averted its gaze from her. She suppressed the urge to shiver. "Have a care of becoming involved with this abhorrence, Crea. Beware the ramifications for the other smallsky denizens, not just yourself." The shrouded gaze stayed on Crea for several moments. But Aébhal also kept a huge red finger pointing at Eimear.

Finally, without another word, Aébhal dropped his arm, before turning and walking back into the tree line.

"Do not speak," Crea said as she watched him leave. She stood still, searching the trees, where they stayed in silence for a long time. Eimear could see Crea's knuckles were white, holding the bow tightly, just as she realised she had balled her hands into tight fists. A strange bird flew near them and squawked. It made Crea flinch.

With a whooshing sigh, Barragh produced his waterskin and sat, offering it up to Eimear. Eimear drank deeply and sat beside him, returning the much lighter skin. After what seemed like an age, Crea turned to Eimear. The intensity of her eyes made it hard for Eimear to hold the gaze.

"You are in danger. If you go back through the portal, Aébhal will soon discover and no one in your world can protect you. If you continue your path here, he will surely kill you both at the first opportunity."

"Can you protect us?" Barragh asked.

"I can. But I do not know if I should. The arrival of this child could signal the end of the peace. We three smallsky denizens are bound to neutrality as we monitor our assigned portals. It has been our task since the beginning." Pausing to observe something in the distance, she held up one finger to them. Eimear tried to make out the focus of her attention, but nothing was obvious. After a moment, Crea continued.

"I do not understand what is happening, child, but you are being used." She pointed at Barragh. "You will need to bring her away from the portal dolmen and away from the settlements—especially your own. You must watch her carefully. Our land ruins almost all who arrive here—some very quickly. It may not matter that her father was a gruagach."

"I will mind her, Crea. Don't you worry."

"Barragh, without the support of your settlement, you are in bother. And should you seek their assistance, Aébhal may make you rue that decision. Get to the court of the Fand quickly. I must consult with my brother and sister at the longshore. I will be back to speak with you both."

With that, she unfurled her wings and flew away towards the black crease above them. Eimear marvelled at how quietly she moved through the air.

"Well," whispered Barragh. "This is not good." He started walking toward the tree line on the opposite side of the clearing to which the giant had gone. Eimear moved to follow but sensed another set of eyes watching her. She turned towards the trees once again. Though she could not see anything, she knew something was watching her. Not the malevolent gaze from beneath the cowl. Something different. Her eyes narrowed as she searched.

"Come child, will you? Fast," Barragh growled.

Another quick scan revealed nothing.

She turned and followed Barragh quickly.

WATCHER

***

***

DRAWING HIS CLOAK around himself, he couldn't help but smile. As Aébhal passed, he made sure the giant couldn't see him in the undergrowth. Like a grazing animal, he herded Aébhal here without his knowledge. Tildhe's reports of the draíocht amassing around the child were not exaggerated. Even from the distance he observed her, it was as clear as the crease from the other

59

side of the world. Yes, the land would ruin her, but before then she would be more powerful than any from Faneside or Fandside. The danger was clear.

Still smiling, he watched the child and her protector disappear.

I have much to do, he thought.

He made sure to leave by the same route he had taken to arrive. Crea missed very little. He was counting on the recent arrivals to keep her mind occupied so he could travel back to Faneside.

It was time.

Time for the two sides to crumble and be rebuilt.

Time for the changes that would ensure the Fae world became all it could be.

The putrid state of things could not continue. A weak Fand and a weaker Fane had ruled too long.

He broke a leaf from the Wellan tree before him and inhaled the scent. He was one with this place as he was with his own side of the crease. It welcomed him as the Faneside would welcome him home.

The crease.

He thought of himself being thrown over the edge and his breathing became rapid.

I will fall for eternity if my plans are discovered.

He shook his head.

No time for weakness.

Weakness was the root cause of ill on both sides; weakness that was left to fester. It was time for the deep well of strength he knew only he possessed.

It brought him no joy to be the cause of the chaos that was sure to unfold. While none would thank him during the chaos, his children's children would reap the benefit of the seeds he had sown. He had buried them deep, but the seedlings were forming. He walked under the low branches and put his hand on the tree trunk, enjoying the rough feel under his fingers. The dark brown bark of the tree mirrored his skin. This tree had been a seedling too. It had grown tall and strong without a protector. His seedlings would grow to become mighty trees one day.

He had finished his preparations. It was time.

The time of the Fae. The sídhe.

His time.

DUILLECHÁN

***

Bliain le duine agus bliain ina choinne.

One year with you, one against you.

***

THIS IS NOT good.

Many of the aches and pains Barragh suffered in the other realm had eased upon his arrival home. He had even felt a little taller with his hunch relaxing. Now they were all back. Worse.

This is not good.

Aébhal. Aébhal had come to greet them—no wonder the aches were back.

62

The aches are back, and the back's aching.

He should have said no, but he could never say no to Mirdhí. She was so beautiful even though she had no time for him.

"Mind her, Barragh," she had said. "Keep her away from danger. The Fand will try to use her for some scheme or other. Present her and bring her back to us if there's any way to do so."

"I can only do my best."

"And don't forget to come back with her."

"Would you miss me terribly if I didn't?" he asked.

"Don't I miss you already, Barragh," Mirdhí replied with a wink.

Maybe when he got back, he would summon the courage to tell her how he felt after all their long years together. He realised he couldn't hear the girl behind and spun to check on her. There she was, a few paces away, regarding him with her big eyes. *She could have been a duillechán creeping so quietly through the brush.* A little sense of pride warmed his heart.

"Come," he said, and she moved to walk beside him.

"Barragh," she said. "Why does my head feel strange when we walk together outside of Crúach? The same thing happened with Mirdhí when I met her first?"

He cursed himself for a fool. It had never crossed his mind that she did not know of the haze. How would she? They had taken her in but explained little of their ways, choosing instead to shower her in their affection.

"The duillechán's draíocht is stealth. When we travel, we can do so in a bubble... no... more like a place where only we can move. Just out of the consciousness of those around us. On the periphery of their senses. We can be seen, of course, but only by those focused on finding us. Even then, those same few will not find us easily. We call it the haze. It serves us well, for we are not warriors."

The child raised her eyebrows. "Can you teach me to use it?"

He paused. Barragh had not considered the possibility. "I don't know, child. I don't know. We'll have to give it a try someday. For now, when you travel with me, you can enter the haze by my side. As long as you don't crash around like a bullock, that will do nicely."

She nodded once, seemingly happy with his response.

Scanning before him, he considered his options. Fleeing back through the portal would be no good. No one there could protect the child, Crea had said. She was right too. He wondered who could protect her in this world because he could not. Getting Eimear to the Fand was unlikely if Aébhal put his mind to stopping them, even if Crea was watching.

How is he being allowed this side? The giant was breaking the rules. That said, bringing Eimear to this side wasn't allowed either, even if the Fand demanded it.

I knew this would happen. I knew there would be trouble. What can I do against him? I should have insisted Crea stay with us. She surely could have kept the girl hidden from danger. What the Fand didn't know wouldn't harm her.

Hitching his pants, he tightened the string holding them up. He wouldn't be long losing his fine lump of a belly with all this haring about.

Barragh turned to the little girl beside him. Determination etched onto her po-face endeared her to him more. How could her little face be anything but that? He had noticed her demeanour change in her days with them. Her eyes grew wider as curiosity had bubbled out of her. She had listened to stories and asked questions. She had helped with the work and was a quick learner. Things came naturally to her. The draíocht saw to that.

The poor little pishkin. How terrifying the world must be for her. Her life as an orphaned slave had been grim, even if they had tried to protect her from afar. When she arrived in the duillechán's clearing, they all felt a sense of righteousness, a change for the good.

Good, my arse. We've made it worse.

Now she was here, her short, grim life heading towards a violent end.

As he spotted the battered scabbard hanging over her shoulder, a thought flitted into his mind.

Perhaps it's better that her life does come to an end. There's no future for her, only pain.

He stopped dead in his tracks, shaking the thought out of his mind.

"Why am I here, Barragh? Why does the Fand want me?" Eimear stopped walking to kick at a tuft of silver grass.

"Well, I'm not sure if I know, Eimear," he said truthfully. "Politics or some such."

"Why must I go to her? Why do you do as she says? What about what I want?"

A note in her voice made him wonder.

"What about what you want, Eimear?" he asked, a lump rising in his throat.

Eimear stood, tight-lipped, eyebrows raised.

"We never asked you," he continued. "What is it you want? For yourself?"

She stared into the trees, brow furrowed, then up at the lands closing over her as a cloudy sky would in her world. It must have been mind-blowing for her to see; the world inside a sphere, yet she had hardly even gasped. When she spoke, he strained his old ears to hear her.

"I want to go back with you, back to Mirdhí and the others. I want to stay there. At Crúach. I want that to be my home."

"Aye," he said. "I know that." *It was a stupid question.* "What about altogether, though? Not just for now. For your life, I mean. Do you get what I mean?"

"For so long, I wanted to be a child," she sighed, sitting on crossed legs. "That is what I wanted for as long as I remember. I did not get what I wanted then; I don't think I will get what I want now."

"What, my petal? What is it that you want?"

Her mouth opened to speak, then closed again, then opened once more.

"I want to be me."

Barragh stood, neck craned to listen. He had expected something else. More. Her back straightened, and she sat bolt upright. Something passed between them, a significant moment perhaps. He stood on his tiptoes desperate to make her feel right.

Think of something, would you, you fool?

Barragh realised that both her mouth and his eyes were wide open. Eimear searched his eye briefly and then looked away. Knowing no more would come, he cursed himself for missing his chance.

Nothing. That's what I really offer her.

He sat across from her, basking in his own uselessness.

"It will get better, you know," he said, reaching out to pat her hand. "Your life. From here on. It will get better every day."

She nodded, and her sad eyes made his heart ache.

Neither of them believed it.

"We should go," he sighed. "Keep moving and what have you. We'll find somewhere better suited to rest."

Another blast of old-duillechán noises accompanied his awkward rise from the forest floor. He reached down a hand and made more noises as she took it and pulled herself into standing.

He made a go at a reassuring smile and set off once again.

This is not good.

He became aware of her flagging as they went. He cursed himself for a fool. He had been setting a relentless pace that must have been hard for her. She would need food and rest. They would. He was old. Everything happening to him was strange, especially now that he was old. He had led such an unremarkable life up until this point.

He spotted a relatively pleasant-looking clearing and veered towards it, bringing them out of the haze and back into normal time. Several small animals and birds scattered upon their approach. The large trees surrounding them cast enough shade that Eimear might find it easier to sleep without a roof. Moss covered the clearing floor.

That should be damn near comfortable, he tried to convince himself, knowing full well how his back would disagree entirely.

"Let's stop and rest. You can eat and we'll sleep for a bit. Are you hungry?"

She nodded. A loud grumble from her stomach seconded.

"Right then. You do whatever you need to do and get settled, and I'll get us something ready."

As he busied himself making a small fire, he watched her from the corner of his eye. She didn't have much, only that sword that was far too big for her. He watched her lay it flat before her and sit cross-legged to study it. She straightened out her clothes and ran her fingers through her brown hair a few times. He realised he was smiling at her.

"So now. We'll have a go at a bit of sleep. It will be strange for you to get used to the brightness, but hopefully, it will happen quick enough." He threw his food bag at her. "You can put that over your eyes if it helps?" He added a wink of support.

"I will not need anything. I am perfectly capable of sleeping where I please," Eimear huffed. "There is no need for you to baby me, Barragh."

Cock-sure of herself. Not a blind notion of how much danger she was really in. He couldn't help but poke her a bit to see how she would take it. *See what stuff she's made of.*

"That said, we'd best sleep lightly here," he whispered.

"Why?"

"Ah. Staying away from settlements is not an easy thing. There aren't many who do it lightly and fewer who do it unprepared as we."

"Why?"

"Why. You ask me that a lot. A lot of why questions indeed."

She did not respond.

"Well, there are many things in this world that can kill you. Leaves, insects, reptiles, spiders, animals, creatures, monsters, spirits. And other things too. Dark things."

"What other things?"

"Well. For one example, there's Caen!"

"What is Caen?" She shifted and lifted her head to rest it on her fist. Now he had her curious.

"A beast," he said, leaning towards her. "A creature. He roams far and wide, some say on both sides of the crease. There have only been two or three that have survived his visit. Many a set of remains have been discovered with signs left from the work of his great jaws. Those who have lived talk about how they heard his voice in their minds."

"How big is it?"

"Hard to say. Those who have seen it are usually scared witless and don't make much sense. It comes when you're at rest, not making. a sound. Quick as a flash, with no warning or any such thing. Attacks and kills so quickly that none have a chance to raise a bow or a sword."

Eimear sat up again, then moved onto her knees before him. He noticed her taking a deep breath. She was right to be afraid here; that was probably enough of the poking.

"I think I would like to see it."

"What? Why?"

Breaking out in a near-smirk, she tilted her head.

"Sometimes why is a good question after all."

He chuckled, despite himself.

"Why, it is, after all, ya shite ya."

"I wish to meet it and know why it kills as it does. I want to speak to it."

"It kills because it is hungry, I suppose. It is huge. A big lump of a thing. It must need lots of food. And because we are tasty-looking things, we'd both be gobbled up quick enough."

He saw her glance at her sword.

"You'd want to be an awful lot handier with that yoke to be thinking of trying to scrap with Caen. I'll tell you that. A young slip of a thing as yourself would hardly be worth eating for him."

"I would give it a pain in its belly." Something changed in her face, and he felt uneasy for a moment. Her young eyes had gone steely; her chin raised in defiance.

A guffaw left him without his bidding.

"I'd take off like a weasel, as would you. Give it a pain in its belly and your arse, ya shite ya. Anyway. That's only one creature. It might be one of the fiercest, but there are little things that can get you here too. So, be on your guard, and we will only sleep here a short time."

With that, the child put the bag on her head, rested it on her arm and was snoring in moments.

Barragh chuckled again and lay down to do the same.

CHILD

***

*Is deacair ceann críonna a chur
ar cholainn óg.*

It's hard to put an old head on
young shoulders.

***

THE FOREST WAS densely packed with beautiful trees.
Colours and hues that Eimear had never seen sprang
from lithe branches. Lush undergrowth reached out to
meet them eagerly as they moved deeper in. Scents that
she had never experienced, some pleasant and some
less so, assaulted her nostrils. This strange world
around her teemed with animals and insects both

71

familiar to her and utterly alien. There was something about this world that could not be confused with her own. It was slightly neater, a bit more serene. It was… leaner.

Barragh beckoned to Eimear to follow closely, and his fingers danced a little. As they walked, the world fell out of focus into the haze.

"We'll make it hard to be followed. We can travel faster too. We're good for something, we duillecháns," Barragh whispered with a nod.

Eimear tried to focus but could only just make out the trees through the blur. She was beginning to love the feeling of haze travel.

As they walked, Eimear's mind began to wander. Her eyes had focused as best they could on his diminutive back. His hunch signalled the frailty of his age. Who was he to her? Why had she followed him at all? The rest of her life recently had been a blur. This blurred place seemed like the only thing she had done of late that gave her a chance to focus. Why was she here in this place?

I am here, said the sword.

But I don't know what to do with you.

Cut, said the sword.

He cannot scream. There would be no music.

Cut the Fand, said the sword.

Eimear nodded slowly. "I will."

"You will what?" whispered Barragh over his shoulder.

"I will burst if I do not make water soon," she said, conscious that her face was hot.

72

"Oh. Blast it. I had not thought. Over here," he fussed, and her eyes started to refocus almost immediately.

They stopped to rest near a stream and ate from Barragh's provisions. The trees here were thicker than before, their leaves darker. The world in the distance almost blended in with the treetops, and Eimear suddenly found it hard to catch her breath; so vast was the scene, yet all before her. She could see the most distant parts of the world by simply looking upward.

"You should stop doing that. It will melt your head thinking about it. This place is backways from your place. Backways and arseways. Take your time before you start trying to figure it all out. Here. Drink this and focus only on the liquid," he said, handing her a skin.

The water was cool, refreshing. Eimear closed her eyes to try and settle herself. *I am here. The world has always surrounded me. Seeing it makes no difference. I am here.*

As she drank and took deep breaths, the growing sense of panic left her. *I am here.*

"Help me fill these, will ya?" Barragh whispered, as he handed her a waterskin. They both filled their skins to bursting. Barragh chewed on his lip as he sat back on the bank, watching her.

"Eimear. Were you talking to your sword back there? Do you talk to your sword?" he whispered.

She regarded him as she drank. He knew. He held her gaze. She loved the ugly smile that would break out on his face when he watched her. An icy fist grabbed her heart at the thought of him not doing it anymore.

"Does your sword talk to you, maybe?"

She stoppered the waterskin and wiped her face dry. *What can I say so that he will not think me strange?*

He shook his head. "Don't trouble yourself with an answer. I suppose you haven't had much in the way of company over the years. Maybe talking to your sword is an excellent idea. In fact," he held his waterskin aloft, "I think I'm going to start talking to this lovely waterskin. I will call her Philomena; she will have a beautiful singing voice."

Eimear rolled her eyes up at him, full of fondness for the old creature. He gave her a nudge of his elbow and a wink.

He opened his mouth to speak but snapped it shut as they heard a growl.

Searching for the source of the strange noise, Eimear grunted in surprise when she saw three large creatures a ways downstream from them. All resembled ferocious hounds but stood on two legs and had long taloned hands ... claws. They were all staring at Eimear and Barragh with glowing red eyes. Eimear could sense the malevolence leak from them, the hatred. Their low growls made their way upstream, momentarily masking the diligent sounds of the trickling stream.

"Child. We must go very quickly. We must get to my home settlement so they might protect us there."

The beasts started to move upstream towards them, eyes never leaving their prey. Eimear felt a wash of emotions. Was it fear? She did not know anymore.

I am not afraid, she told herself.

Let them come, said the sword. Cut them all.

"Go," whispered Barragh and bustled her into the undergrowth. "Move your arse."

They ran as quickly and quietly as they could. Barragh pushed past her to lead the way. It seemed, to her, that he knew the direction he was going. Eimear could barely tell her up from her down. Chancing a backwards glance, she could see no signs of pursuit. Barragh stopped to listen, and then changed course towards his right.

Shortly after their change in direction, they burst into a large clearing where some people were working– chopping down trees and cutting them into boards. Eimear examined them more closely. They were not people as she knew them.

Are they people at all?

They were broad-shouldered and barrel-chested, hugely muscled, and bull-necked. All were hairless except for long pointed beards from the tips of their chins. They roared alarms at each other as Barragh and Eimear burst from the treeline. Many drew weapons– clubs and spears mainly.

"Stop," roared a voice louder than any Eimear had heard before. "What business have you here?"

"Hoodoons," Barragh's voice strained. His face was red, and he gulped back a deep breath. "Coming here."

"Hoodoons," roared the closest to them.

The bald figures reached for weapons and moved forward into a defensive line, Barragh and Eimear moving quickly behind into relative safety.

The hound creatures arrived from the treeline slowly, surveying the clearing before them.

"Twarvs. Spears," roared one of the bald brutes. As several of them hefted spears to throw, another three hoodoons appeared from the treeline, advancing ominously.

Eimear noticed another three coming from the other side of the clearing. The twarvs started to falter, a gasp or two escaped from the members of the line.

"Twarvs. Circle," commanded the same twarv. They formed into a defensive circle and raised their spears at the approaching creatures.

"This is not good," whispered Barragh. Eimear couldn't tell if he was talking to her or himself.

Barragh took a piece of discarded wood and shook it like a weapon. It was almost comical how unintimidating he was.

His knuckles were white where he held it. His other hand came to rest on Eimear's shoulder. Her hand drifted down to the handle of her sword. It did not need to speak. Her face softened as she drew it. It should have been a heavy burden for her, yet she could hold it loosely in one hand. She inhaled deeply and shut her eyes. The ripples in her stomach were not of fear but of excitement.

As if given a signal, the hoodoons attacked, leaping towards the Twarvs. Twarvs lashed out at them, fighting with skill, but the powerful beasts quickly knocked and savaged many of them.

Eimear's head swam, and her heart leapt as the screaming started. She gasped, slowed herself and took a deep breath. *It's so beautiful to hear.* Eimear started humming the sad song, and the world made sense.

Twarvs and hoodoons exchanged blows. The ferocity of the beasts matched the cunning attacks of the twarvs. Yet the thick hide of the hoodoons made it difficult to inflict serious injury. The lead twarv's voice boomed orders, which mired Eimear's enjoyment. She moved towards him, hoping for a chance to cut him so that he might use his powerful voice to satiate her. However, Barragh stuck to her protectively, standing between her and the nearest threat.

He wants to stop us, whispered the sword, feeling light in her hand.

No. He is trying to protect me. We must protect him against them. He cares for me. The acknowledgement felt out of place in her mind. It was not the time for such thoughts.

The twarvs continued their well-organised defence. There were only four hoodoons left. Although eight twarvs remained, at least fifteen lay dead or dying on the ground. They surrounded the hoodoons, two of whom were injured. They had likely won the day. And Eimear's sword had not made a cut. Her grip on the hilt tightened.

Let me play them for you.

When three more hoodoons appeared from the trees, a ripple of panic washed from the twarvs and Barragh. The beasts attacked on both sides, and the twarvs died quickly. Two hoodoons broke off the attack, turning toward Barragh and Eimear. Eimear basked in the fresh wave of screams. She watched a spray of blood shoot skyward. She could almost taste it as a wet crimson sheen bathed each combatant.

The hoodoons attacked. One leapt into the air towards her.

Belly said the sword. Open it.

Stepping forward and down quickly, she lifted her sword towards the creature's soft belly, and the blade did its hungry work. The creature folded into a ball mid-air, and she ducked away as it landed. As it howled in pain, Eimear knelt beside it to listen closely. Insides escaping, the hoodoon writhed. Eimear put her hand beside the wound and pushed so the entrails came out quicker. The creature's shrieks turned to rasping gurgles. Eimear moved her face beside its head, pushing the sword against its neck in case it tried to bite her. She hummed the sad song for the creature as it died. Its glowing red eyes faded and darkened.

She saw blood covering her hands, running from the creature's wound, and dripping in globs from her sword.

***

"Eimear," came Crea's voice.

When did she arrive?

Eimear shook her head and tried to make sense of the scene around her. The remnants of the battle in the clearing were horrific. All but one of the twarvs lay dead. The hoodoons that the twarvs had not killed, lay dead or dying, pierced by one of Crea's enormous arrows.

The smallsky denizen was watching with a twarv, whose torso bore the marks of both claw and fang; the only twarv to survive the savagery. Both seemed unnerved by her actions despite all else that had just happened. She frowned. *Where is Barragh?*

"Where is Barragh?" she whispered, her heart pounding when she could not see him.

"I am sorry, child," said Crea. "I was not in time to save him."

She gestured towards where a hoodoon lay on top of her small friend. Eimear's shoulders sagged.

Barragh.

Waves of anger and pain washed over her. She felt small, useless.

"No," she said, her voice cracking.

I should have been there to protect him.

"Please. No."

She stumbled over to where he lay, Sword heavy in her shaking hand. Her eyes stung as she saw Barragh's staring vacantly at her. The hoodoon had started to gouge into his chest and neck before the great arrow had skewered it. Eimear saw then that the arrow had passed through the hoodoon and into Barragh's stomach.

A cold feeling went through her to replace the other emotions. The flying creature had not tried to save Barragh. *She had killed him. Not the hoodoons. Her.*

She killed Barragh.

Cut her open, make her scream, urged the sword.

Eimear hefted the weapon. She grimaced, lips trembling as she tried to grasp what she was looking at. She felt like screaming her rage but didn't want them to hear it. Her mouth opened as the pain threatened to carry her away.

"We must go, Crea. There may be more." The twarv wiped the sweat from his shining brow, creating a singular area of skin not wet with blood.

"I must recover my arrows, Arthmael," she said quietly to the twarv, the one with the booming roar. "Take the child. We must go."

"The child? Why?" he asked, bloody face aghast. One of his arms hung limp at his side. "We must warn the settlement."

"The Fand has called for her."

79

"Crea, I must return to my settlement and tell them what happened. Then I must help with their burning. My people... my friends... look at what has happened to them. This child is nothing." His voice raised into a roar.

"Arthmael," she turned to him. "Aébhal is this side. There is a chance he sent the hoodoons."

"Sent? Hoodoons sent by Aébhal? What madness is this?"

"My love," said Crea as she went to him and touched his injured arm. "There is something wrong. Terribly wrong. This child is born from a gruagach and a cailleach. She is here from the open sky otherworld."

The twarv eyed Eimear suspiciously. His emerald-green eyes were breathtaking, yet cold and cruel.

"Her? So, this is her fault? What about here? Do you not see the slaughter?" he asked, frowning, eyes harrowed.

"Arthmael, listen. She must continue on her way to the Fand. We must bring her, for this was what she bade. I will tend now to your wounds." She focused her gaze down his body as if gauging their severity. "Then I will fly to your Settlement and tell Serrisa what has happened." His sudden grimace at the mention of Serrisa did not stop her. "When I return, we must bring Eimear to the Fand..." Crea hesitated, looking at him imploringly. "If you need to return to the Settlement, so be it, but I will need help."

He searched her face for a moment. "I have a duty to attend to. Even if I do not help to tend to the bodies of my people, I must tell Serrisa what happened here. Come with me. Bring the child. I will help you to protect her if you need me to. But more twarvs may die if they are attacked unprepared. Come with me to talk to Serrisa. We can take time to enlist help of some strong spear arms for a journey to the Fand."

"The twarvs fought bravely, Arthmael. There was honour in it, and we will not forget. This girl needs to be brought before the Fand quickly. Her presence has the potential to reopen old wounds."

"Let us be quick then. Serrisa first though, then the Fand. That is, if you are sure it the wisest course."

Eimear watched Crea. She was staring absently at the fallen twarvs, lips pursed.

"Perhaps you are right, Arthmael. We cannot leave them like this so easily. Serrisa, then the Fand."

Eimear's head was swimming, memories of the screaming, the blood on her hands, and the cold feeling in her stomach vied for her attention. All while these two talked as if she was nothing, incapable of making her own decision.

They mean to leave Barragh here.

She shook her head and hummed the sad song to herself.

I will not leave him.

As the twarv approached her, Eimear adjusted her hand on the sword hilt.

Under his beard, his neck is unprotected.

Yes. I will let him come to me and attack.

Yes.

The twarv stopped to stand over her.

"Crea, my love," he said quietly, without taking his eyes off Eimear. "This child means to kill me with that sword in her hand."

Crea stood.

"Eimear," she said. "Is it true?"

81

"It is," Eimear hissed at them. "I will cut you both, and you will make music for me." Her face softened; sticky blood trickled down her cheek. Barragh was gone. They were nothing to her.

"I see," said Arthmael. "Are you going to do it in front of him?"

He nodded behind Eimear. Before she could turn to see whom Arthmael was referring to, something hard hit her head.

WATCHER

***

Ciall agus míchiall - dís ná
gabhann le chéile.

Sense and nonsense - two things
which do not go together.

***

HE SHOOK HIS head. The child was already changing.
Her naturally adept sword work on the creature was a
show of that. For one so young to kill one of them was
astounding. For her to continue to cut the creature
afterwards was perplexing. She was something to be
reckoned with, indeed, and would surely become a
formidable warrior if her basic skills could be extended.
She was not yet strong enough to easily best the
hoodoons, however.

He considered the three dead beasts at his feet. Even
he had not found it easy to kill three, especially without

being seen by the twarvs. Crea had been slow to arrive, and he could not risk the child being killed by the hoodoons, so killing the creatures had been necessary.

Still, the beasts could be controlled. They had done his bidding. A thought struck him that made him breathe a long slow sigh. *No one will ever know of the incredible things I have done. I am alone.*

His thoughts strayed back to the child. With her pale face and rounded ears, she could just as easily have been one of the sídhe as the mangblood that she was. Her skin was a lighter hue than his, her nose and lips somewhat thinner, but there was no way to miss the commonalities. Many of the sídhe had skin the same colour as hers. It was a source of constant irritation that those people through her portal could seem so much like his people. She could be one of them. The oldest stories told how the sídhe were the first to inhabit their world and that those people came from his.

Little did most of the Fae know they had come from different far-reaching worlds through the portals. All searching for the draoí and their gifts.

There was no doubt about it. He was right to want her here. The draíocht illustrated that more than any conversation could. His gaze moved across to the Faneside. The crease would always be, but two halves could become a whole. He had waited many years for a key to open the doors of possibility.

The child, it seemed, could be that key.

Whatever she is, she is not one of my people. She is a tool I will use to craft and shape the future of my people. The Fae. The sídhe. My people are here.

For now.

Carefully looking for those who might be watching him, he moved back along his recent path to return to the Faneside.

TWARV

***

Is lú ná fríd máthair an oilc.

It takes very little to cause
trouble.

***

ARTHMAEL LAID THE child on one of the stout tables in
Serrisa's long hall and took to pacing up and down the
straw-covered stone floor. Serrisa tutted loudly, gaze
flitting towards Crea. As her arms crossed tightly, the
array of arm greaves, bangles, bracelets, and beads
made quite a racket. She tapped on her knees where
both legs ended and signalled to old Páidí to move her
wheeled chair over so she could inspect the mangblood.

"This child? You feel that she has something to do with the attack?"

"I do not know, Serrisa," Arthmael admitted. His undying respect for her meant, as always, that as much honesty as possible was the best way. "Have you ever heard of such a number of hoodoons attacking so many twarvs? It has never happened, surely. Yet almost immediately after her arrival, it happens?"

He crossed his own arms. He knew it was unwise not to tell her straight about Aébhal, but he needed her thoughts on the child first.

"Who is she?" asked Serrisa.

"She is half Fae, half human," answered Arthmael. "Neither Crea nor I know much more. Her name is Eimear. The duillechán, Barragh, brought her through the portal. His body is with the others."

"Which are where?"

"Where we were making trestles near Sceachbeag."

Serrisa's square jaw tensed. She tied back her long sable hair with a leather tie. Páidí made a move to help, but she tutted him away. His stocky shoulders slumped.

"Why have you brought her here?" she asked softly, checking over the unconscious child. Arthmael knew of her struggles because she could not have children. She would have made a fine mother.

"I needed to warn you about the attack. Perhaps we are mistaken. Perhaps this is something new. Perhaps more hoodoons might attack. Also, I need her to be asleep until we get her some of the way, at least, to the Fand."

"Perhaps, perhaps, perhaps, and also," she snorted. "What good is perhaps to me over a mound of dead twarvs." Her eyes narrowed. "We, you say. Why is the smallsky denizen with you?"

"Crea can answer for herself, Serrisa."

Serrisa's bushy eyebrows knitted together, green eyes burning. Though her attention did not stray from the child, Arthmael knew well enough that he had overstepped.

"I have no doubt that she can, Arthmael. But why is she not at her post? I find her presence here as strange as anything else you have said to me. It is difficult to digest."

"It was difficult to comprehend even as it unfolded," Crea shook her head slowly.

The twarv leader's hands gripped the rests of her chair, knuckles white. She signalled Páidí to bring her before Crea.

"So, you did not see the danger? Did not see these creatures as they approached?"

"I did not. I cannot see everything that happens," Crea stood, hands open by her sides. Arthmael frowned at Serrisa's tone. *She asks too much of Crea. Expects so much.*

"Yet, you arrived as it happened. Why is it that you managed to spot it unfolding, then? Luck?"

Crea's pale face coloured. Arthmael spoke before she could. Her discomfort was his.

"It was a good thing that she did, or we would not have bested them."

"I see," said Serrisa, her gaze boring into him. "What of this young thing? Is she so important that you must both leave? Without helping us to find and burn the dead? Do you know why the Fand would want her here? Knowing it will defy the long-standing wishes of the Fane?"

"I have no answers. It is the will of the Fand. That is all I know. You must help us to ensure that she does not wake before Arthmael and I can take her to the Fand," Crea turned to Eimear and brushed a strand of hair from the child's face. "She is troubled. It is likely that that will become more prominent while she is here."

"Arthmael is wounded. He will not leave before being treated," said Serrisa.

Arthmael rose to speak. Serrisa's raised finger silenced him before he could. "Bring me over to her again, Páidí." The twarv positioned his wife in front of the mangblood, the one who never spoke, pushing the other who never walked. Serrisa placed her hand on Eimear's forehead and whispered words of rest.

"Crea, this is not our concern. This child is not our problem. Many of our kin have fallen. We need to send them away in the flames of a pyre. The child will sleep for a few more hours. You may take her."

"The Fand has summoned this child," Crea said, moving beside them. "You must aid us in seeing her wishes done."

"I must?" Serrisa chuckled, the laugh not reaching her eyes. "The Fand wishes to use this child in some courtly scheme or other. She has allowed bands of hoodoons to walk the forests unfettered." She pushed Eimear's hair away from her face. "The needs of this settlement will have my undivided attention until I have assessed the threat and until the bodies are recovered and honoured on their pyres. I hope I am speaking plain enough for you, Crea."

Crea's wings unfurled to stretch out wide; the upper tips brushed off the rafter holding up the earthen roof, then folded slowly behind her again. Arthmael, grim-faced to match his mood, shrugged. *Serrisa can be wrong, just like anyone.*

"Most certainly, Serrisa."

Arthmael felt himself growl. One of the many thick tapestries adorning the long hall caught his eye. Some hero or other was fighting some villain or other. "I will not be so quick to abandon an ally in a time of need. Not when I have seen the danger Crea would face on her own."

"Crea has dealt with hoodoons before, Arthmael. I am sure of it," she pointed, and Páidí wheeled her towards the entrance to the lower tunnels. "She will manage."

"Aébhal is this side, Serrisa. He came to meet the girl and her duillechán guide at the portal. He has taken an interest in her."

Serrisa froze in her chair for a moment before signalling to a guard, who nodded curtly.

"Send out a band to burn the bodies where they lay. Let their woodwork be their pyre. Tell the digger crew to cover us in. Twarvs to the lower tunnels." She turned back to Crea. "Take the child with you and go. You," she said to Arthmael, "You follow me."

"I need assistance, Serrisa. The Fand will not be pleased that you turned your back on me," said Crea.

Serrisa almost fell forward from the chair, causing Páidí to reach out towards her. "You failed to tell me about Aébhal," she hissed. "Neglected to mention his presence this side. If he were to come here…" Her face had turned pale. "You failed to tell me about whatever is happening between you and Arthmael. Few settlements will aid you until things become a lot clearer. For now, do as you will; but do it elsewhere. If the Fand does not understand my reluctance, I will deal with her wrath later."

With that, she nodded, and Páidí wheeled her out the polished wooden entrance to the lower tunnels.

Arthmael stopped Crea, who was preparing to leave, with a meaty hand on her lithe wrist.

"I want to go with you, Crea."

"Against the will of Serrisa? You are not talking sense."

"I cannot allow you to proceed alone."

"In truth," said Crea, turning to stand before him. "Perhaps it is the best way to proceed. As you say, I am likely to meet with the same reaction in any of the settlements between here and the Fand's palace. Aébhal is this side. The hoodoons rising is secondary. I will carry her. She is small enough, so I should manage."

Arthmael gazed into her eyes, struggling, as always, to comprehend how beautiful they were.

"You are brave, Crea. I will not be able to help you if you fly. But I do not wish you to leave."

"I cannot stay away from my duty for long spells. Yet, I do not wish to leave your side with your injuries."

"I would have thought the underground to be uncomfortable for you."

She smiled, and he could not help but smile back. His stomach fluttered wildly.

"Here, I am always happy to leave," she said. "You? Increasingly less so. Dare I say it, your company was worth a small skirmish."

"I will follow you when I can."

"Good," said Crea, and she turned to recover her bow and pick up the child.

CHILD

***

*Námhaid an cheird gan í a
fhoghlaim.*

If you don't learn your trade, it
becomes your enemy.

***

WHEN EIMEAR WOKE, it felt like she was floating. The
sensation was difficult to process. Her hands and body
could feel something underneath, but it was soft and
comfortable, like a fat bed of moss in the woods or thick
grass growing back after reaping. She sat up quickly,
kicking off some kind of coverings. Upon inspection,
she realised that they were soft blankets. Her
experience of blankets up until that point had consisted
of harsh feelings: strong-smelling, threadbare, rags.
There were cloth sheets under her, stretched across a

huge bag packed full of softness. Her fingers prodded it.

"It is the down of large birds that we have in this world, Eimear. We put it into sewn cloth bags. It is called a mattress."

"A mattress?" Eimear mumbled. Her body felt rested; her mind, anything but.

Sitting back on the mattress, she stopped to examine the girl who had spoken from a chair across the room. Her skin was as brown as the bark of an oak tree, her hair tight to her head. She had deep brown eyes, almost black. Eimear guessed her to be sixteen or seventeen winters old. Eimear's breath caught when she saw Sword was in the girl's lap.

"Tell me, Eimear. What do you feel?"

"I feel nothing," she lied. "Who are you?"

"I am Doireann. Crea carried you here. It was no small feat. Her wings were only made for her. To bear you such a long way must have been hardship indeed."

"I did not ask her to carry me," Eimear shrugged.

"That is true. Why do you think you are here, I wonder?"

"The Fand wants to see me." Eimear pretended to smooth out the blankets on her legs as she tried to better judge how far her hand was from Sword.

"Do you know why?"

"No." Eimear felt Sword in her thoughts. It was ready for her. She shuffled forward a little.

"I will tell you a secret. The Fand dreamed about you, Eimear. A long time ago, when she was young. She dreamt that you would come and change things here, end the division and bring unity of purpose."

Doireann stood and walked through a wide archway to a place outside. Eimear clenched her teeth. An opportunity missed.

A stone barrier was just outside to stop people from falling, and Eimear could see they were up in a tall building. It was difficult to judge from where she was. Eimear rose and walked to join Doireann. They stood on a stone platform that jutted from the tower where they stood. Eimear felt fear creep through her at the thought of falling. When she considered the black line of the crease in the distance, the fear made her want to get back into the relative safety of the bed.

A breeze ruffled through Doireann's clothes, as she spoke.

"In the dream, you helped her to bring the two sides together as has never happened before. The Fand believes that that time is almost upon us." Doireann leaned on the barrier, unwittingly holding Sword precariously close to the edge. Eimear sat, bolt upright. She felt a sudden ache in her shoulders as she stared at the weapon.

"She believes that we can become one if there is a common goal. We can build more bridges over the crease and build a world here without the incessant conflict. We can create, Eimear. Create harmony, strength, and lasting peace. We just need a way to bring us together, and the Fand has seen it in her dreams. We must go to your world as conquerors. We must make it our own and allow the Fane to impose his will upon that place."

Holding Sword up as if to present it to Eimear, her face came alive, eyes bright.

"You had a different name in the dream, but your face was the same, and this ..." She brandished Sword. "This was in the dream too."

Seeing Doireann's hand shaking as she held Sword confirmed a suspicion.

"Why did the Fand tell you about her dreams, Doireann?"

"Why do you think, Eimear?"

"I think you are the Fand, maybe?"

Doireann smiled and patted Sword.

"You are as bright as a wenflower."

"You look very young to be a ruler of anywhere," Eimear said quietly. She followed Doireann back into the large, airy room. She had never thought a room could be so large. A beautiful set of intricately carved, polished wooden chairs was on the other side of the room. The Fand moved to sit on one of those chairs. A large, beautiful tapestry hung behind; the image of the same portal dolmen she had recently passed through.

The Fand followed her gaze. "I can still remember the day we opened the gateway to your world. I felt sure that the way signalled a future of prosperity for both worlds. Such things have not come to pass. Therefore, it is time for a new future."

"You did not answer my question," said Eimear, entranced by Doireann's smooth, brown skin.

"You did not ask one." Doireann's smile was all teeth.

"How do you look so young?"

"I am in a position whereby I can look how I would choose to as I see fit; depending on how I feel. Does that make sense?"

"No. Can I have Sword back?"

"Yes. But not now. Now I would have you learn how to use it. And I need to know that you will not try to harm anyone with it. Could you promise that to me?"

"No."

"I thought not, Eimear. There is something about you. I do not know if it is the draíocht here or if it was in you before you arrived. It gathers around you in a staggering manner. To what end, I cannot tell, but you are in danger of losing yourself, I think. Do you understand me?"

"I do, but I do not know what to do."

"Will you let me try to help you?"

"Why do you want to help me? Why should I let you? Am I to be your servant?"

The Fand paused to consider this. She leaned forward on her chair.

"Yes."

"Do I have to?"

"Yes."

Eimear became distracted by her hands, which felt suddenly alien to her. Someone had cleaned them and trimmed her nails. She also wore a white dress. Eimear had never seen any clothing so clean. She raised her eyebrows as she noticed that her hair smelled clean and brushed. She could not remember the last time that had happened. It must have been a difficult task. *How long have I been asleep?* A wave of indignancy rippled through her.

"Can I have it back now?" she said to Doireann, nodding at Sword.

"No, Eimear. I think you might make bad decisions if I give it to you without the correct training; and the discipline that training would provide. Crea told me about what has been happening since you arrived. The hoodoons are terrifying creatures for anyone to behold. Crea told me that you killed one. Is this true?"

"It is."

"I see."

Eimear thought of Barragh. In the short time they had together, she had become fond of him. Her lip began to quiver, and she shook her head so that tears wouldn't come.

*****

A loud knock at the entrance to the room shook her from her sadness. She turned to watch a large male creature duck in. His top half was that of a normal man, his furred bottom-half, that of a two-legged goat. He wore a loose shirt and held a strange conical hat in a tight fist, running the other huge hand through his dark, unkempt hair and wispy beard.

"Come, Hógar." The Fand stood. She held Sword in one hand, with the hilt pointed towards Eimear. Eimear judged the distance to be too far to reach quickly. She shuffled a little down along the mattress.

"Hógar," said the Fand. "I have asked you here in secrecy, and you must swear a secret to me too."

Hógar nodded, brow furrowed. His hairy face was handsome but grim, scarred from some conflict or other. His brown-eyed gaze fixed on Eimear, and she stared back at him.

"Do you swear it, Hógar?"

"I do," he said, hands wringing the hat. Two of his fingers were missing from his left hand.

"Hógar," said the Fand, "This is Eimear. She is daughter to your brother, Bégha."

Hógar's face became a series of moving pictures. Eimear could not make out what he felt the strongest, finding herself feeling very little.

"I want you to watch over her while she is with us. My son Aébhal is on this side. He is going to kill her if he gets a chance. She will need protection. You and the other gruagachs will provide it, and since she is practically one of you, it seems suitably fitting. I wish you to teach her with spears and swords, Hógar. Will you swear it?"

Eimear's ear pricked when she heard he was to train her to use Sword better. Her face softened, and her eyes closed. *That is what I need. I will learn quickly.*

Hógar bowed stiffly. "I will see your words followed. Or, that is, your orders done. So, yes, I will, My Fand." His gaze flitted over to Eimear as his cheeks reddened. Shaking his head to himself, he stood tall and said no more. As he straightened, Eimear noticed a huge, jagged scar along one of his flanks. He had seen his share of war; heard the music too. He would do nicely.

"Leave us and allow the child privacy so she may dress." He did as commanded, and the Fand turned to Eimear.

"You will go to the gruagach settlement, but before you do, I want you to stand before my court. I want to introduce you to them. They will be very curious about you, Eimear.

"Why?"

The Fand stopped for a moment at the entrance of the strange room. "Do you know that I have not been asked so many questions in a long time? I have quite enjoyed it." Her dark stare was penetrating. "I am the

Fand, Eimear. You will do as I say. Dress yourself. I will have someone come for you shortly." With that, she left.

Eimear noticed someone had left a beautiful dress of yellow and green on a small stool. Beside it was a pair of leather slippers.

Eimear dressed, humming her sad song and wondered how she might cut the Fand and what music it would make.

After dressing, the walk through the palace left Eimear's head spinning. A timid, human-looking Fae had accompanied her through the place, a network of long straight rooms with doors to other rooms now and then. Sets of stone stairs offered even more strange places to discover. The stone was a polished white, with beautiful threads of colour running in strange patterns throughout.

There were windows, not covered with hide or wood, but some material so clear she could see through it. She put her hand on one to see if it was cold. A warm smoothness met her fingers that made her feel closed inside this strange place. The outside world seemed distant, alien.

Eimear could see she was a distance above a huge square with colourful flags and stalls. She could not see what the stalls contained but was curious and wanted to visit the place immediately. She could not imagine what the building she was standing in could be like from the outside.

"Follow, please," said the Fae. She turned and shuffled on. Eimear obeyed. It was a long walk, through long rooms with long staircases; her guide turned a series of lefts through several thick wooden doors.

They arrived in a room filled with benches and chests, tall cabinets, and shelving. There were scrolls and parchment stacks. There were other small boxes that seemingly only opened on one side. Eimear carefully pulled one open to find it full of countless leaves of parchment. There were strange markings on each leaf.

"What are these?" Eimear said.

"Books," said the Fae.

"Books?" Eimear had not heard the word before. A cacophony of alien smells made her head spin. Coughing gently, Eimear stood tall and tried to move her head away from the books so that she might find cleaner air.

"Please attend," said the Fae, whose brow was sheened with sweat. "Do not speak unless asked. I will bring you to a place and point where you will stand. Do not move unless someone tells you to move. It might be that no one addresses you. When I return for you, you will follow me without a sound."

The Fae peeked out between a heavy curtain. A waft of strange smells leaked into the room with the books, causing Eimear to sneeze. The Fae adjusted her skirts as she spoke. Running her hand through Eimear's hair, she adjusted her dress a little too.

"You look very pretty, child," said the Fae. "What's more, you have a gleam in your eye. Stand tall for yourself. You will do well."

She seemed to want to say something more, eyes darting around quickly but instead turned to push back the curtain for Eimear to pass through. Hearing the voice of the Fand speaking inside, she paused.

"…now that you are aware of my intentions, it should be clear to you that you are not in a position to

101

treat this through to a satisfactory end. The draíocht goes to her. It surrounds her and everything she does. I must treat with the Fane himself. Though my desires may not make sense to him yet, I hope given time he will see them for what they are: a new way forward; progress."

I am not afraid, thought Eimear as she moved forward, but her tummy fluttered wildly, tendrils of doubt growing within her.

She walked into a great hall and could not help but gasp. Her mouth fell open as she saw the arched ceiling that reached upward impossibly high, held aloft by giant pillars of the same white stone.

There was a large space in the centre of the great circular hall. On her right, a raised wooden platform in the shape of a tree had long, bare branches reaching upward and outward. Nestled amid the branches was an ornate chair, upon which sat the Fand.

Eimear was immediately confused. She was clearly the same person, but Doireann appeared ten or more summers older. Jet-black ringlets were tied back to reveal long, pointed ears.

"Be still, Aébhal," she said, angular face stern. Eimear followed the Fand's gaze to look upon a monster. The cloaked fathach she had met at the portal dolmen had removed his cloak. His skin was apple red, stretched tight, over a muscular bare torso. From his forehead grew a single black horn, sharp and threatening. His eyes were black apart from two tiny white pupils fixing his hatred on her. He had his massive fists clenched. Two enormous hooves adorned thick, squat legs, larger than the mightiest bull that ever lived.

I am not af… Eimear could not finish because it was not true. Half turning, she searched for an escape. The curtain through which she had entered was closed and lost in a soft wall of folds. A tear escaped from her eye to trickle quickly past her nose.

There is nowhere for me to go. I have nowhere else to walk, only the way ahead.

There were dozens of creatures in attendance. More. Hundreds. Of all shapes and sizes, colours and hues. Some were familiar from legends, some as human looking as her escort, some utterly alien. Each one of them watched her walk to her spot. A hush fell over the already quiet hall. The Fand turned towards her.

"Move forward, Eimear."

I am here. I have nothing to lose. I have never had anything.

Something within her changed. The twisting in her stomach stopped. Her lips no longer twitched downwards. She took a step forward and then another. *Here I am.*

She felt the Fand and all present watch her as she walked to the hall's centre.

There was a long silence before the Fand spoke.

"Born of two worlds, your kind has long since been turned away from our lands. Detested by many here as an abhorrence, you will likely make few friends here. However, change can bring growth; growth brings prosperity. I present to you all this child of two worlds. I say to you all that she is under my protection."

The Fand leaned forward and spoke directly to her son, the fathach, Aébhal. "If she is harmed in any way or taken from this side, those responsible will feel the keen sting of my fury. Aébhal, you, of all, have learned what I mean. Without Cromm at your side, you cannot match me. And you, of all, should take heed as you take the message to the Fane. What I propose is not without uncertainty, but the Fane is brave. It will not be without challenges, but the Fane is wise. It will require vision and a firm hand of guidance, but the Fane is, above all, a leader to his people, to our people."

The audience began to shift in their seats, some rose to standing. Whispers rippled through those gathered. The creatures here did not appear to believe what they were hearing. The red giant spoke.

"O, my Mother, my Fand. I would not have thought you would ask such a thing, yet I am your servant, as I am the Fane's, so I will see it done. I would ask you, however, to take hold of your senses in one thing. This future may be possible if you say. Still, I beg you, let me slay this abomination before the court so they may know a spell of poor judgement has abated. For it to be standing here, in this court, tarnishes the very ground on which it stands. We must destroy it. Then I can go to the Fane and tell him of your proposal. He and I will know you do not seek to use this most heinous thing without a true need."

His urgency dripped venom; his fury barely held in check.

"I did not ask to be here," Eimear told the fathach. "But I am here now."

There was an audible gasp of dismay and the fathach roared. Many of those in attendance started to shout. A growl escaped from the Fand, who curled her lip in distaste.

"Do not speak unless someone tells you to," said the Fand, voice cold.

"This has gone on long enough. Its words are poison. My love for you is too strong to observe this foul act," roared Aébhal and charged towards Eimear.

Guards, whom Eimear had not noticed, leapt to restrain the creature. Gruagachs, twarvs, duillecháns and others all sprang into action with ropes and hooks, nets and staves.

Eimear felt an arm wrap around her waist, Hogar's, and he summarily dragged her from the fray. She watched, open-mouthed, as the fathach became entangled in a web of ropes and nets.

Hógar took off running, with her under one arm, through one of the long narrow rooms. Eimear struggled to catch her breath as he ran. Each of his strides knocked a little wind from her under his firm grip. He placed her on the ledge of one of the windows to peer through. The court's defenders dragged the enormous red-skinned fathach into the courtyard below. In places, there were two or even three pulling at the same rope or net to bring him away from the Fand. Eimear found it strange that no one was using any weapons to attack him, nor was he lashing out at them. She watched him move as unbridled fury coursed through him. He was powerful beyond words, rage fuelling that power. There was something else, too, something familiar. She could almost taste the aggression flowing from him, and she wanted more. She wanted to feel it.

I feel it already.

No. Not feel it, Eimear wanted to release it as he did, release all her years of turmoil and sadness, abuse and despair. She wanted to roar as he did, to bellow at the gods and tell them of her anger.

Hógar stood beside her, breathing heavily.

"Do you know what you are?" he said, head shaking. His conical hat sat crooked on his head.

"I do not know what you mean. I am a child."

"No." The gruagach watched as they finally dragged Aébhal to his knees before the arriving Fand. "You are him."

"I don't know what you mean."

He rubbed his stubbly chin.

"You will."

The courtyard outside filled with creatures of all shapes and sizes, going about all manner of tasks or chores, had ground to a halt. Aébhal had gone suddenly still, watching the Fand's arrival. She appeared small before him, yet Aébhal bowed his head. She placed a delicate hand on his shoulder.

The Fand spoke to him then. Eimear could not hear the words, but as they were delivered, Aébhal's strange and terrifying gaze found her sitting at the window ledge with Hógar. His cold hatred for her pricked her like a thousand wooden needles, sharper than any Seasún could have carved. Hógar ducked to hide, but Eimear sat, staring back. For all his hatred, there were no wounds from a stare, no pain from a glance. She had heard him scream and wished to hear it again.

Here I am, she thought to the giant.

She smiled her first ever smile at the giant who sought to kill her.

GRUAGACH

*Níl leigheas ar an gcathú ach é
a mharú le foighne.*

There is no cure for regret but to
kill it with patience.

NEITHER SPOKE AS they travelled. Guards had escorted them from the Fand's settlement as far as the lush meadows of the near-sídhe. The guards were clearly nervous as they accompanied the unlikely pair. They were visibly relieved when setting off back towards the palace.

Hógar shaded his eyes as he surveyed the way ahead. The distant hills would bring them into the mountain range beyond.

Still a fair ways to go.

Half-heartedly, he had tried to make conversation with the child, but her tight-lipped, one-word answers had delivered them back into silence—hours of silence. His talking to children was rare, and he was happier in the main, to avoid it. This mangblood was a greater mystery to him than any he had faced before. After the recall from the fighting unit, his life was simple. Teach. Train those sent to him. Show them how to fight and kill.

The arrival of this mangblood turned everything he knew upside down. He hawked and spat.

Bégha. The fool.

His brother would surely delight at the thought of this awkward journey.

Or would he?

He had been a shit-stirrer whose sense of humour Hógar had long found tiresome. However, Eimear was his child, his daughter. Here, away from the world she knew, in danger from many enemies who she did not know to exist.

She bore many of his features too, which was worse. Her dark eyes mirrored her father's, yet in place of his arrogance, her eyes were cold, hidden. Finding someone who might take her in and relieve him of the burden would be difficult.

I will, though. I'm not keeping her.

"When can we stop? I am tired." Her voice broke the silence and his mulling. He turned to her.

"What?" he said.

"I need to rest. I feel unwell," she said. There were tears in her eyes.

His head felt hot. He hadn't considered her needs. She was a small thing, frail. He surveyed the terrain

108

around them. There was brush and some small woodland areas that would do.

"Let's rest then," he said. Hógar had been marching at a warrior's pace for hours. It must have been gruelling for the child. He cleared his throat and tried again, trying to sound softer. "I'm sorry. I hadn't thought about you."

A lazy tear globbed down her cheek.

Pointing towards a dell between them and the foothills, he said, "There. We'll go there. Seems fine and safe to me."

He checked over the pack the Fand's people had given her, containing clothing and rations. It was hefty for a slip of a thing like her.

"Give me that, and I'll carry it for you," he said. He tried a smile, but it felt like a grimace. Eimear nodded and swung it off her shoulder. There was a wet patch on the back of her cloak, where she had been sweating under the weight.

A thought struck him while lifting it onto his shoulder next to his own. "Do you need me to carry you?"

She wiped tears from her eyes and straightened up with a curt shake of her head, then started walking towards the dell ahead.

Eimear. That's her name.

"Eimear," he said. "Wait." Taking his waterskin from the side of his pack, he held it out to her.

"You'll be needing water."

Nodding slightly, she came to him, took the skin and drank deeply. It sounded like a sucking calf that had strayed from its mother.

"How are you unwell?" he asked.

109

She shrugged and kept drinking.

"I mean. Do you feel faint or what-have-you?"

She shook her head and kept drinking.

"Easy now, or it will all come back up."

The child stopped and belched loudly, causing Hógar's eyebrows to rise. She went to drink again, and Hógar shot his hand out to stop her.

"Easy, I said. You'll make yourself sick."

She belched again, but this time some of the water came back up with it. She was shivering, though the day was not cold, and there were dark circles under her eyes that he had not noticed.

"Is it morning?" she whispered.

"What?"

"When is it?" she said, just before she collapsed.

He hawked and spat.

Bégha, the fool. Hógar, the bigger fool.

***

The fire took quickly, and he debated hunting for something to stew. Seeing the child lying on her cloak, breathing rapidly, he decided against it and instead took some time to find chamomile growing among the nearby trees.

The dell itself was ideal. There was a shallow, almost surrounded by trees that would allow them decent enough seclusion. Hógar knew well enough that these lands were not truly wild.

A memory tried to break into his consciousness, bloody horror from some battle long ago. He shook his head to resist it taking shape in his mind's eye.

Even the true wilds of this world are nothing compared to the wilds of war.

Sitting beside her, he settled in to deliver regular dribbles of chamomile infused warmed water into her mouth.

Dehydration was something he had seen plenty of in many campaigns. Those same campaigns that had left him stiff and sore from a score of poorly healed injuries.

Sleep and regular trickles of herb water would help.

Despite his best efforts, the memory of bloody horror broke free of its prison. He groaned, covering his face with a hand. It had been during a lull in a fierce battle where he was gulping back water, fighting dehydration. He remembered spotting birds around a ditch, going to look and finding the bodies of the vanir children; their chests hollowed out where the scavengers had been busy. His eyes had stung, first from the smoke of a scorched village and then from his tears.

Hógar hawked quietly and spat.

The child was sleeping well enough now. Her breathing settled, and she was in as much shade as possible.

He allowed his eyes to close.

***

Hógar awoke to the sounds of movement. Reaching for his spear, he sat up quickly. His breath caught in his throat. The child was sleeping soundly, but a clan of badgers had joined her, all huddled around her, fast asleep. Two cubs had found their way up to her neckline, and it almost seemed like the child had grown a fine beard since they had stopped.

His breath caught again when he saw a tiny creature flitting through her shining brown hair—a sprithsídhe: a creature from folktales thought to be a myth. As Hógar watched, he saw more of them flying around her, weaving in and out of her hair.

What is she?

"It is unusual, is it not?" The voice jarred him from his awestruck state, and he spun to find one of the smallsky denizens standing across the dell from him. Crea. The Fandside watcher. Hógar shook his head. He was sure his mouth was wide open but did not feel quite ready to close it yet.

"She is unusual," Crea continued, voice low.

"Crea," he bowed. "I... I am honoured that we meet."

Her eyes focused on him momentarily before turning back to the child. His breath caught and released almost at the same moment. "It is kind of you to say, gruagach. What do they call you?"

"I am Hógar."

She moved towards the sleeping child and her visitors, hardly bending the grass underfoot.

"Hógar," she repeated, clearly preoccupied.

"I had thought them only to exist in stories," Hógar said as he tried to focus on the buzzing sprithsídhes; each could be a tiny version of Crea, with similar wings and lithe forms.

Crea shrugged. "I am as shocked as you."

"What is this girl? I did not know mangbloods to be the cause of such things."

"They are not. Though some have come to our world, they have not been as strong. The draíocht everywhere," her wings flashed open for a moment. "It shudders where she walks. It comes to her as if knowing something about her future that we cannot yet fathom. She is going to be the cause of great upset should it continue."

"Perhaps it might be best to dispatch her then? To set the draíocht right."

She turned to him; eyebrows raised. A sudden movement of her hand revealed a dagger, which she presented it to him, her eye's boring into his.

"Dispatch her then, Hógar. Save us from her." He searched for humour in her huge eyes, but they were unreadable. "Take it, Hógar. You will need to do it as she sleeps."

There was an urgency in her voice.

"I was not saying..." he started. "I was thinking aloud, you know. I wasn't suggesting that I..."

"Then who?" Crea stepped towards him. "When?"

Pressing her fist against his chest, she pushed the hilt of the dagger towards him.

"I was thinking aloud. I have no interest in murdering a child. Mangblood or not."

"But you have done it before." She hissed. "You can do it again. This one, Hógar gruagach, has sprithsídhes playing in her hair. She has Aébhal crossing from the Faneside to kill her. She has the Fand wishing her trained. She has the draíocht of our world twisting."

A strange scent filled his nostrils as she leaned in close. "Dispatch her."

The place around them went so silent that he could hear the soft buzzing of the sprithsídhes, the heavy breathing of the badgers and the child.

"This is a test," he said, stepping back. "You are testing my loyalty to the Fand and her word."

Crea hissed gently; lips curled. "A test?"

"You would kill me before I got near her." He hawked and spat. "I might be a fool, Crea, but my loyalty is unquestionable.

Once again, the place grew quiet.

Crea stood tall, towering above him, and the dagger disappeared. "A test. Yes, Hógar. That it was."

She unfurled her wings, the midsun light causing them to glisten.

"Do not speak to anyone of this. Of the meeting, or the sprithsídhes. Or the test. Train Eimear as the Fand commands. She will become whatever it is that she will become. Fare well, Hógar." With that, she was gone.

Hógar took a deep breath, his unease damn near itchy. Shaking his head, he went to mix some warmed water with more of the chamomile. She would be thirsty.

MANGBLOOD

Maireann croí éadrom a bhfad.

A light heart lives long.

EIMEAR DID NOT hear Crea leave, but Hógar's relieved sigh was enough of a sign that she was gone. She kept her eyes closed and breathed deeply, so he thought she was still asleep.

The sprithsídhes had stopped whispering to her when Crea arrived, but they resumed when Hógar went to tend the fire. The same message over and over again.

They do not know. The draíocht is a poisoned cup. Do not drink. They do not know. There is a plot that leads you towards their demise. They do not know. The draíocht is the feverish dream. Wake. Wake, Eimear.

Like she had killed Barragh, Crea wanted her dead. That Hógar could not see it was irrelevant. He was a fool. Eimear longed for her sword, knowing she would need it.

The animals that had come to rest with her stirred and scuttled away. The creatures who had moved through her hair and whispered in her ear flew away.

That she was alone here was in no doubt.

That she would forever be alone here was likely.

I will train, she thought, *because I don't know what else to do.*

"Wake Eimear," said Hógar. "You need to drink."

And when I am done, I will kill Crea and the Fand.

She opened her eyes to find Hógar standing over her, face hard.

I will kill them all.

***

Eimear found Hógar's care surprising. He was almost tender towards her, carefully helping her to drink and eat as she regained her strength. Her thoughts turned to Barragh and his wizened old face. He had tried to care for her too and now he was dead.

Crea.

She tried to recall his responses to Crea's request. Had he considered it? Would he consider it again? It was difficult to know. Yet it was also difficult to remain suspicious of him as he went about the business of preparing for a march.

"Have you always been so aware of yourself?" he asked from his knees as he tidied his things into a pack.

"What?" she asked, knowing what he meant, but not how to answer. Or if to answer.

"You heard me," he said. "Answer me if you want. Or don't. But you don't need to play games with me. My place in the world is of no consequence to anyone.

I suspect that's one of the reasons they asked me to mind you. I'm no one. Just old Hógar."

"Are you so old?" she asked.

"Yes. I am. Compared to you, anyway. Stop avoiding the question. More games—shite I can't bear. If you don't want to answer, fine." He tightened the pack quickly to accent his last word.

"I have," she said. She did not want to play games either.

"I know you have. I'm asking you about it." Sitting back on his haunches, he spread his hands. "We will need to get to know each other. Here's a way to start." He made a kind face, the first time his face had been anything but hard towards her.

Did he consider it?

"Why? Am I not to be your servant? Am I not a mangblood?" Eimear's voice was defiant. "You nearly marched me to my death not so long ago. Do you suddenly care?"

He made a horrible noise and spat on a nearby tree. A glob of his spit stuck tight to the bark. Standing, he started pacing as if considering.

"Eimear," he started. "This is all new to me. I'm used to being by myself. Not used to dealing with people up close." He shot her a glance. "Like you have been, by the sounds of things. And yes, you are a mangblood. But you are not just a mangblood. You are more. How much more we are yet to see."

He picked up his spear: a well-oiled blade on a sturdy wooden shaft. Gently running a finger along the edge of the blade, he grunted in approval. The way he studied the thing, made Eimear wonder if he could ever regard her with such a caring gaze.

Expertly, he twirled it around him; the spear becoming a blur; leaping and tumbling, he turned and threw it. It flashed across the dell to pierce the bark exactly where he had spat.

"I'm not sure how to care for you," he said, moving to his pack and putting on his silly hat. "But I'm willing to try if you give me the chance. And no," he said, offering her a hand to lift her. "I didn't consider it. Neither did Crea. Now let's go."

Eimear struggled to contain a gasp, allowing him to lift her to her feet. "How did you know what I was thinking?"

"Because your face looks like that's what you were thinking. You're not so mysterious, I'm beginning to realise. We'll take a while to get to know each other. Won't be too long before you can tell what I'm thinking too."

Looking at his hard, almost cruel face, made it hard for Eimear to imagine such a time.

Taking the two packs and his spear, he scattered the fire with his foot. "And no," he added. "You're not going to be my servant. But if you want to learn, you'll do well to listen. Not learning is the easiest thing anyone can do. I can teach you, child. Your gruagach heritage means you should have the warrior way within you. We just have to unlock it."

He looked towards the ominous black of the crease and she thought she saw him shiver and avoided the temptation to look at it.

"Eimear. The Fand gave me a task, yes, but you need learn about the world; to train and to understand how things work. To fly into your own mind. To explore it as you would another world."

"I want to learn."

"Come on, so. Go and make water before we go, or whatever you need. Then let's find somewhere to fill the waterskins. I'll have a mind on catching something to eat, and we'll stop again in a few hours. I want to learn too, Eimear." He flashed her an awkward grin before setting off. "I'll wait for you up ahead."

"Wait. Will you help me to get my sword back?" Eimear surprised herself with the question.

Hógar lost his grin to be replaced by stone.

"There are lots of swords. Once you have mastered the art, I will get you a sword."

"No, Hógar. I'm not asking you to do it now. If there is ever a chance to get my sword back. The one I came with. Will you help me?" He raised his eyebrows and his face twisted. It was not easy to know what he was thinking.

She spoke slowly, so he might understand. "It is the only thing I ever owned. The only thing I brought with me to this place."

He shrugged. "It's in the palace, Eimear. Who knows where in the palace. I think it's best that you forget about it. Forget about your world too, for that matter."

"If there's a chance," her voice near a whisper. "That's all I'm asking.

He was silent for a moment; then he shrugged again. "If there's a chance."

Nodding once, she stood tall to signal her readiness.

"Come, little one," Hógar said. "It's time for you to meet the gruagachs. Your people. It's time to go home."

GRUAGACH

***

*Ní bhíonn an rath, ach mar a
mbíonn an smacht.*

There is no prosperity unless
there is discipline.

***

HÓGAR HAWKED AND spat as he watched the girl train.
He had taught many other warriors with a slew of
different weapons, each of which he had mastered over
decades of practice, duels and wars. In each one, his
skill varied. His spear work always left his left flank
open. With sword and shield combined, his footwork
suffered. Though he could find openings in the most

cunning warrior's defence, while his own defence tended to suffer against shorter opponents.

After five short years of training, this girl had no weakness, no flaw to exploit. Whatever weapon she used, whether it be a spear or a wooden spoon, she could beat any one of her sparring partners. Hógar still used trickery and cheated to beat her and keep her honest. Yet his chance to do either lessened each time they sparred. The girl, he had come to realise, *was* the weapon.

A chill passed through him as he remembered her smiling at Aébhal. He thought about it often. It must have been a terrifying sight to her eyes, yet she smiled. Was she really his niece? Perhaps. Was there anything in her that he recognised? No. That was the only time he had ever seen her smile.

Have I tried hard enough to make her smile? He had never been good with others. He did most of his talking with a spear or a sword. Training ones, more recently. Yet, the girl had found a way into his heart, for he had no defence against her innocence, perseverance, or bravery.

Her training had been nightmarish. In the early days, she had been trounced, battered and bloodied. She would appear the following morning to face it again without complaint. Tight-lipped nods signalled respect from her sparring partners but did not lessen the punishment they gave her, time and time again.

As she grew in age and, more apparently, skill, he recalled how she would soundly beat those same sparring partners and then add an extra blow or two to cause them pain. When they cried out, her eyes would close in her delight. Soon enough, no others her age would spar with her. They would rather take a beating for defiance than train another second with her. Hógar had had no choice but to put her sparring against the adult warriors. Over the years, all but the strongest or most stubborn among them had refused to train with her as their children had—hardened warriors, afraid of the child.

Hógar rubbed his finger over the three knuckles the child had smashed with a club. He had refused himself a yelp of pain, remembering her feverish eyes as she landed the blow.

"That surely hurt you," she said.

"Stick it in your ear, you little goat," was his reply.

He grimaced. Eimear would kill him one day. Probably soon.

As he watched, the two gruagachs attacked well—one feinting and flanking, the other feinting and flowing into an actual attack. Their fight travelled the length and breadth of the fenced paddock. Some of the settlement's inhabitants were sitting outside their huts, watching the sparring, as was oft the case. Most of the large number of huts crowded around the paddock, so a view of the sparring was always available. Hearing about decent tussles second-hand was a painful thing to a gruagach. Less and less of them came to watch Eimear these days. Few but Hógar stayed for long, especially when Eimear was being hard on her partners.

The sound of a throat clearing signalled that Dristan had come to watch.

"There'll be no draíocht left after her," said the gruagach.

It was hard to argue the point. It gathered around her expectantly as if it sensed her potential for incredible deeds.

"What are you going to do with her?" asked Dristan, placing his grey-furred hands on the fence.

Hógar shook his head slowly. "I've run out of things to teach her. I did so a year ago."

"I have watched her, Hógar. She is creating her own style of combat, making up her own rules. The draíocht lets her do things she should not be able to do. She has surpassed any of us here. I am the eldest. I have never seen the like of her."

"Yes."

"I have also seen how you cannot control her moods."

"Yes."

As he watched, she stood and bowed to the two Gruagachs before her, loosely holding a quarterstaff as if the thing bored her.

"I'm helping her to control it herself."

"Are you? Are you really? Or are you telling yourself that?"

Hógar's mentorship had turned towards reflection and discipline. Without both, she was in constant danger of losing herself to deep anger. He had decreased her weapons training and taught her to fish and gather herbs instead. To hunt and swim for exercise—to run without rest for a day and a night—to be silent as a gentle breeze and to learn of the other Fae. He tried to have her sit and listen to her arms and legs, to pay attention to her fingernails and the tips of her hair—to try to understand the working of her breathing and the thump of her heart—to watch the dance of spiders, hard at work. She listened when she pleased, speaking little. Her actions spoke loud enough.

"Was there something you wanted, Dristan?"

A breath whistled through his bulbous nose. "I want her gone. Many here do. She is not and has never been one of us, regardless of what she may or may not mean to you."

Hógar closed his eyes. *What does she mean to me?*

Dristan tutted. "We have seen her eyes turn and fear a terrible wrath is coming. We will discuss it at the command table over the coming weeks. I wanted you to know it will be happening. If you cannot get rid of her in the meantime, we might send the two of you away." Dristan turned to leave. He paused, stretching his old back slowly. "A good retreat beats a bad stand, young Hógar. You've always been a stubborn one. Be careful."

"I don't recall you saying such things when she fought off the hoodoons, Dristan. The same ones who would have eaten me had she not charged." His throat stung for some reason. "I don't recall anyone at the command table fearing her terrible wrath when she brought down the Olpéist with a spear through its wing. In fact, I recall the whole settlement cowering as she strode out to meet the beast."

"Be that as it may—" Dristan continued before Hógar interrupted him.

"When your granddaughter went missing, I don't recall anyone searching harder or farther than Eimear."

He turned to face his old mentor.

"Perhaps the command table needs a palm of a hand and an angry eye."

Dristan brushed something off his cloak. You've always been a stubborn one, Hógar. Be careful." Hógar turned back to the sparring as Dristan left.

Eimear was toying with her two sparring partners. Light taps of her quarterstaff served to unbalance, offset, disrupt, and injure a little. Her mind was possibly elsewhere because her opponents had suffered from minimal contact.

Hógar chortled as one of the warrior's clubs managed a rare contact with Eimear's wrist. She glanced at him as he did, eyes narrowing, causing him to avert his gaze.

Hógar's goal was to get her to search inwards—to spread wings as Crea would and fly into her mind and heart. He felt sure the young woman needed healing. Whether she knew it herself was in question.

A sudden crack signalled that Eimear's play fighting had taken a menacing turn. She masked the change in her face with a twirling staff. One of the gruagachs was down, cradling his arm; the other was backing away. Both knew well enough not to make a sound.

"Hold up," shouted Hógar, putting as much authority in his voice as he could. Eimear did not heed him and began to move forward in attack, staff cracking suddenly off the standing gruagach's furred shin. He grunted and fell.

"Eimear, hold up," Hógar roared, climbing over the fence and walking towards her, fists clenched tightly. As he leaned to pick up a fallen club, his hat fell into his hand, and he threw it towards the girl. Eimear lashed out with her staff again, this time across the gruagach's knee. He gasped loudly in pain. Hógar heard a hiss of delight escape from the girl. He lifted his club and walked towards her. "Eimear, you're going to be running for many days if you don't..." He stopped when he saw her face.

It was cold. As were her eyes. Eimear's pupils faded behind a white fog.

"Eimear," he said, afraid. She stalked towards him, raising her staff, and started to twirl it menacingly.

"Eimear. What are you doing?" he asked, raising the club before him.

"You laughed at me getting hit."

"I did not laugh. I enjoy you being challenged."

"Ah, is that so?" She continued towards him, constantly twirling the staff. Hógar retreated until his back touched the paddock fence.

"Of course, that's so." He hawked and spat, a strange taste in his mouth.

"And me being challenged makes you laugh?" She stood before him, legs planted, showing off with the stick.

"I didn't laugh, child. I was just enjoying the exchange."

"You are calling me a liar."

"Eimear. You're goading me for a row and acting like a child. I thought you'd grown out of this."

"I don't care what you think I have grown out of."

"You're angry. Fine. Be angry. But don't act the little shite with me, girl."

"Or what?" She tossed the spinning staff in the air and caught it without so much as a glance in its direction.

"Eimear. Put it down and get a drink. That's enough."

"Or what, Hógar? What will you do? Try not to scream as I beat you?"

"Eimear... what are you doing?" He went to spit, but his mouth was too dry. He grasped hard on the club, which suddenly felt very light.

"What am I doing? I think I will do that thing we have both known I would do. How will you cheat your way out of this, do you think?"

Hógar felt the blood drain from his face. The other two warriors, who had been standing, mouths agape, limped off towards the settlement for help.

He lowered his club.

"This is how you repay my efforts, Eimear? These moods of yours are happening more and more frequently. Is this the way you want to be behaving? Can you not see how you need me the most?"

Flicking out the quarterstaff, she knocked the club from his grip.

"I do have needs, Hógar. But I do not feel that you truly understand them. I think it is time to show you."

Using her quarterstaff, she deftly broke his nose. Stumbling backwards, he shot a hand to the leaking break. Eimear's eyes glazed over as droplets of blood landed at his feet.

"You were useful, Hógar. But it was so, so long ago. Since then, you have become increasingly irritating with your trickery. Thinking I cannot see every possible action you can take? Every possible threat you can conceive. And you laugh. You laugh at me getting hurt. I am tired of this. I am tired of you."

"Eimear. Control yourself for the sake of the gods."

"What will they do to stop me?"

127

Another voice answered. "They do not care about you, Eimear. Hógar does."

Crea stood on the other side of the training yard, her bow in one hand, an arrow in the other.

Eimear sneered, causing Hógar to reach for the fallen club. Hardly recognising her, Hógar's bloody hands shook.

"Bird, have you been sitting on your shit heap watching me? Waiting to kill me as you did Barragh?"

"Eimear, I did not kill Barragh. The hoodoon did. If you cannot see that, you have lost whatever sanity you were clinging to. I will ask you once. Put down the staff and leave here, or I will use the bow."

"I wonder could I get over to you before you nock your arrow, Crea? Murderer," Eimear challenged.

Shaking her head slowly, Crea tutted. "You may surmise all you wish, pretty child; only deeds will end the need for speculation."

"Would you dispatch me then, Crea?"

Crea stiffened, and her mouth opened.

"Or will you have someone else do it, as you asked Hógar to?"

"That was a test, Eimear." Crea seemed uncertain.

"A test? Do you still mean to cover your true intentions?"

Hógar thought back to the dell, and his blood froze. Eimear had been listening.

"Child, you cannot comprehend my true intentions, and I will not explain them to you until you are in some way my equal."

"I understand." Eimear became a blur as she attacked, crossing the distance between them in a heartbeat. Hógar gasped as he tried to process what was happening. Crea brought her bow up to block Eimear's vicious staff strike, smashing her other fist into her face. Eimear landed on her back, stunned. Hógar ran club overhead and brought it down on the child's head.

***

The court of the Fand watched in silence as she leapt to her treetop throne. Hógar sat with Dristan, the gruagach representative. He was curious about why she summoned him. The child had raged before. Not to the same extent, no. But to be summoned before the Fand over it was an extra worry. After being brought before the scribe, Hógar had been forced to report Eimear's turn, in great detail, to the elders and then to the Fand herself, finally delivering his niece to the dungeon.

He had done his duty as well as he could. Yet as he considered Eimear sitting alone in the dark, he realised he had left a part of him down there with her.

Who is she to me? What is she to me? Why do I feel this way? Desolate.

He thought about those times he had found her hiding somewhere, teary eyed, thinking of Barragh, or the duillecháns, or her own world, and he knew the answer well enough. The child was his kin. She had been given to him to protect.

Across from him sat Crea. Alone. For her to be away from the portal dolmen for any length made everyone uneasy; however, they used the portal increasingly less often. The other two smallsky denizens, were not present. They would surely be watching the other two portals.

He caught Crea exchange a look with a broad-shouldered twarv and was puzzled. The exchange was

129

affectionate, almost intimate. Hógar rarely found twarvs to be anything except brutish. When she turned towards him and caught Hógar's gaze, he narrowed his eyes at her, and her cheeks coloured. He hawked and spat, grimacing when he saw the glob land on the marble floor. Glancing around, he was relieved to see no one seemed to have noticed. As he considered trying to wipe the glob with his foot, the Fand spoke.

"Fae kin, it has finally happened. The Fane has responded to my request for a meeting. He is willing to make plans with me. Plans to guide us to a new place in our history. A place of power and unity." Gasps echoed into the upper arches. "Such a thing has not happened in our history. At the next full turn, our horde will travel to the crease. We will meet the horde of the Fane and there, we will unite as one band. I intend to convince him that I am right in what I desire. What I crave."

She stood and grew taller as she did. Her long green hair spilt in ringlets down to her shoulders. Her face became feline, and her skin soft, charcoal grey.

"We will go, prepared to make war—not on our kin. There will be no battle with Aébhal or Cromm. They will fight alongside us. Our brethren. Our kin. I know this in my heart because they are from my very insides and have heard my heart beating.

"No, we will go to make war on our true enemies, and in doing so, we will unite and become strong. We will go to the land of Éire. From there, we will conquer the world of the human folk. I will lower the bridge and invite the forces of the Fane to cross to our side. It is my wish that the bridge will be left down."

Gasps and shrieks nearly lifted the roof.

Several settlement representatives stood to speak. Others sat brooding or whispering urgently into the ears of their compatriots. Hógar turned to watch the Fand. She was smiling broadly, arms held aloft towards the vaulted ceiling. She clapped her hands abruptly.

"Attend me. We must do another thing. Eimear, born of two worlds, is to come with us. The Fane has asked it. Though I do not know why, I know that the Fane is wise indeed. She will travel under my banner and protection, for I feel her destiny is at my side for this great meeting."

She paused for a moment, pink tongue licking around her fangs. Hógar felt his stomach knot.

"While we must still be on our guard for potential trickery. We have all learned that our hopes and reality seldom intertwine. We must, in fairness, consider the need for compromise. It is known to me that the Fane wishes to cast Eimear into the crease."

Hógar's mind reeled. To be cast into the crease was a source of terror for all the Fae. He could not bring himself to consider Eimear falling. He tried to focus on what the Fand was saying.

"We must consider that that is the extent of her role in this thing; to become a symbol. To be the offering I make that will see this agreement come to fruition.

"Seeing this mangblood attacking our people as she has done, I am increasingly inclined to consider it, at the least. Such a gesture would certainly improve the air of trust between the two sides." The Fand paused for a moment. "There has been so much conflict. Is it not right that there is peace here? Conquest and ambition have their place in any society. Yet, wisdom and vision allow us all a wider view, a chance to delay our need for constant bursts of gratification in this place. Consider our past and present. Think of our future. Two sides, no longer. One world. We are all from the same womb. Let us open a portal and turn our immense power to other worlds."

Crea stood. Most of the other would-be speakers had returned to their seats, so the Fand saw her immediately and narrowed her eyes. "When Crea smallsky denizen rises to speak, my curiosity demands that we attend to her input."

"My Fand. I am yours to command. I will act without question. Yet, I wish to present my point of view for your consideration if you would have it?"

"By all means. Continue."

Hógar noted a crease beside the Fand's eyes in place of the usual smoothness.

"The girl came to us as you bid. She has stayed here, though we never asked for her wishes. Hógar has been working with her, and in many ways, she has excelled. Yet, my Fand, as I have watched, I have seen a change in her. The draíocht seems to collect around her still. This place is ruining her, even though her heritage should be protecting her. It is not of her doing that she lies in the dungeon. She is losing her mind. I think, perhaps, that she came to us broken.

"When I hear you say that she is to be cast into the crease to appease the Fane who has never once laid eyes on her, it is cause for my deep discomfort. Can we not leave her back through the portal? Why was she brought here? To be sacrificed in honour of hate? No good will come of her death here. Should we not return her to her people for the time she has left, to fare as they do."

Silence descended on the court. Even Hógar, who stayed away from the palace and fancy places, knew that to question the Fand in public was folly.

The twarv stood and began to speak. Many observers' faces told the story of their shock.

"My Fand, I am Arthmael. I saw the child kill a hoodoon during the early days of her arrival. She was dangerous then. The child has been in training. Her skills have drawn draíocht in ways unseen in any land. Any who have laid eyes on her can see it is so. There is a perilous nature to the notion of bringing her to a place where tensions are so high. There may be a price to pay for it. I concur with the sentiment of the smallsky denizen."

The Fand's crease changed to a full sneer, lip curled in contempt.

"I wonder why it is," she said, "that a twarv and a smallsky denizen would plead for the life of a mangblood? Perhaps something about the merging of two separate races appeals to the two of you. Can it be, that your two sympathetic viewpoints might be rooted in familiarity? You think you are the only one who sees, Crea? You think me to be as half-witted as your people are reputed to be, Arthmael? No. Surely there can be nothing forbidden taking place right before all our eyes. The consequences would be something indeed, would they not?"

She turned to Hógar.

"What say you, Hógar? Is this girl a danger to the stability of our whole world? What training have you given her? I suspect that the collective sum of all the fighting knowledge ever possessed by the gruagachs would not educate a mighty warrior enough to pose such a threat to the realm, so I am curious to know why Crea suddenly frets. I do believe she will help change our realm for the betterment of us all. Either fighting by our side or dying for a greater cause."

Hógar sat, mouth agape. There was surely no correct response here except silence. He closed his mouth, and the Fand continued.

"I feel that I have lost focus on who best should be in this side's higher echelons of power. Perhaps I should give the duillecháns or the sídhe settlements a more favoured place at my side. It seems that the twarvs and gruagachs have lost their sense of place. As for one of the three smallsky denizens acting so rashly, that is another issue. One that might require a quest into the old world to find a replacement?"

Neither Crea nor Arthmael responded. Both sat back on their benches.

The Fand smiled, teeth clenched. "These matters will all wait, of course, until after the meeting at the crease. The mangblood will join us. Three representatives I have chosen to chaperone her. Crea, Arthmael, and Hógar. Should she become the cause of any problem, the three can accompany her, as she falls forever in the black depths of the crease."

A shudder passed through the audience.

"Now, is there anyone else who wishes to advise their Fand on matters of state?"

No one spoke. Falling into the crease was a nightmarish end.

"Alert your settlements. I will light the beacons when I need your warbands." She stood stiffly, cast a gaze across the court, and left.

HÓGAR

Is leor ó Mhór a dícheall.

You can only do your best.

As THE PREPARATIONS commenced, Hógar found it
easy to disappear into the hustle and bustle. Many
souls, drunk with single-minded loyalty, went about
their duties. Few of them focused a gaze on him, guards
included. People milled about the corridors, ignoring
him as he moved deeper into the palace.

Spotting a decorative suit of twarv armour, he took
the helm and put it under his arm, not stopping to see if
anyone saw him. He marched towards the steps leading
to the tunnels, the cells, and the stores.

As he moved to the quieter areas, the number of
workers in the halls decreased. Some gave him sidelong
glances, but he spoke to no one. Finally, he spotted
what he was looking for: an elderly manach woman
shuffling along in front of him. She had a strange odour,
which reminded him of something or somewhere. He
smiled as he remembered the manach's draíocht
included subversion of the senses.

"If I might stop you for a question?" he asked, keeping his voice low. He rarely came across manach's, so it was always jarring to see them unhooded: her large translucent eyes, clear liquid swirling gently inside them; her sagging ears drooping on each side of her pale round head; her tiny mouth tight-lipped, under her bulbous nose. Whatever manachs might be, they were a thing to behold, that was for sure. She bowed her head and went to pull up her hood.

"No need," Hógar said as he laid a hand on hers. "I won't be annoying you. Can you show me where this helm needs to go? The Fand wants it stored with her other precious trinkets." He chortled. "I don't want to be getting anyone to do jobs for me, so I said I'll take it there myself, wherever it is."

The manach had stopped walking, and he turned away from her stare.

"Who are you?" she said, barely louder than a whisper.

"I'm up for the gruagachs. Sent with the mangblood, Eimear. Hógar is the name. May as well be of use now that she's staying here."

"Are you trying to get to the cells?" she asked, her head swinging from side to side. Was she searching for someone to alert to his presence?

"No. I don't want to be anywhere near the mangblood bitch. She tried to kill me, last time I laid eyes on her. I tell you now, stay right clear of her."

She touched the helm with a spindly hand.

"What is this?"

"Can't be sure," he shrugged. He had done enough talking. The less said now, the better.

"Give it to me. I am going below."

136

"Can I go with you? They'll just send me running for something else if I return to the great hall."

"This is not the way these things happen. Who are you?"

"Look," he whispered as he checked the corridors on either side. "I have displeased the Fand twice now. If it happens again, she will have me cast into the crease. The Fand told me to bring this to her stores. If you help me, we'll be done in a flash. If you don't, I'll be falling. I told you already. My name is Hógar, and I'm just trying to stay out of trouble. Help me."

After a moment, the manach continued on her way. Hógar checked around him and followed. "You're a treasure," he said. "What's your name?"

"Pe." She whispered.

"Pe?"

"Pe."

"Thank you, Pe. I won't keep you."

After descending the chiselled steps and following a series of twisting, nondescript corridors, Pe pointed to an unguarded door in the torchlit gloom. She drew back her hood and scratched around one of her eyes. It was unsettling to see. The manachs needed no torches; as they lived most of their lives deep underground, their strange eyes had grown accustomed to the dark.

"There's more than one way to displease the Fand. I will have to tell the others you were down here, so I do not find myself party to any trouble." She turned to leave. "Have a care, Hógar. Though your lies are well meaning, your life could be forfeit." Saying which, she disappeared into the darkness.

The door ahead of him was nondescript.

Why are there no guards?

So close to the underground tunnel system that ran for miles around the palace, it was unusual to think there was no security protecting the Queen's precious commodities.

He smiled despite himself as an obvious answer struck him.

Who would dare steal from the Fand?

No-one. Not one singular soul. Except for Hógar.

Fool Hógar. All for a silly promise to a girl who tried to kill you.

Approaching the door slowly, he spotted it was slightly open, with hopeful torchlight reaching out from inside.

This is not wise, he thought checking the way back. He considered turning back and following the manach. It would be easy enough to find his way out. Picturing himself being flung from the longshore by a fathach, he nodded.

Time to go.

The sound of a raised voice stopped him.

The Fand.

Two halves of Hógar went to war. One half, urging him to run back to his settlement and the training paddock, away from this madness. The other made his eyebrows rise and his ears hot with curiosity.

There. Again. The Fand's voice escaped through the crack in the door.

If she is in danger…

Curiosity demanded that he move towards the door. He threw the torch on the ground nearby so that he wouldn't draw attention to himself and pressed his ear to the opening, but the voices were no clearer. They were a distance away. He pushed the door open slightly, trying to get a look at those speaking, but large shelves of dark wood blocked his view. The shelves were laden with boxes and artefacts, each resting on a label. He choked back a cough as a multitude of scents assaulted his nose and throat.

As the voices, two of them, rose and fell, he decided to push further into the room. They surely would have stopped if they had noticed him. He moved inside and left the door as he had found it.

The voices were coming from deep in the large store. He tried to make out recent signs of passing, but the pale stone floor was spotless. There were recently lit fatted torches on brackets along the other wall.

Hógar swallowed his rising anxiety. Staying low, he began to weave his way through the fortress of trinkets towards the voices.

"...all of this is for nought." The speaker was a male, his tone soothing.

"For nought?" asked the Fand. "You were the one with the vision. You were the one filling my head with prophetic nonsense. If you can't even promise she would fight on our side?"

"I never promised anything. You chose to believe in my visions. To claim they were your own. I have only ever spoken the truth. I can only say it so many ways. To destroy her as a token is folly. The draíocht that would go with her would leave this place starved."

"It would return soon enough."

"You do not know that, Doireann. You know very little."

"I have warned you. Be careful how you would speak to me." Her growl brought the hairs on Hógar's neck to standing.

The other voice growled back. "All I do, I do for your glory. I must speak to you as an equal, for us both to be clear."

"Yet you are not."

"I grow weary of this."

"*I* grow weary of *your* games," The Fand's voice had changed. It was a good bet that her form had changed too. The thump of his heart in his ears made it difficult to hear the hushed tones. "You insisted that she be brought here," the Fand continued. "You insisted it was the will of the draoí that she be brought here. It seems obvious that her purpose here is to be a catalyst. Nothing more."

"I will leave you to think on it," said the male. "Unless you decide to gobble me up and be done with all this?"

"How do you know I have not decided to do just that?"

"Because, Doireann, a full mouth means you wouldn't be able to talk. And we both know how much you love that. I will not be here for a time. I must watch him to make sure he is where we want him. As for Eimear, you have heard my view. You have heard my logic. I will not repeat myself anymore."

There was no sound except for a creature breathing heavily. Hógar held his breath and hoped his heartbeat wouldn't give him away. After a time, the breathing stopped, and he heard tiny footsteps moving through the store, the door opening and closing.

Sitting back against one of the stout shelves, he calmed himself and began to think.

***

Hógar went to the dungeon and found Eimear. She was back to herself, if somewhat sullen, sitting on a bench in the darkness. Stern iron bars stood upright between them.

"Am I here because I attacked you?" she asked. She appeared so young in the shadows. Helpless. Her training clothes, which were practical and well-worn in the light of midsun, were tattered, stinking rags here in the dungeon.

"No. You are here because the Fand wishes it," Hógar said, hands squeezing the bars. "I did not know what she wanted of you."

"What does she want of me?"

"To use you." His voice sounded as cold as the bars felt.

"Hógar. The rats, here in the cell with me, knew that." As if to illustrate a point, something skittered in the darkened corner behind her.

"She means to throw you into the crease if the Fane bids it, which he will. You will be an offering." His lip started to quiver.

Eimear shook her head. "It does not make sense to me. When we met first, she told me that she had seen me in a dream and that I would bring about a great change."

Hógar shrugged. "If you never did another thing, Eimear, you have done that already. The Fand has not been consistent in either her thoughts or her actions. It is like she is listening to voices that align with her when it is convenient for her. It is not the sign of a strong leader, but she has been plotting either way.

"She knows of the Fane's hatred for the mixing of races. She knows that he will accept the offering as a gift, and she will use it to curry favour with him. Perhaps even unite the sides, as she suggests. The Fand has been planning this for some time, I fear. Eimear, you are the peace offering."

"I am not afraid," Eimear whispered.

Hógar stood, trapped, at the cell door.

"Do you feel this place is corrupting you?" he asked.

"There has always been something wrong with me," she murmured, finger tracing along the stone walls.

"Oh. Is it worse the longer you stay? Or better." He searched her face. Hógar knew that now, more than ever, he needed to connect with her.

"I do not know. I feel like it is easier for me to do bad things." She stood to take a step towards him but stopped short of the bars.

"How does that make you feel, Eimear?"

"Curious," she shrugged.

Hógar shook his head. As always, when she talked like this, his thoughts went to changing the subject. This time, he did not.

"All of the things that you've seen here. All of the bad things. You were not the cause of any of them, child."

She stood silent in the darkness for several moments.

"I know." Her voice was flat when she spoke.

"You remember how we were working on you flying into your mind?" he asked.

"Yes."

"To gaze down on the valleys below and know them?" He nodded.

"I do. Yes," Eimear nodded back.

"To visit the deep dark caves and the highest peaks in equal measure?" He raised his eyebrows.

"Hógar. I was there. I remember," she barked, raising her eyebrows too. He bit back a smile.

"It is more important than ever, Eimear. Far more important." The smile faded as he took a deep breath.

"There exists in all creatures a desire to right themselves when they fall over. It is the same in our minds. You have fallen over in your thoughts at times and will need to right yourself."

She turned from him, kicked at something, and spun back to face him; teeth gritted.

"Why? Am I not to be cast into a hole so that I fall forever? Has the Fand not said as much?"

Hógar regarded her in the shadows. The child had become a beautiful young woman. She had tied her tousled brown hair on either side of her face. Her brown eyes were black pools in the shadow. though she scared him to his core, he had become very fond of her.

"Would you kill me?" he asked.

"Do you wish it?" She frowned.

"No. I mean, if you stood on this side of the cage— if you stood beside me. Would you... do you want to kill me?"

"No," she whispered. "Hógar. You are my only friend. What happened back on the sparring grounds ... it was not me. At least, it is not what I wanted. There is a part of me that craves, yearns, for slaughter. I cannot help it being there, but I had been getting much better at concealing it."

Hógar nodded grimly. "This place wants that side of you. It will draw it out of you while you are here."

143

Eimear went quiet.

"Eimear, I have had no one that I care for. Maybe that's why she paired me with you, not because I am related to you. I have no one who depends on me. No one who will mourn my passing."

"I will," Eimear said.

"Didn't you almost cause my passing quite recently, never mind mourning anything?" he huffed.

Eimear's face softened in the dark.

Hógar produced a key. "She will cast me into the crease for this, and I will fall forever. You must not let that happen. I will release you, but if she catches me, you must promise to kill me. I do not want to fall forever. I cannot imagine it. However, I care about you, Eimear. So, I am going to help you get home."

"I have no home," Eimear whispered, eyes wide.

"Well. I will return you back to your world, and you can build one."

Eimear moved to grasp the bars. Her hands came to rest just below his. "I care for you too, Hógar... when I'm not trying to kill you. I did not know my father. You have been as one to me." She paused and made a face. "I hope you understand me. Killing aside."

"We are agreed? Have you sworn it so?"

"I have, though I feel uneasy at the thought."

"Well. Stay uneasy for as long as you can." A thought struck him. "Wait. Hold on. You're not to do it unless she catches us. No Hógar killing until we're caught. With no escape. You understand? Will you swear to that, too?"

She stood back from the bars and dropped her hands to her sides. "Hógar. I promise I will not kill you until I have to, and then I promise to kill you."

Hógar's eyes narrowed as he processed her statement.

"I wonder has any other daughter said that to her father before." Before she could answer, he produced the scabbarded sword she had brought through the portal. Finding it in the Fand's treasure room had been no small feat. Whatever trust he had built for himself in the palace over several years was now a thing of the past.

Eimear leapt to the bars of the cage.

"Sword," she hissed, black pupils unnaturally large.

"Stand back. I will open this, and you can have it."

"I can have it? You will give it to me?" Her eyes narrowed into slits. His back suddenly felt itchy, a place that he would not easily reach to scratch.

"Yes. Move back."

Twisting the key, he stood back and held out the thing. She came out and took the sword from him, drawing it to inspect it. Hógar closed his eyes and waited for her to run him through. The sword might scratch the itch.

"You can open your eyes, you goat." Her voice sounded unusual. He did and saw she was smiling. It was the second time he had seen it, but where the first was malevolent and chilling, this was warm and beautiful. She sheathed her sword and buckled the belt around her slim waist.

"May I?" she said, suddenly standing awkwardly.

"May you what?"

"You know. Ehm. May I … embrace you?"

"Oh… Of course, Eimear," he said, straightening up and opening his arms to welcome her. Such a thing had never happened.

Eimear moved into him and wrapped her arms around him tightly. He did the same. She felt frail in his arms, and he felt hugely protective of this other-worlder the Fand had thrust into his life.

He had wanted to hold her when she wept over Barragh or when she had broken her wrist. He had wanted to hold her when that young gruagach had broken her heart with a few words. She had put on a brave face, but Hógar knew she had felt kicked in the heart. He had wanted to hold her when her blood had come, and she had no one to guide her. Kindly Imelda had told him it was coming soon, but he had been useless. He couldn't help, though that was what he wanted.

He had wanted to mind her and show her affection and love, but he did not know how. Love. In a life so devoid of it before her arrival, he realised now it had arrived the day she had.

"Come, Eimear. We can't have you fall so quickly back into your needy ways."

She stood back, her movements suddenly stiff. There were tears in her eyes.

"Hógar," she said. "Thank you for everything you have tried to do for me. And thank you for letting me embrace you. I have not had one before. I had always imagined it would be very nice, and it was."

Hógar's eyes were watering too.

"You have had a hard life, Eimear. Let us hope that this very moment is the change. An embrace and a smile have marked the change. We will see it done."

He watched her mind work behind her passive face. A gentle nod signalled her agreement. He smiled at her.

"Come. Let us be very quick and very quiet. It will not be an easy thing."

"Will Crea not see us?"

"She will, Eimear. Let's see if the gods favour our plan."

He turned to walk. After a few steps, she spoke quietly, as if explaining to someone.

"No. He is like my father."

"What?" said Hógar.

"Nothing. I am just getting used to saying it."

"Oh," said Hógar, eyes narrowed. She was not convincing. Her hand rested on the hilt of her sword. "Oh," he said again and turned his suddenly exposed feeling back to her to begin their escape.

EIMEAR

*Chonaic mé cheana thú, arsa an
cat leis an mbainne te.*

I saw you before, the cat said to
the warm milk.

EIMEAR FOLLOWED HÓGAR quietly as they marched on
the forest path. The butt of his spear made a satisfying
thump on the packed forest floor. They had evaded
pursuit—for now at least, and Eimear could nearly feel
a sense of contentment. The only barrier to contentment
was the hairs on the back of her neck standing tall—
someone was watching them. Her hand rested on
Sword as it often did, though she knew, at least, she felt
that the watcher was not malevolent. She chided
herself, knowing that she could never understand the
intentions of whoever was watching.

"Hógar?"

He hawked and spat. "Yes, Eimear?"

"Have you ever felt that someone, or something, was watching you? From afar, I mean?"

The question caused him to shoot her a puzzled look.

"No. Why? Have you?"

"Yes."

"Why didn't you tell me before now?"

She shrugged. It seemed obvious. "We were not so close then as we have become now."

He broke into a grin. "I suppose. Do you feel like they're watching us now?"

"Not us, Hógar. Me. And yes. I feel like they are."

He slowed a bit and threw glances in all directions, hand tightening on his spear. "Are you jesting? I cannot tell."

"No. I do not know how I know, but I know. Someone is watching me, as they have since the day I arrived."

Hógar stopped. "How do you know this? In which direction are they? Are you sure someone is there?"

"No," Eimear admitted. "I am not sure of anything."

He tutted loudly and wrung the neck of his spear.

"Then it's probably best if we keep walking and leave things like that to your imagination?"

"It's not my imagination."

"If you say so," he said, setting off again, this time with a longer stride to quicken the pace.

"Hógar. I am not making it up. I feel it."

He hawked and spat. "Perhaps it's just that you need to pass wind. I get strange feelings when I hold it in as well."

149

Trees surrounded them, squat red-leaved trees with gnarled, ancient trunks closed in around them as they went. If it was difficult to see beyond the wall, she felt sure it would be equally difficult to see into where they were walking. Yet, the feeling remained.

She shrugged again and continued behind Hógar.

Was it a creature? One of the Fae? At times she hoped beyond hope that one of her duillechán friends had come from Crúach to watch over her from a nearby haze. At times it filled her with a sense of hope. Over time, when none of them ever came to see her, her hope faded.

It was a mystery she did not feel she could solve.

She followed Hógar, focusing on his pack-laden back.

Will you not cut him?

Never.

Why do you resist me? Why must you hold me back?

What else can I do?

Use me.

To what end?

To find out why we are this way. We have never had answers—only more questions.

They are trying to help me. I cannot dismiss their efforts for mindless violence.

You feel that I am mindless? Have I not served you loyally?

There are times when you help me, and there are times when you make it harder for me.

150

What am I to you?

You are my sword.

What are you?

I am a girl of two worlds who has not found her way.

What if I am the way?

Violence?

I am not violence. I am a sword. What are you? Why do you need me?

I am... I feel...

You feel what?

Anger.

Anger?

Rage.

Fury?

Yes.

Controlling your fury is what makes it hard. Not I.

Perhaps. Yet you do not offer answers either. You offer only more questions.

Indeed. Here is another. What is it you desire?

I do not know.

Yes, you do. You want me to make the music with you. Staves and practice swords cannot make it as we can together.

I do. We will.

When?

You never have to wait too long.

I will wait. For now.

You are my weapon. That is all. You can only do as I wish.

Sword did not respond.

You will do as I wish, Sword.

For now.

Eimear moved her hand from the hilt.

"Are you well?" said Hógar, who had stopped to check on her. His face was strange.

"I am well, Hógar." She tried to soften her own face, when she realised that she wore a scowl.

He nodded. "We must move quickly from here—fewer trees. Your watcher will be delighted. Are you happy enough?"

"For now," said Eimear.

He hawked loudly and spat into the branches of a nearby tree, nodded to her, and they set off at a trot.

***

After hours on the go, they stopped to rest.

Eimear grunted as she tried to make herself comfortable. The knotted ground underneath was insistent on her feeling its knuckles. It had been a while since she had to endure sleeping outside like this. The prison cell had been wretched, but there was something wonderful about being in such a dark place for a while. It calmed her mind, and she slept deeply there.

Here, it was a tree being stubborn in not wanting her to sleep at all. Sighing, she sat up and surveyed the area.

Hógar was in a heap of snores and grunts at the foot of a vast rowan tree. A rasping fart leapt from him to greet her, and she wrinkled her nose.

Flat meadowland had disappeared to become long rolling foothills. The mountains were close, and the land around them was more challenging terrain than they had passed.

As she searched for a more suitable place to find comfort, the tingle in her neck started. The watcher was back. Eimear searched the distance: hills and small woodland areas, boulder formations and the banks of a nearby river.

As always, she felt no fear. Instead, the ever-growing curiosity urged her to search a little further, a little longer. Maybe this time, she might be able to see who it was who had been watching for many years.

As often she would do, she raised her hand to wave. Sometimes it would make the feeling disappear, and others not. Eimear walked to the top of the nearest hill. As she did, she glanced at Sword, lying on her pack. It never spoke when the watcher was around. It could stay where it was.

TWARV

*Is fada an bóthar nach bhfuil
casadh ann.*

It's a long road that has no
turning.

ARTHMAEL STOOD ON the trail, stroking his beard, and
waited for the mangblood child and the gruagach
donkey: potentially, to become his new charges. Even
after the child's admission that she intended to kill him.
No wisdom in it, nor good sense neither. Just his love,
following her heart. Hard to argue, he supposed. She
had chosen him of all the faces on their side. He had
never really figured out why. A simple and plain-
hearted twarv he was. That was the brunt of it. All she
had to do was ask. Yes, was the answer. Yes.

The Fand knew. Did it matter? Relations between
the races were beyond frowned upon. They were

forbidden. When it happened, the punishment was always final. For Crea and him to walk that road could only lead to one end. Yet they had. They had fallen in love over many years; the attraction had been irresistible. No wisdom in that, nor good sense neither.

Working against the Fand's wishes meant death. But falling in love with the smallsky denizen did too. The two roads ended in the same place, and they had chosen both. He checked through a crack in the copse towards the distant peaks for her. It was unlikely she could see him here. But she knew where he was. And she loved him.

He watched them as they approached. The two made no sound upon arrival. Though impressed, Arthmael gave them his meanest look. That should keep them honest. Hógar's spear came up defensively.

"I would talk to you both," he said to them.

"Arthmael, is it?" asked the gruagach. "Have you been sent to stop us?"

Arthmael noticed the mangblood cur reach for the sword she once again carried. He drew back his lips in a snarl.

"Call off your hound, Hógar," he said. "I've been sent, yes, but not by the Fand."

Hógar lowered his spear and raised a hand to signal the girl to stop drawing her blade. She did not heed him.

"Crea sent me," said Arthmael. "To help you both. Hoodoons fill the Forests and outlands. More than we knew existed. Something has happened to drive them from the marshes. Crea feels that the Fane's draíocht might be the cause. Hógar, tell the bitch to put her sword away, or I will knock her down again."

The gruagach turned to face the mangblood. His hands went to her shoulders, and he whispered urgently to her. She stared at Arthmael all the time, and it became challenging for him to maintain his meanest face. There was something about the hunger in her eyes that unnerved him. He could still remember her defiling the hoodoon she had killed when they met. She was a monster.

Though her eyes had become feverish, Eimear became focused on whatever Hógar was saying to her. She nodded, putting her sword into the well-worn scabbard. Arthmael was shocked to see them embrace. Not as lovers. Hógar held her gently as a father would hold a child with a hurt.

Hógar turned back. The mangblood's head bowed, and she stepped back.

"Why are Crea and you helping us? And what is your name?"

"I am Arthmael. Crea has decided to help you because she feels the cause is just."

"And you? Do you feel it is just?"

"It remains to be seen. I know only one single truth concerning this matter. Either by her hand, her actions, or through our affiliation with her, this girl will cause all our deaths." Arthmael took a deep breath.

"The Fand's hunt will set off the moment they miss the mangblood. They are faster than we are, so we must cover a fair old distance before that happens. Crea will know when they leave. I would have you know that neither of us will raise a hand against our people over this child. But I have promised to protect you from whatever else hinders your escape. We are heading for the portal dolmen. Let us go."

Arthmael led the way. He knew many of the trails through the Stolen Forest well enough. Tasked with forestry and hunting, the twarvs were ramblers; Arthmael was a principal figure among them. His neck felt almost itchy with the mangblood walking behind him, especially after she whispered to her sword when Hógar made water behind a tree. Crea and Hógar seemed convinced the child could be saved once back in her world. Arthmael knew it was too late. She had already been a monster on the day they had fought the hoodoons. Now she was a monster more ruined by draíocht—a monster who wanted to kill Crea.

A thought struck him that made him slow his pace. *I'll have to kill her*. He could deal with Hógar after. As a well-trained Gruagach, Hógar would be a formidable opponent; likely, he would kill Arthmael. If not Hógar, the Fand would surely execute him for disobeying her. But Crea would live. How had he not seen it before? They did not both have to survive this, just Crea. Her heart would be broken, yes, but she would live. A wave of relief passed over him—a sudden sense of calm.

He started to formulate a plan. If he spun suddenly and crashed into the gruagach, he could have his spear through her belly before she could react. After that, he could try and convince Hógar or fight him if there was no choice. He offhandedly glanced to his left as if checking for a sound, trying to catch the girl in his peripheral vision. He could see Hógar walking behind him but could not see the girl. He would need to know her exact position in advance of his attack. If she had killed a hoodoon, she was dangerous. Deadly. He needed to be deadlier. After a few minutes of trying to spot her innocuously, Arthmael was perplexed. He could not correctly identify her position.

His answer came accompanied by his gasp. In the branches of a tree up ahead sat the girl looking down at him.

"We are not likely to be friends if you plan to kill me as we walk, Arthmael," she said. "Or worse, while I sleep?" She had not drawn her sword.

Hógar seemed as surprised as he was to see her up there. "What are you doing in a tree? Come down. Arthmael does not plan to kill you," Hógar said, a strain in his voice.

Eimear leapt down from the tree, landing without a sound. "My mistake," she said.

As she walked past Arthmael, she stared deep into his eyes. Her pupils were specks nearly lost in the brown.

"Shame upon me for even thinking such a thing," she said. Arthmael swallowed. Her gaze bore into him as she had returned to her place behind Hógar.

She is a monster.

***

Crea landed before them near the River Gaoth. Arthmael had kept them from the traditional points of crossing. Though the river was swollen, it was slow moving, and they could cross using a simple raft that he had almost finished constructing. Arthmael had hastily lashed it together, but for most other races, it would be considered a fine vessel. It would likely not keep them dry but would shuttle them across. He could tell from Crea's face that she was anxious.

"Arthmael, Hógar, Eimear. I am pleased you have made it to the river without difficulty."

Arthmael stole a glance at the mangblood. She was staring at him. He flinched and looked back at Crea. Unease weighed heavily on him, but she hadn't realised.

"You seem bothered, Crea. Have they sent the hunt?"

"Yes," she said. "But there is more. The Fand is accompanying them with a warband of many races. It seems she wishes to draw many eyes upon us."

Arthmael feared as much. The Fand always did relish an opportunity.

Crea continued, "I am also torn between my duty at the portal dolmen and our pursuit. Hoodoons surround us. They have kept to the shelter of forests and divided into packs. They have never acted in such a way in my memory. When they hunt, it is and has been groups of three. Yet now, they are acting as a collective. Someone is directing them."

"How many?" Hógar asked.

"As far as I can tell for now, all of them."

"I do not understand," said Arthmael. The most he had seen in his life had been the day when Eimear, Crea and himself had last been together.

"There are hundreds. Perhaps thousands."

Arthmael mouthed the word. Thousands. So many of the creatures would be able to destroy this side and maybe the other if the way was open. His mind boggled. Thousands?

"Someone has found a way to control them. It is beyond my ken. They have always been considered little more than savage creatures of opportunity.

159

Perhaps there is a way for us to use this situation to our advantage," continued Crea. "The Fand needs to be made aware of the hoodoon infestation. And the infestation needs to be dealt with. The creatures will have surrounded us soon. If they do, we are finished. The Fand's hunt will surely destroy the hoodoons if they discover them. We must make the Fand aware of our presence here."

"How?" Hógar said. "Can you fly to them and tell her."

"No," said Crea. "No. I suspect I have fallen far out of favour and have a deal further to fall if the Fand catches me. We must attract her with a powerful show of draíocht."

Draíocht did indeed bathe Crea, but Arthmael did not know how her power might manifest itself.

"Your smile might do the trick," he said, forgetting himself.

Hógar pretended not to have heard. The child raised her eyebrows. Crea flashed a grin at him, and Arthmael felt a smile creep across his face.

He thought of their meeting; him wandering into a cave where she had gone to be in darkness. Her fear that he would tell anyone that she was not at her post, watching the portal and the Fandside. He had made a promise to her then as he had stared at her in the shadows. A promise with one condition: that he could sit with her the next time she went to the dark.

He shrugged at her. "I don't suppose it matters much that they know about our true feelings now."

"I knew already," the gruagach said with a brief shrug.

"So did I," Eimear said, nodding.

Arthmael smarted. Walking over beside him, Crea leaned down and kissed him. He didn't care who knew. There was life and death in her kiss: bliss and agony—made more so by the forbidden nature of such a love. It didn't matter anymore. Forbidden meant nothing to such feelings. Forbidden was swept aside like a twig in a spring flood by such feelings. Neither words nor thoughts could encapsulate them—no place vast enough, no crease deep enough.

Crea moved away; he smiled once more. He could not help but look at the other two to gauge their reaction. Hógar had moved away and was rummaging through his pack. Eimear stood watching with a strange look on her face and tears in her eyes. Arthmael did not understand, nor did he want to.

"My smile notwithstanding, we will need a feat of truly dazzling draíocht."

"How?" Arthmael said.

"Her," said Crea, looking at the child.

Arthmael looked at Eimear, then back at Crea.

Hógar hawked loudly and spat. "What would you have her do?"

"I have been watching you over your years here, Eimear."

"You have. But you are not the watcher. I think I would know."

Though the others might not have realised, Arthmael could sense Crea's confusion. He knew her well enough to read the tiny changes in her perfect face.

"I am not the watcher?" Crea asked.

"Never mind. Continue, please?"

"I have watched you, Eimear. At times, when I should have been watching the portal dolmen, or the longest shore, or for the Fand's safety, I watched you from my perch. I could not help myself. I have seen something happen that no one here has seen before. You have attracted such draíocht that it dwindles in parts of this world. It has gathered around you as if the draoí themselves returned to watch you practice. Few in any of the worlds have had such an effect, none without a lifetime passing. Something has happened with you, Eimear. Something is happening. Something difficult to fathom. Do you feel it?"

"Feel what?" Eimear asked quietly, clearly alert.

Crea moved quicker than a blur. The rock she threw at Eimear moved quicker again. Eimear took it from the air before her as if it was stationary. Crea threw another and another. Barely moving, Eimear dealt with them with ease.

"Do you feel it?"

"I feel as I always do."

Crea attacked again using her bow and an arrow. Before Arthmael or Hógar could gasp, the child had taken the arrow from the air. There were no more feared warriors on either side than the smallsky denizens, other-worlders without peers with their bows. Arthmael's shock made his head shake.

"What do you always feel, child?" Crea asked, outwardly calm. Arthmael wondered what she was really thinking.

"I feel that I can do what I please," Eimear answered, "but I stop myself to protect those around me."

"From what?" As she asked, she loosed three arrows at the child; so quickly that Arthmael could only be sure by the rattled twang of the bowstring. When he looked to see how Eimear had fared, she was not there. Crea closed her eyes, head bowed, with a smile.

"From me," Eimear said, appearing from behind the smallsky denizen.

Arthmael gasped.

How?

There had been no sight nor sound to mark her movement.

"Eimear," Crea asked without opening her eyes. "How easy would it be for you to kill us all?"

"Hógar and the twarv pose no threat. You move well, but your bow would not protect you from Sword."

"Eimear, can you leap across the river?"

The girl took a moment to judge. Arthmael reckoned the river a furlong wide or thereabouts. He had seen Aébhal leap over the crease once. A longer distance perhaps, yet Aébhal was surely the most favoured by draíocht that the Fae world had known.

"I don't know. I have never thought to do such a thing."

"Try it."

"How?"

"Leap, Eimear. Leap and trust the draíocht to lift you."

Eimear stroked the hilt of her sword for a moment. Arthmael saw her nod almost imperceptibly. He looked at the sword too. The weapon was a dark part of her. A dark part indeed.

She turned to Hógar, eyebrows raised.

"What do you think?" she asked him.

"That would be something to see," he said, shrugging. "But it's probably best if you start with something smaller."

163

While looking at the distant riverbank, she shook her head slowly.

"I don't see how I can make it across. I cannot swim. So if I don't..."

Crea went to stand beside her.

"I can fetch you from the river."

"Why should I trust you?"

Arthmael suddenly saw Eimear for what she was. A child. A scared child.

"She can be trusted, child. You can already sense that yourself. Surely?" he said. He threw his spear onto the ground and opened his hands. "You're the one we should all be worried about."

Eimear stared across the water once again for several moments. She was considering.

"You will not see if you do not try."

Arthmael realised he was holding his breath. He wanted the girl to try. He also realised that he wanted her to succeed.

Apparently, Hógar did too.

"I think you can do it, Eimear," he said, voice thick with pride. Eimear turned towards him, and her face softened. Arthmael felt a warmth from her towards the gruagach.

Strange ways in strange days.

"I will try for you, Hógar," she said, her voice almost a whisper.

As she turned towards the river, Arthmael had a thought.

"Child, leave the weapon aside," he said. "It may hinder your efforts."

There was a cold light in her eyes when she turned to him.

"You are transparent in your efforts," she stretched her neck from one side to the other. "You do not need to fear Sword unless you plan to try and kill me as you plotted to in the forest."

Arthmael felt a hot hand of shame grasping at his neck. Crea gazed across at him with loving eyes, but she would not approve. He would need to explain to her and felt anxious that it would have to wait.

The girl leapt. His jaw dropped. As he watched, she landed on the far side of the river, turned to them and waved. Hógar burst into applause and whooped loudly. Crea smiled, nodding to the two.

"Come across when you can," she said and flew off to speak to the child.

Hógar clapped Arthmael on the back.

"She is something special, isn't she?"

"You are not aggrieved that I was thinking of killing her?"

"Arthmael, you could not harm her if you had the neck of a bullock and a month to plan it. I am not aggrieved because she was never in danger from you. Come. Get me across to her."

Arthmael shook his head. Events felt increasingly like the makings of a saga, yet he felt no different. The girl was extraordinary, to be sure, but that did not make being in her company any less dangerous.

Shaking his head once more, Arthmael dragged the hastily lashed raft onto the river. He pointed to Hógar, who had retrieved his gear.

"Cut two straight branches. We will use them to paddle across."

Dropping his pack and spear, Hógar went in search of two suitable branches. As he did so, Arthmael pushed the small raft onto the river and checked it for worthiness. It held together well, as he knew that it would. Across the river, the two were talking. Heads bowed together as if sharing secrets. Arthmael put his pack and spear on the raft and checked Hógar's progress. The gruagach's search had brought him into the trees. As Arthmael waited, he heard horns in the distance. Crea had been right about Eimear's draíocht. The hunt was upon them.

"Hógar," he called. Turning, he thought to call Crea. However, if the hunt were close their spears would knock her if she flew nearby. *No. Leave her safe on that side.*

"Hógar," he called again, moving into the treeline to look for the gruagach. His breath caught in his throat. Three hoodoons were sitting around Hógar's body, eating various parts of him. He glimpsed a movement to his left. There were more than three. The others were moving towards him through the white-barked trees. Arthmael turned to find one of the black-eyed creatures blocking his path. He tried to scream, but the creature lashed out at his chest, knocking him backwards. Wind whooshed from his lungs. It leapt to attack his neck, but he caught the creature's wrists and flung it aside. Arthmael's head spun as he tried to catch his breath. As he got to his knees, another hoodoon landed on his back, talons clawing. He jumped backwards against a tree, throwing back his head to smash against the creature's maw. Its grip lessened, and he swung it in front of an oncoming attacker. Arthmael felt himself flagging. He righted himself, preparing for the next attack but was too slow and tired. He was knocked to his back once again. Two creatures stood, poised above him.

Arthmael was confused to see a spearhead burst from one of their chests. He shook his head to clear it as the other turned, and a hurled spear pinned it to a tree.

The hunt had arrived.

Arthmael staggered to his feet, trying to gulp in a deeper breath and made for the river, fully expecting to be knocked by hoodoon or spear. As he broke from the treeline, he saw that Crea and Eimear had marked the two males absent and were anxious. Crea saw him running and flew towards him.

"No, no," he gasped, unable to shout as he wanted. He leapt onto the raft and started paddling with his hands. As he watched Crea come to him, the battle spilt out of the trees, hoodoons and Fae clawing and cutting each other. A spear or two were hurled toward Crea and again, Arthmael tried to warn her back. Eimear shouted to him. He could just about make out the word Hógar. He waved her back.

"Run," he gasped. "Go."

Crea was over the river, dodging the increasing number of spears. She called breathlessly to him. "Go," he mouthed, knowing she would see.

Eimear suddenly drew her sword. She intended to leap back over to find Hógar. Arthmael paddled with all his might. He had to warn her. Too late. She leapt. This time, she fell short. Halfway across the river, Eimear landed and quickly started to drown. He looked to see if Crea could help. As he watched, a spear lanced into her leg. He howled as frustration washed over him.

Crea flew to where Eimear was struggling, another spear passing beneath her wing.

Arthmael paddled and kicked, urging the raft forward. Crea tried to pull Eimear from the water but could not manage, the panicking girl dragging her down. A spear hit the raft in front of him, almost knocking him off. He cursed and steadied himself. The girl went under. She grabbed Crea's foot with one hand. Crea was bleeding into the water and losing control, wings flapping frantically.

At last, Arthmael arrived beside them. He batted at the girl's arm to release Crea. As she did, Crea flew away towards the far bank. Arthmael, pulled Eimear onto the raft, where she spluttered and gagged. He saw that the sword was still in her hand and shook his head. She held onto it even when it was quickening her death. She curled into a ball, cradling it.

"Where is Hógar?" she gasped.

"Dead. Hoodoons."

Arthmael's arms were like frogspawn, but he ploughed them into the river to get to Crea on the other side.

SMALLSKY DENIZEN

Más olc maol is measa mullach.

If it's bad on the flat, it's worse
at the summit.

CREA LANDED HARD, gasping for air, cursing their luck. She had not seen Hógar emerge from the forest but had seen the numbers of Fae and hoodoons engaged in battle, so could imagine his fate. She lay on her back, gazing up at the distant mountains of the other side. The cold solitude of her perch sang to her. Scanning the smallsky around her she could not see the two other denizens, Cern or Dalla.

What does that matter? A Fae spear had wounded her. Fae from the Fandside. Her people had attacked her, by order of the Fand.

She heard the oncoming splashing and someone calling her name. Arthmael. She loved him to the tips of her wings. She no longer cared that it meant their end. To help the child was a cause that was just. They could not produce a child. It would never have been allowed, even in the strictest secrecy. Eimear would be their child. Her life and her safety would be a tribute to their love.

The splashing grew nearer and the calls more urgent. Crea gritted her teeth and rose to sitting, the now-broken spear lodged in her thigh. Her blood dribbled onto the yellowing grass beneath her. She noticed a streak of mud along her shin and tutted. Rolling to one side, she slowly got to her knees and then her feet before limping over to assist.

"Crea," Arthmael cried. "You are hurt. Oh, by the gods, let me see you. Do not fret. I will make you well once again."

"Arthmael. I am well enough. Let us get her into the trees."

Crea looked across at the far bank. There stood the Fand, just outside of the blanketing trees that stretched to her left and right. Her large, fanged mouth was open, panting. Tongue lolling and bloodied. She was watching Crea. She stood as tall as a fathach, grey fur covering her torso. In her taloned hand, she held the head of a hoodoon. One of her taloned feet stood on the creature's body.

"Come here," she commanded, her voice sounding in Crea's mind, as if she was standing an arm's length away.

"I will not, my Fand."

"Did you know the hoodoons had come?"

"I did not, my Fand. Someone has compelled them to act like this. There is treachery afoot."

"There is treachery all around me. Some as a result of my slipping vigilance and some the work of others, unknown to me. I never thought that you would be the culprit. I will cut your wings from you and cast you into the crease. There is no other way."

"She must be sent back to her world, my Fand. She is something the likes of which we have never seen, as if she is draoí herself. More perhaps. Whatever your plans for her might be, you cannot control her."

"I felt the draíocht from her as you meant me to. She is a curious one indeed. That said, where there is unity between the two sides, there is strength. Where there is division; where there is treachery, we must cut the poison from the wound."

Hoodoons were appearing in greater numbers around the Fand and her hunt.

"I must attend to these animals. I will come for you soon."

"I am sorry, my Fand."

"I am sorry too, Crea."

***

The girl was quiet as Arthmael tended to Crea's wound. Crea made sure not to cry out, though the pain was excruciating.

Eimear sat, staring into the fire that Arthmael lit when he deemed them far enough away from the battle at the River Gaoth. After they ate in silence, Arthmael lay down to sleep. Crea also felt the need, but not before talking with the child.

"Eimear, I am sad for your loss."

"It is all I have ever known. He said my smile and our embrace would mark the change. I think there will be no change unless…" she paused, lips pursed.

"Unless what, Eimear?"

"Unless I change things."

"What do you have in mind?"

"I think I have no home here. I have no one to care for or who cares for me. I think I have been brought as a plaything because they do not know what I am."

"Do you know what you are?"

"Yes, Crea. I do."

"What are you then, child?"

"I am rage."

"I do not understand. You are angry; I understand that entirely."

"No, Crea. I am rage. I am fury. Draíocht created me this way. Not by the people in this world or the world where I once lived. Don't you see it? You will die too. Arthmael will die. I will be left, and the draíocht will come to me. Sword has told me these truths, which I see to be true. I am rage."

"Sword… It has told you?" A cold shiver passed through Crea. "What do you mean to do?"

"I do not know—nothing for now. The draíocht did not let me jump back across the river. It will lead me to where I must be to do what it means me to do."

172

"Eimear, you are young. Your heart has been broken many times, and you feel angry about it. It has all been so unfair on you. Arthmael and I will get you to your world. You can learn to feel joy again. Learn to live again. You must not abandon hope."

The child looked at her, flames reflecting in her eyes.

"I have never felt joy, Crea." She hissed. "I will make music. I will make music, and all who hear it will know."

"You cannot let your rage control you, Eimear."

"I will not. I will let Sword control me. He knows. He understands what is needed."

She smiled then, and Crea's blood ran cold.

"I must sleep, Crea. I thank you for what you are trying to do. I hated you once. I wished to cut you in many ways. I have changed my mind. You are a creature of goodness, so Sword will not bite you."

She lay down and was soon snoring softly, the gentle breeze lifting a strand of her hair to dance gently over her ear. The child's words, troubling as they were, were not the main source of disquiet in Crea. There was something more. Something that Crea could not comprehend outright. A sense. She felt her gaze drift to the distant island in the smallsky on which the portal dolmen of the old world stood.

Angry heat from the firepit reddened her cheeks.

Crea watched the girl's hair dance. Perhaps the wind was trying to signal to Crea that Eimear was asleep.

"What does the wind want me to know?" she whispered.

***

The smell of food woke Crea. Eimear was sitting by the smouldering fire, eating some of the rabbit that Arthmael had roasted. He brought her over some of the meat on a stick and checked her wound, nodding approvingly.

"You are an ox," he said proudly, sitting back down to eat.

"And this is something that appeals to you?"

"Everything about you appeals to me," he said as he spat out bone and gristle. "Even the tough bits."

Eimear watched them. Her scabbarded sword nestled snugly in her lap.

"Did you sleep, Eimear?" asked Crea.

"Yes, thank you."

"Do you still intend to come with us to the portal?"

"I do. Though I would like to know what you intend to do once you get there."

Crea shot a sidelong glance at Arthmael.

"When you are safely through the portal, I will carry Arthmael to the mid-portal. We are going to go to the old world."

Arthmael's face was unreadable.

"Tell me about the old world. Hógar would rarely speak of it."

"The old world is as alien to here as the Fae realm was to you, Eimear. None but the Fane and the Fand are allowed to travel there, and none but the smallsky denizens have ever been allowed to travel back from there. Even for me, who was born there, it is a place steeped in mystery." She winced as pain lanced through her for a moment.

"One thing about the place and the gate there is that few who step through ever return. Time is not fixed as it is in the other worlds. One particular cruiticheán who stepped through came back before he had stepped through in the first place. The two versions of the same creature fought and killed each other in confusion."

Crea did not intend to return. She would go there with Arthmael, with his dashing smile and stout heart, and they would carve out a life together, whatever lay ahead.

"I hope you will both be happy," said Eimear, solemn face filled with sincerity.

Arthmael stopped eating and spoke slowly.

"It will be hard, I think. Or rather, there will be hardship. But we cannot be together here. So, yes, we will go to the wild place and tame it with our love and persistence. There are plants that grow in the desert— some animals that can live in the water and on the land. We will go and be a part of the land around us. That is where there is happiness. I only hope that the time there allows us to live together forever and a day. That is all I truly want."

The two listening considered his words. Crea loved his poetic soul. She agreed with his every word.

"It will be a great adventure," she said.

"For now," the twarv said as he stood to shake off the remnants of the food. "Let us go. If they catch us, we will look like some fools after all our talk."

Turning to the child, Crea tried to gauge her state of mind. It was far more likely that Eimear would make them look like fools. Their efforts would teeter between failure and success, depending largely on whether she would try to kill them. The young lady was beautiful in her solemn-eyed complexity. There was such innocence about her. She had been led from one miserable existence to another, experiencing little of the world of her own volition. Sighing, Crea stood and walked to her to extend a hand.

"Will you come with us to the portal, child?"

"I will. I do not have another place to go to."

"What about your own world? Where will you go there?"

"I could try and find Mirdhí and the others. Perhaps they will let me live with them."

"Will you leave the sword on this side, Eimear?" Crea felt uneasy asking about the weapon, avoiding looking at it directly.

"No," said Eimear, taking her hand and standing up. "I know better how to control my pangs, Crea. You do not need to fear me; or Sword."

"Well then," Arthmael said. "If you are going to keep it, you need to look after it more than I've seen you do. Did the gruagachs not teach you how to sharpen it or oil it? Even the scabbard looks in need of repair. May I?" he asked.

Eimear's face darkened a little. She seemed to consider the request very carefully. Without speaking, she lifted the sword slowly for him to take.

He drew it, examining the blade expertly. His thumb gently passed along the sharpened edge, and he jerked it back quickly. Crea noted his expression changing to one of unease, suspicion.

"I have never seen you sharpen this, Eimear. How is the blade so keen? And no rusting either?" A drop of his blood landed on the blade. Even a gentle touch had cut his thumb.

Eimear's face had softened. Was there a hint of pride in it? The child raised her chin as she accepted the sword back, sheathing it quickly.

"At least wipe my blood off it," Arthmael said.

Crea suddenly felt the urge to leave. "Let us just go and hope that that is the last blood that ever touches this strange blade."

Arthmael nodded, his bright eyes inspecting the child.

They broke camp and left it with barely a turned blade of grass to mark their presence. Crea tried to hide her limp. Arthmael would fuss if he realised how much pain she was in. She gritted her teeth and walked with them. Though it was more effort than flying, she wanted to be close to Arthmael. Her rock. Her true perch. Those piercing eyes that would try to find her in the mountains when the rest of the worlds busied themselves around him.

Though the hunt had crossed at the Bridge of Wild Horses, they were still surely a comfortable distance behind them. Crea judged that she and her two companions would accomplish their first objective. She wondered about their second.

She looked towards the distant island of mid-portal. She had been doing so more and more frequently of late—more since the arrival of Eimear than she had for an age before. It was calling her. To make it there meant two certainties: Cern and Dalla. Her brother and sister would see her approach and confront them. Cern, responsible for portal security, would stop any of their attempts to pass through.

Would she try to kill them? Would they alarm Fane, Fand and Fae to their approach?

Yes. We are doomed. Crea did her best to suppress her increasing morosity.

***

As Crea was scouting behind, she heard the snarls of hoodoons and Arthmael's war cry from under the thickest trees, warning her hoodoons had ambushed the others. She scrambled back to them as quickly as she could manage, cursing herself for not seeing the attackers, though they had concealed themselves well before the attack. She had been focused on pursuit, as well as monitoring the portal dolmen.

Reaching the woods, she found an unusually still scene. The hoodoons had severely bloodied Arthmael. A circle of a dozen or more surrounded them. There were six on the ground already, which confused Crea. She had only heard the commotion moments prior. Two of those felled still lived and were groaning in pain.

The creatures circled Eimear, whose face was smooth; eyes clouded over, standing with a bloody sword by her side. Arthmael's spear was clean.

One of the creatures noticed Crea's return and growled a warning. As Crea reached for an arrow, the creature dropped to the packed earth below, as did those beside it. Crea gasped. She had only seen a blur. Arthmael issued a roar in challenge and attacked the hoodoon nearest him. Crea loosed two arrows as quickly as she could with any accuracy. She reached for a third arrow, but there were no longer any targets. All the creatures were lying on the ground. The eerie chorus of the injured hoodoons' howls was terrible. Eimear's eyes had disappeared behind a veil of white except for two tiny black dots. Then she closed them fully. She walked among the hoodoons, drawing her blade across their bodies to elicit further cries. Crea could make out the sad tune that Eimear hummed once again, and her blood froze.

One of the creatures tried to defend itself from further suffering with tooth and claw. Eimear caught it by the scruff of its neck and dragged it behind her as she went. Her voice, humming from behind bared teeth, rose in intensity. Her shape had changed. It was difficult to look at anything except her sword, even though it was plain to look at.

Arthmael turned to Crea, open-mouthed, then back to stare in disbelief at the girl. Crea knew what he was thinking. He had voiced his thoughts enough to her. Crea saw her then and knew what he had often said was true.

She is a monster.

FANE

*Níor chaill fear an mhisnigh
riamh é.*

The man of courage never lost
it.

THE FANE, FERRAGH, sat drinking in his great hall—the
mead going straight to his head. It was too sweet for
him after so much meat. He wiped a belch away from
his mouth. The wet lacey sleeve got caught on his lip,
and he spat it out. His oaken throne complained loudly
at the jerking movement, and he rested back against the
stout backboard.

"I will have grape wine," he said to the young sídhe
girl. "No more mead."

He sighed and closed his eyes briefly as sleep tugged
at his other sleeve.

"My Fane," Aébhal said, standing at the edge of the furthest tables.

"Aébhal," he said. The giant seemed particularly animated, even at a glance. "Come and join the festivities. Girl," he hailed. "A fathach-sized mug for the red-skinned fellow."

Perhaps he would join this time. There was always more mead. Ferragh watched the sídhe servant hustle to prepare the drink. He eyed her rump in her skirts, and his lip twitched. No twitch from anywhere below. Time caught up with all.

"My Fane," Aébhal said. "We are preparing to leave and could use your leadership and renowned impetus."

Ferragh grimaced inwardly. Had his son stopped just short of saying impotence? *Can he read my thoughts?* He hid the surprise that tried to break out on his face. No. Surely, he was being paranoid, which was unlike him. Ferragh Fane was, among many other things, sure of his stead. He knew his place well. His son, however, still had lessons in that area.

Aébhal's ambition and increasing impertinence were galling. Still, he would surely remember his place as a subject, as all should on the Faneside. Ferragh was not a ruler to be taken for granted. If his son had forgotten, he would need to remedy it.

Not yet. Let's see what he is up to.

The Fane allowed the sleep to drag at his eyelids a little. As Aébhal grew inexplicably stronger every day, it seemed best sense for Ferragh to appear at his weakest. He needed Aébhal to continue to underestimate him.

He regarded his red-skinned offspring. The draíocht that continued to gather around him had swollen once more. Ferragh had asked Dalla smallsky denizen to watch the prince's movements to see if they could deduce what had caused the recent, rapid growth in power. She had not even been able to keep track of his whereabouts, not to mind his undertakings. What was worse was that Aébhal had a look in his eyes, a look of arrogance, of insight. Whatever plans Aébhal had devised were serving him well.

Yawning theatrically, Ferragh feigned a look of utter disinterest.

"Ah, the exuberance of youth. A joy to behold at all. A treasure to see in one's most loyal kin."

The words caused a slight narrowing of Aébhal's eyes. *Treachery it is.* Ferragh was increasingly sure of it. Since Aébhal had arrived back from the other side, his manner had changed markedly. Whether the visit to the palace or his interaction with the mangblood was responsible, Ferragh could not fathom. For now.

"My Fane, it has taken you years to decide. Since you have decided, however, we must see it through." Aébhal's zeal was apparent.

"You are quite right," Ferragh said. "Send word to the settlements, Aébhal. It is time to leave. Gather the great horde of the Faneside so that the ground rumbles under its united march."

Aébhal nodded slowly but did not move.

"Was there something else you require?"

"The mangblood child, my Fane," Aébhal said, fangs gleaming.

Ferragh grimaced. The mere mention of the thing was sobering. Irritatingly so.

"What of it?"

"I have had word from my spies."

182

"And?"

"The creature has absconded … with Crea."

Ferragh stood, the stout table screeching indignantly as his belly pushed outward.

"What? What has the Fand done about this outrage?"

Aébhal's fist smashed onto a table, breaking jugs and plates alike. When he drew his hand back, black blood dripped from a self-inflicted cut. He raised his clawed hand to examine it. Ferragh watched as his son bit a flap of loose skin from a knuckle and spat it perilously close to the Fane's throne.

"Not nearly enough. She chased them with a hunt," Aébhal growled.

"Crea? Crea seeks to betray me too?"

"Too, my Fane?" Aébhal's head tilted a trace of blood still wet on his lips.

Ferragh's eyes narrowed.

"Too. Yes. And the mangblood child, Aébhal."

"Ah yes, of course."

"I need to know what is happening over there. It seems the Fand cannot properly control her subjects."

"Indeed so, my Fane. A true leader rules their subjects wisely but without allowing dissent. Perhaps I should leap over to the other side once again. To ensure the Fand attends to the task appropriately. She will not be pleased, but should you command me to do the thing, then of course, I would do your will, as is right."

Ferragh pursed his lips. He found it hard to care about the mangblood child. Perhaps, in his youth, such a thing would have caused him to rage. It was important to do what was expected of him, though–especially while he weeded out disloyalty. His thoughts strayed to mead.

"Not for now, Aébhal. We do not wish to raise tensions before the meeting of sides. I would have you act as my close advisor in these times. Cromm, I will require your presence at my side. I wish to know what your spies report. Until the mangblood is no more, I will not be able to feel at ease. Only then can we truly engage with what the Fand has suggested: a new world to be conquered and ruled in my name. The takings to be shared among the Fae kin to mark a new age of power. We will conquer a place ripe for the taking: Éire. Where is my wine girl?"

Aébhal bowed curtly and left. Ferragh called for the flag to be raised for Dalla as his hand reached for a nearby goblet. He needed to find out what she knew, where her loyalties lay. Relations with the three smallsky denizens had always been trying. Crea betraying the Fand was an ill omen indeed.

***

When Dalla arrived, Ferragh had the great hall cleared of guests and his table moved away. After the servants had finished and left, he turned to her.

As always, the sight of her amazed him. Her large yellow eyes framed by the short owl-like hair were unfathomable. Her rounded butterfly-like wings moving constantly behind her added a mystique. Reading her would be difficult for most, yet he was Ferragh, the Fane. None could easily hide from his probing gaze.

"Have you heard?" Ferragh asked.

"I have. Quite probably not all or near all the story. I know that Crea has left with the mangblood child."

"Do you know what her intention might be?"

"No, my Fane. How would I?"

How would you, indeed?

"If you were in her position, what would do?"

"I would not be in her position, my Fane."

Ferragh let out a chuckle. She was as aloof as ever. Whenever they had spoken, he enjoyed that side of her the most: no-nonsense, a succinct report and back to her duties.

"I will need you to be at your most candid. Strange things are happening around us, Dalla. You have prepared me for none of them. To be honest, I fear there is a side of me worrying that information is being kept from me deliberately. If I was to be at my most candid, I might propose a notion to you. The Fane has need of a new smallsky denizen. While she travels to the old world to obtain said services, perhaps I might join her to engage the services of another of your people in your stead?"

If Dalla felt shock or dismay, her face did not change to show it. She did not blink or swallow anxiously. Ferragh could not help but be impressed.

"I eagerly await your decision, my Fane," she said.

"Will you watch the other side for me?"

"I cannot."

"I command it."

"That does not change what is and what is not forbidden. In the same way, the mixing of races is forbidden. Your subjects visiting the old world is forbidden. I will obey your commands, my Fane, except when they breach the contract."

185

"Crea does not seem to have your commitment to the same."

"I am not Crea, and she is not me," said Dalla, slight colour rising in her cheeks at last.

Ferragh's gaze landed on the ebony blood left on the table by his son.

"Dalla, where has Aébhal been going?"

She pursed her lips.

"I do not know. He still manages to evade me. It is rarely for any length of time."

"Rarely?" Ferragh was getting tired of this. "Rarely?"

He walked to her, close enough that her alien scent filled his nostrils. He stared into her enormous eyes.

"What good are you to me when my need is so keen?" he hissed at her. "Is Cern so careless? Was Crea? I want you to find out. I do not care what you have to do. I also want you to watch the other side. I forbid you not to. Report to me on the subject regularly. I will meet your refusal with a level of finality to which you are unaccustomed."

She went to speak.

"Be silent, wasp," he growled, head starting to ache. "I suddenly find your company tiresome. Leave."

She turned abruptly and left the great hall.

Ferragh's mind raced. How had he become so blind? So out of touch? The great hall sat in a musty haze—leftovers on the benches and floor. Broken pottery lay in pieces, drowning in a mix of wine and mead. Jaded tapestries clung for their lives to the dilapidated wall, shedding plaster as if disrobing in disgust. A pile of weapons lay in a heap by the main entrance. Discarded by revellers in advance of merrymaking, forgotten upon leaving.

Where are my servants?

He shook his head. He had sent them away.

"Mura," he called. The sídhe head servant rushed to him. "Clean this filth. This place is a disgrace. I will cast you into the crease if it is not in order next time I check. How have you let it become so vile?"

Mura bowed her head and left to assemble the other servants.

Ferragh set his chin. Aébhal was correct, indeed. It was time to show this side his leadership and renowned impetus.

"I will bring order back to this place," said the Fane. He finished the contents of his goblet, stepped over a puddle of wine, and walked from the great hall.

***

Ferragh gazed out from the walls of his palace, and his heart sank in his chest. The warband had gathered already as if plans had been in place for months. It was the warband of the Fane in name only. Wherever his gaze landed, he saw more and more clues to the actual ownership of this campaign, if not necessarily the real intention behind it. There were marches from the hairless fir buí, the hump-backed cruiticheáns, the reptilian dragans, and the shrouded manachs. Ferragh's head shook slowly. All of those settlements had fallen out of his favour over many years. Indeed, he had forgotten the dragans even existed. And here they stood, all looking to Aébhal for orders. None looked to Ferragh. He, the only duillechán Fane in history, watched helplessly as the scene unfolded before him.

There were more fathachs here than he could count, each with unique and brilliantly coloured skin and armed with spears the size of flagpoles.

A steady stream of representatives queued to speak and be spoken to by Aébhal. Everyone in the valley could see him, standing tall atop the Whittling Mound. Aébhal's gaze met his. Ferragh feigned an approving smile. His son did not return it.

Dubhaltach cleared her throat behind Ferragh.

"What did you find out, Dubhaltach?"

The human-looking sídhe servant sniffed loudly. Her slow drawl, which normally amused Ferragh, was tinged with a venomous edge.

"You are correct in your suppositions. Aébhal has been busy making preparations. He has enlisted the help of all the settlements on this side, no exceptions, all under your banner."

A spark of hope ignited in Ferragh. "All of the settlements? All of them? Under my banner? How did this come to happen without my knowledge?" Perhaps his son really had worked tirelessly on his behalf, for the good of this side.

As I would have myself and did before him.

It was not the time for paranoia. It was the time for glory.

Dubhaltach shrugged. "We have been feasting for many years, my Fane. Aébhal never partook, though you urged him to join us."

Ferragh nodded. Aébhal had been sombre company all his life, never leaning towards merrymaking. He had busied himself with draíocht and its way. Asking always about the draoí themselves; seeking the eldest of the Fae to teach him; his thirst for knowledge on the subject: insatiable. Ferragh watched his son issue commands and listen to a stream of issues. Had he misjudged Aébhal's motivation? Perhaps betrayal was not his path. What did it matter if he disappeared? Perhaps it was solitude that Aébhal sought. What did it matter if he did not revel in the great hall? Ferragh could once again revel enough for the two of them after this campaign reached its end.

"I must admit to feeling a large sense of concern, my Fane. I worry about Aébhal's aspirations," said Dubhaltach, as if she had listened to Ferragh thinking. *Or have I been talking aloud?*

"Dubhaltach," he said patiently. "You said it yourself. Aébhal has united them under my banner and is merely getting a start on what I was bound to do myself. I must admit, his inclusion of the lesser favoured settlements is something of a jolt, but it had been on my mind to do the very same myself. Indeed, I recall telling you as much quite recently."

Dubhaltach said nothing. Ferragh knew that Dubhaltach was not as sharp as he once was. He was probably trying to recall.

"Where's that wine?" Ferragh muttered to himself.

"All of the serving staff are scouring the great hall, my Fane. I must say, it is a welcome event. And since you are out of the place, perhaps I could go through several matters of state that require your wisdom and keen eye."

"Yes, yes, Dubhaltach," said Ferragh. "You do not need to fuss. I will check on progress there, and you can tell me everything you want me to resolve once I have wet my whiskers a little."

Dubhaltach was apparently searching for words of gratitude as Ferragh moved past him. *Things are progressing as I planned.*

It was time for a drink to celebrate.

WATCHER

Béarfaidh bó éigin gamhain
éigin lá éigin.

Someday some cow will bear
some a calf.

THE WATCHER EXAMINED the harpoon points from his cross-legged position in the knee-high grass. He had sharpened them to perfection and nodded in appreciation of his work. He thought about naming the weapon, as warriors oft would do. Someone had named it *Greim Tapaidh* or some such nonsense. *Quick grab?* It galled him that they could not think of a more suitable moniker. Someday, he would give it a title worthy of the weapon's past and future deeds. The thought flitted away as it tended to.

Not today.

Catching a glimpse in a prong of where his short, black hair met his brown skin, he twisted the shaft slowly. His square jawline appeared on the blade. When he twisted again, the black and brown of his eyes came into view. He sat for a moment, with his eyes asking him questions as oft they would do. Questions that changed with each answer that he would provide.

Resting the ferocious weapon across his lap, he leaned back into the rock and stretched his legs out on the grass. He looked up along the visible length of the crease. The world never ceased to amaze him with its dynamic beauty. Yet, the impenetrable dark line that divided the world in two always drew his gaze. *Would my mind quiet if I fell there? Would it mean peace at last? Peace forever.*

A movement at the bottom of the hill caused him to look. Gurtle shuffled towards him, her head shaking as if she was struggling to hold in her news. The sight of her lifted him, as always, her skin as dark as his own. Streaks of white ran through her thick woolly hair.

"What is it you wish, Gurtle?" he called, standing into a stretch of his limbs.

Shuffling on towards him, she continued to shake her head. He bit back a smile. *Important news.* His stomach turned a little as his mind began catastrophising, and his smile disappeared.

Bad news.

Gurtle was panting when she reached him, wide nostrils flaring, her wrinkled face a mask of concern.

She peeked over her shoulder and leaned into him as he stood.

"A challenge," she whispered. "There is a challenger at the door of your tower, so there is."

Cromm felt his eyebrows rise. There had not been a challenger for an age. He put away the whetting stone and reached for his cloak.

"I have been too busy everywhere else," he said.

"What?"

"I was speaking to myself, Gurtle. I was thinking aloud. I have been neglecting my settlement while trying to achieve loftier goals."

"Hadn't I said it to you on many occasions, hadn't I?" She adjusted herself with a loud sigh. Her face was a picture of unhappy thoughts.

"We will not rush back, Gurtle. You do not need worry about that. I am happy enough for him... is it a him?"

"It is, so it is."

"Well then. He can wait. You deserve a chance to get your breath back, and I am in no mood for a fight. Perhaps by the time we get back, I might be more inclined towards it."

"You'll need to be, so you will. This one looks frightening."

"Gurtle, are you not frightened of everything?"

Her reddened face twisted into a scowl. "I'm not afraid of twisting your ear, so I'm not. Like I had to when you were a cheeky pup."

Putting the harpoon between his legs, he fastened his cloak pin. "You tell me how you used to twist my ear, Gurtle, but I can't recall you ever actually doing it. Tell me of my foe. Why is he so frightening, do you think?"

"The Hooded One. That's who it is. The Hooded One. Here. To fight you and maybe kill you."

"Gurtle. Who is the Hooded One?"

"Too busy off fiddling with the world, you've been. Too busy. The stories of the Hooded One are not new. He has been making his own name. He has been whispering promises across your lands. He has fought many ferocious warriors and bested them with ease."

"How have I not heard of him?" Cromm said as he started to walk in the direction of his settlement and his tower.

"What?"

"I was talking to myself once again. Wondering to myself how I do not know these things."

"You've been off whispering to that denizen, so you have. And off doing things in other places. Leaving me to do everything here. How do you think I'm supposed to manage?"

He looked at her when he heard a plaintive note in her voice. There were tears in her lavender-coloured eyes. Cromm stopped and rested the harpoon in the crook of his elbows so he could hold her shoulders.

"You have always managed. Everything. You are the real leader here, Gurtle. I did not mean for you to bear so much responsibility; however, I am not convinced that is the real problem here."

She sniffed loudly, thick lips tight.

"Gurtle. There will always be challengers. I will have to fight them and kill them. One day, one of them will kill me and take my place. It will not happen soon." He released her shoulders and took the harpoon in his hand. "I feel so strong. The draíocht comes to me. There are none who can equal me here."

194

"Well. I can worry about you anyway, so I can. Especially if you're up to things you shouldn't be up to?" The last word rose in query.

"You wouldn't want to know, Gurtle," he chided. "You're worried enough already."

"Oh, you mean hearted scut," she growled, curling her fingers.

He stopped himself from laughing when he heard the voice behind him.

"Cromm, I would speak with you. I have news."

He turned to face Dalla, who stood, face serene, twenty paces away.

He made his face hard, knowing that she had probably watched the interaction between Gurtle and him and that Dalla needed to see him without weakness.

"Gurtle, let him know I will be there shortly."

"Oh," she fussed. "I think you should just come with me now and never mind talking to that creature. She should be doing what she should be doing."

"Gurtle," he hissed. "Do as you are bid."

He could feel a cold glare from behind him, undoubtedly directed at the denizen. Gurtle's presence faded into the distance before he spoke.

"Speak, Dalla."

"It has begun. Aébhal is undertaking his plans. He has been going through midportal. It seems he took your advice. I suspect he has killed one of the Draoí, killed them and taken their power."

"I have often wondered about the possibility," Cromm said, his mind reeling. If Aébhal could do this, then he could too. He just needed a brute on which to test his theory. "His ambition will swell with his power. He will not be able to resist killing our father now."

195

"I have said it and will say it once more. He will be too much for you to control. You have made a mistake." She stood stiff-backed, frowning.

She doubts my scheming.

The smallsky denizen continued. "The warband of the Fane has gathered. Your visits to the outer settlements have proved successful, as you proposed. They have all sent warriors."

"All? Even the manachs?" He could not mask the surprise in his voice. He had sent out his warriors a week before. The manachs had been concerned about how he used them; their draíocht; to control the hoodoons to invade the Fandside. It mattered little now.

"All of them. I have never seen it done."

"What of the Fand and her mangblood pawn?" They both knew he had been watching her grow and of his fascination with her. Perhaps she did not realise the admiration that had been growing in equal measure. Her face gave nothing away.

"Crea has taken her from the palace. The Fand has followed with her hunt. The world has been shaken."

"Keep me informed. We have much work to do. But first, I must attend to matters here."

SMALLSKY DENIZEN

Is sleamhain í leac an tí mhóir.

The big house has a slippery
threshold.

THEY RESTED BY the banks of a fussing lake.
Cantankerous waves launched wet splashes into the
wind. It was not an ideal spot for them, but Crea could
go no further.

Arthmael was clearly preoccupied with Crea's
wound, watching her constantly with a look of growing
concern. She toyed with the idea of revealing the extent
of her pain but decided against it. His fussing was as
useful as the lakes.

Crea looked at Eimear. An admission of suffering might also bring about the change in the child. Crea had seen many wars, killers and killings, many who got lost in battle and committed terrible deeds. She had never seen anything or anyone like Eimear. It was also becoming increasingly apparent that the child was now attracting all of the world's draíocht to her – at times, it was nearly overwhelming to be in her company. The discomfort of flying meant she had no choice but to stay in that company often.

Crea was vigilant and made the best use of her time in the air to check for pursuit and potential ambushes. The tears of pain made the task more difficult, but she did it. They were coming closer to the portal dolmen. Roving bands of hoodoons had harried the Fand's hunt. They still followed, but not so close that would hinder Crea's plan. With the girl returned to her side, all Crea would have to do, was to lift Arthmael to the old-world portal.

A tiny voice inside screamed at the thought. The pain would surely be too much. The idea of it was unbearable. Unimaginable. Yet there was no choice: the old world or the crease. There was little else she could control. She turned at some sound or other and could not help but flinch.

Arthmael stood before her, his eyes boring into her.

"You have not been straight with me," he said. He took her hands.

Crea's eyes darted to Eimear, sitting a distance away, who was conversing quietly with her sword again.

"You must not speak of it. If she realises how much pain I am in, it could turn her to a frenzy. For all our sakes, let us deliver her to her to safety and then we can consider the wound more seriously."

"My love," he said. "How did it all get like this? Did we ever really have a chance?"

"No, Arthmael," she whispered, reaching out to touch his face. "Yet, I would not have it any other way than this. I cannot resist you; you know?"

"Nor I, you."

She jumped a little when she realised Eimear stood an arm's length from them.

"I should check the wound," she said. "There will be no frenzy. You are both safe. I have developed an interest in wounds, as you may have guessed. An expertise that Hógar made sure I drilled."

Arthmael moved to stand between Crea and the child.

"She is right, my love," said Crea, pushing him gently aside. Crea felt nauseous, unsure whether the wound or Eimear's suggestion was the primary cause.

"Please lie down on the ground, Crea. I will be able to examine it better."

"No," Arthmael said. Crea heard the strain in his voice. A gust of wind blew foamy spray onto the banks around them.

"You are too dangerous, Eimear. You cannot control yourself."

Eimear paused, her face close to his.

"I swear to you that I mean her no harm," she whispered. "There was a time that would not have been true. Now, it is. You may hold Sword if that will make you feel more at ease."

Arthmael's face wrinkled in disgust, but he nodded curtly. Eimear unbuckled her sword belt and handed him the thing. As always, Crea felt it hard to look at it. This plain-looking weapon made her deeply uncomfortable, For something so simple, so ordinary. She noticed Arthmael trying not to look directly at it as he took it between unhappy fingers.

"Will you lie down for me?" Eimear asked.

Crea folded her wings tight and did as she was asked, parting her clothing to reveal the badly wrapped wound. Eimear wasted no time and removed the cloth bandages. Crea watched her for any reaction, but Eimear's face remained emotionless.

A yellowish-white streaked the fresh blood on the bandage, accompanied by a sickly aroma. Crea felt her heartbeat faster as her senses processed the injury. Arthmael's barely discernible grimace caused her to close her stinging eyes.

How was I so foolish to be injured like this?

"It is spoiling. I will need to clean it," Eimear said to them both, her tone almost motherly. "Can you make a poultice?" she asked Arthmael.

Arthmael shook his head.

"Well, you can help me to gather what I need. Find me some honey. I will need some calandúl: the whole plant to the root as much as you can find. Find the cleanest looking clothing that any of us own and cut it up into thin strips."

Her head turned to a worried-looking Arthmael. "I will need those things quickly. Can you fetch them? Please?"

Crea heard Arthmael's teeth grinding, causing his angular jaw to tighten.

"I will," he said to Eimear. "I will be back quickly," he added to Crea.

"Will you need something for the pain?" Eimear asked, patting Crea's hand gently. Crea considered her age.

What a question. She is only a child.

Curious, naïve, impressionable. Eimear had so many childlike qualities that Crea was quick to forget.

"I can stand it," Crea had to hiss between gritted teeth. Her head became light. "I will manage child. No need to worry about me."

Eimear nodded.

A few moments passed before Eimear spoke.

"I'm going to clean out your wound. It will not be pleasant."

"Eimear," Crea asked, cursing herself for having to ask. "What happens if I cry out in pain?"

Eimear pursed her lips.

"I will not lose myself, Crea. If that is what you are suggesting?"

"No. What I am asking you is if you will enjoy it?"

Eimear stood up straight to consider. Her cheeks coloured slightly.

"I believe that I will."

"Why?"

"I do not know," she said, rubbing her eyes.

"Do you not?" Crea leaned in to grasp her wrists and pull the child's hands down. "Have you no sense of why you would enjoy such a thing?"

"No." Eimear's eyes started to tear up. "Hógar used to try to help me explore my mind. He thought that if I could understand myself, I could control myself."

"A commendable thought," Crea soothed.

"I know that I had an … unfortunate childhood. But it does not explain my pangs."

Crea tried not to make her shiver obvious. Eimear focused intently on the wound, but Crea could feel the child's fingers resting limply on her skin.

"My burning desire, need, is to make music," Eimear continued in hushed tones.

Crea was becoming accustomed to being horrified around the girl. She pushed Eimear's hands away from her wound. "What music, Eimear?"

"I have a song in my head—an old tune that haunts me. I do not know where I first heard it. But I have a … need. To hear it," Eimear said, raising her eyebrows.

"Can you not just sing it?"

"It is not complete when I sing it. It remains unfinished without the sounds of despair, suffering, and pain. It is the only thing that I truly desire."

Crea could not respond. She searched the girl's eyes, trying to understand.

"I do not want to be this way," Eimear whispered, an eyebrow trembling with a sudden tic.

"Why do you not change it then?"

"I do not know how. There is no-one left to help me," she said, hunching her shoulders.

"I can help you," said Crea, knowing her words to be hollow. though her words were hollow.

"Why do you say that when you know it is not true?" Eimear's eyes grew hard.

Crea sighed and averted her gaze. "I have tried to do the right thing, Eimear. My life is forfeit. Perhaps it is most likely that I will not be around long enough to help you."

"You could come with me to where I was born," said Eimear. "Maybe I can help you?"

Sincerity thick in the child's voice surprised her.

"I cannot—those Fae who cannot conceal themselves seldom last longer than a few days in your world. Arthmael and I would be hunted and killed. Our hope is to go to the Old World and find a life there."

"What is the Old World?"

"It is where I was born."

"Is it like here or like my world? With a sky and the sea?"

"It is like neither. It is a place without," Crea said.

"Without? Without what?"

"Without much of anything, Eimear.

"It is unfathomably vast. Very little is known about it. To find anything there, one must travel far. That is why many of the creatures there can fly. Smallsky denizens are our name in this world, but the sky there goes on forever. There is only the night, however. A sun does not appear."

Eimear nodded slowly. Now it was she who was trying to understand.

"I do not recall much. I was taken when I was young—given to the Fane and the Fand. I do not know what was exchanged, or the details of the contract. The farsight that is required for survival there is a great boon here. There has been a smallsky denizen watching the portal dolmens for aeons. I might be the first to have sullied the contract."

"Why did you do it?"

"It is you, child. You have been the catalyst. I can see it clearly. As clearly as I can see you drawing the draíocht from around us. Change happens slowly here. You have changed many things in your short time here."

"I did not want to come here."

203

"What did you want, Eimear? And do not say you wanted to hear Fae screams. That is not the case." Crea winced as a wave of pain lanced her.

She noted a conflict of emotions in Eimear. At times, the contrasting extremities were overwhelming, but the more Crea saw of the girl, the less she could maintain those extreme thoughts. The girl never had a chance. Her way, however barbarous in nature, was not her fault. There were other forces at play. Crea felt as insignificant to them as if she were standing on the Plains of Forever in the Old World.

"Mirdhí. The duillecháns. They were kind to me. I wanted to make them happy. I wanted to feel like a normal child. Like a child who had someone to care for them."

A single tear trickled down Eimear's cheek, and Crea believed her.

"I know you do not mean to be the way you are," she said.

The girl nodded solemnly.

"Have you given up on … changing?"

Eimear shrugged.

"I do not know how."

Arthmael busied back to them, providing as Eimear had asked. She cleaned the wound well with water boiled in Arthmael's cookpot. Eimear threw in handfuls of *calandúl*, flowers included, allowing it to change the colour of the water, as Hógar had showed her. She dabbed it carefully as she could in and around the wound. The heat of the water made Crea gasp a little. She shot glances at Eimear who focused on the task at hand. She sensed rather than saw Arthmael's.

"I told you, I am in control," said Eimear, not looking up.

Hearing Arthmael sigh, Crea relaxed her shoulders a little.

"Besides," said Eimear. "I would need to make her really howl to enjoy it properly."

Crea was mostly sure Eimear was joking, though she could not find it in herself to laugh. After what seemed like an age, Eimear gently dried around the wound. She took the wrapped honeycomb and allowed the golden yellow liquid to spill onto the gash.

Eimear lay *calandúl* leaves atop the honey grunting a little in approval. Taking the torn lengths of fresh bandage, she wrapped them around Crea's waist until the wound and treatments were covered and secure.

Crea was about to compliment Eimear's handiwork when she saw a thing that she would have never considered possible. Dalla and Cern flew down to land in their camp.

Eimear held out her hand and Arthmael threw her the sword as he reached for his spear.

Dalla and Cern were contrasting. Dalla was shorter, with tawny hair cut close to her head. Her large yellow eyes were sad. Stretched leather clothing covered her small frame. Large holes were on the back for her jerkin for her butterfly shaped wings to pass through. She had a long whip curled on her belt and a wicked-looking dirk at her hip.

Cern was robed in billowing white, his feathered wings shaped like a bird. Long golden locks fell onto his broad shoulders, and his blue eyes were striking. He held a long silver spear, lavishly decorated in gilt strands of gold. The spear top was smooth and impossibly sharp.

If the child was impressed or intimidated by their sight, it did not register on her face.

Dalla knelt beside Crea to gently test the bandage, avoiding Crea's gaze.

"It seems as though she had the matter in hand. The bandages are on well, sister."

"They are, Dalla."

Cern went to stand in front of Eimear, who was still holding the sheathed sword.

"It is a wondrous thing indeed to stand beside you. To watch you draw all the draíocht from the world around you. Who are you, child? The truth. You are an agent here, sent to turn this place upside down? You must tell us. Enough of the games."

"I am Eimear. They brought me here because the Fand ordered it. There is nothing much more I can tell you."

"Tell me of your parents then." He leaned over as if examining her more closely.

"I did not know them. They were killed when I was small."

"Who raised you then?" Cern asked in a gruff voice. Crea was aware of his brusque manner. She wondered how Eimear would react to it.

"I was raised by many. Cared for by few. I learned much later that a band of duillecháns watched over me, for all the good it did."

"How do I believe her?" Cern asked Crea. "Look at what has happened since she arrived. Even you must admit that whatever feelings you held for the twarv have only truly surfaced since her arrival here."

Crea nodded and then pointed at Arthmael.

"I have loved him from afar for an age. I suspect, however, that you might be right. The attraction has grown steadily from around the time of her arrival. The fact that he and I are together here with her, indeed, signals that something is amiss."

If Arthmael felt hurt by her admission, he hid it well.

"I would have it no other way, Arthmael," she continued. "Though I know you do not doubt."

"I do not, Crea. Eimear being here may be turning the world upside down. But in doing so, she has only set me aright. You had already turned me upside down the first second I laid eyes on you."

"So, what do you hope to achieve, Crea?" asked Dalla. "Speak plainly."

"I will bring the child back to her world, then Arthmael and I will travel to the Old World."

Cern and Dalla exchanged glances.

"Did you think I would just let you both pass through sentiment?" asked Cern.

"I had hoped you might just do that," said Crea, knowing that neither believed it. "What would you have me do, Cern?"

"Take charge of your senses, for the first thing, Crea." He pointed towards the distant Old World Portal Dolmen. "You cannot pass through there. The contract forbids it. And even if you could, the twarv cannot survive there. Even if you were fit to carry him."

"What would you have me do?" Crea repeated, panic rising within her.

"There is only one path for you. You must bring Arthmael through your own portal dolmen."

"Back with Eimear?"

207

"No. Eimear is not going back there. Not now, anyway," Cern said.

"Do I ever get to choose my path?" Eimear asked.

"Not for now, child," Dalla said. "You are too powerful. There is somewhere you must travel. You are being called. Crea has sensed it too. Or are you too smitten by the twarv to see what is right in front of you?"

Eimear pursed her lips, seeming to retreat into her thoughts. Crea noticed her stroking the hilt of her sword as if for comfort.

"Mid portal," said Crea. It must be. That was what Dalla meant. It hadn't been calling Crea at all. It had been calling the child. Eimear started to nod slowly.

"I feel something," she said. "Perhaps it is what the salmon feels. Or the swallow. As if I need to be somewhere."

"Where?" asked Crea. "Where is this place? Where do you feel it is?"

Eimear pointed over the treetops. "There. That way."

Crea exchanged a glance with her brother and sister. The girl was pointing in the direction of Mid Portal Island.

"We three have felt it too, Eimear," said Dalla. "We have felt that pull. But not for us. It seems that our task is to bring you there. Crea misinterpreted her task. Love, it seems, has been confusing her. For a smallsky denizen to abandon their post is a sure sign larger forces are at work."

"What forces?" asked Crea.

Dalla stepped forward. "That is not for us to know, it would seem. We could have tried to resist had we all

208

worked together, yet we cannot change the mess you have made, Crea. In that sense, perhaps the option to resist the calling has passed us by. Eimear must pass through the mid portal before the Fane and Fand arrive."

"I must? You speak above my head though you have not asked my permission. Crea just told me I cannot survive there unless I have wings. What if I decide to ignore the calling? I have been led around like a donkey from one place to another since I can recall. I am different. Do you not see it?" Eimear paused and picked absently at her hands, coloured from dried blood. "I am not a child anymore. I have a power in me. You can all sense it. Can you, Arthmael? Sword thinks you fear me to your core. What of you?" she glared at Dalla. "Do you fear me? Do you think you can make me pass through this gate if I do not wish to?"

A shadow passed across Dalla's face.

"Child, I suspect that none of us can make you do anything should you not wish it."

"Then I do not wish it. I am going home. You two should fly back to where you came from."

"You have no home," said Cern, voice sharp. "What do you go back to? What future have you? You have caused great change here. You can see that clearly, too. Such changes happen once in a thousand lifetimes. We cannot ignore them. Have you not the backbone to see this through to some end?"

Eimear's eyes turned cold, and Crea's blood followed.

"Backbone? Have a care how you speak to me, lest I show you your own backbone."

Cern's hand tightened around his spear. Eimear noted the movement and smiled. Such a smile should have warmed the hearts of those who saw it, for it was filled with joy and delight.

"Come and see," Eimear said. "If that is what you desire."

She leaned her head as if listening. "Yes. Sword is right. It has been too long. Arthmael, perhaps it is time for you to take Crea and move on." Her gaze switched between Dalla and Cern. *Two of you together will provide some sport.*

"What are you doing, Eimear?" Cern said as Eimear's sword slid from its sheath.

"Sister, does she mean to do this?" Dalla asked, her hand straying towards her scythe. "You must help us if she does. She cannot yet beat the three of us, I think."

Eimear glanced at Crea. "After I spent such a time healing her, it would be a terrible shame if I had to wound her further. Crea, I promised you that I would not harm you. I will quickly renege on my oath if you betray me."

Crea stood, arms extended. As she did, Dalla and Cern raised their weapons and flew to a height, ready to attack.

"Stop this," she said to them. "You have no right to come here and disrupt things this way."

"No right?" boomed Cern. "You have left your post behind, your duty unfulfilled. You have lost your mind, Crea. Do not speak of disruption. Eimear will come with us, or we will take her anyway. Strong as she may be, she cannot beat the three of us."

Crea felt control slip away from her. Her wound ached. "Wait," she pleaded.

Eimear looked at her for a moment, head tilted, listening to her sword.

"It appears you were right indeed. We will do it your way."

Crea gasped as a trickle of blood fell from the newly drawn sword to stain the ground below.

WATCHER

Is fearr deimhin ná díomá.

Better to be sure than sorry.

CROMM FELT A mixture of humour and disgust as he stood before The Hooded One.

A sídhe warrior, his opponent stood tall with a long black cloak that covered most of his features. His voice was low, whispered, like a blade over stone, in what Cromm felt must be a considerable effort to maintain for show. Everything about this fool was for show. His retinue seemed taken with the idea of this mysterious warrior, but even fools have admirers.

The Hooded One spoke in maddeningly conceited tones.

"The Faneside sídhe need a true ruler. Not one who leaves us at a whim and shows little or no interest in our needs or the needs of our women and children. Our elderly and our animals.

"You have chosen to leave us undefended and uncared for—anathema for a ruler of our time. You arrive back from wherever and send our strongest warriors away on some damned quest or other. You are not fit to rule. I am here to challenge you, to defeat you and to take your place. As my people and my enemies know well enough, I am the greatest warrior on the Faneside. The greatest leader. The true ruler. Do you accept the challenge?"

Cromm felt light-headed for a moment.

I am weary. Weary of these fools. Is there no equal for me?

"I apologise," Cromm said. "Oh, Hooded One. I could only make out some of what you said. Your mysterious voice was difficult to make sense of. It made me wonder if your wit is as hooded as your features. I would hope it will not hinder your rule. That is, of course, if you beat me in the challenge, which I accept, of course."

For several moments, there was no move from the hooded fool.

"You are unwise to provoke me, Cromm," came the voice.

"You are here to challenge and kill me, are you not? What difference does it make if I provoke you?"

"Come. Let us begin," said the sídhe warrior.

"Do you not intend to remove your cloak?" Cromm asked.

"The Hooded One does not remove his cloak for any."

Cromm looked around at the swelling audience. *Is there no one to speak sense to him?*

"You think to best me with no peripheral vision–knowing that I am Cromm? Faneson. Leafdancer. I fear you are not thinking clearly."

The Hooded One produced a long spear and positioned himself for an attack. His grip on the weapon was loose. He was relaxed. It was already clear that he was an expert.

At standing still anyway.

"Come, Leafdancer," he whispered. "Let's dance together then. I, unfortunately for you, am not a leaf."

Cromm shook his head. His last challenger had been Terraigh. He said very little and fought valiantly, even managing to wound Cromm's thigh, which still bore the scar. The duel lasted a day. Cromm's heart had pounded in his chest in advance of the encounter; his grip on the harpoon felt off; he had been afraid. Terraigh.

Mighty, but not an equal.

He felt only derision towards this whispering fool. *No, not derision. Disappointment. Shame.* This minnow was one of his people. *Responsibility.*

He ran a hand through his soft hair and readied himself.

The Hooded One leapt forward, flicking out his spear. Cromm sidestepped and let momentum carry the challenger past. Leaving his harpoon lowered, Cromm scanned the crowd, making eye contact with several of his foe's retinue. He shrugged at them and turned back.

It took a moment for The Hooded One to readjust. Cromm watched as his head lifted under the hood to try and find where Cromm stood. The glint of purple eyes signalled that The Hooded One had marked his target. As he hefted the spear to attack, Cromm leapt lithely over his opponent's head, twisting in the air to land behind him.

The Hooded One's rising panic was made plain by his hood twisting erratically from side to side. As he spun to find Cromm, Cromm sidestepped to be within a hand of his opponent, making sure to stay in his blind spot.

Most of the world is this fool's blind spot.

"Where am I?" Cromm whispered into the side of the cowl, and then leapt back a distance.

The Hooded One reached up to pull back his hood, and Cromm laughed.

As he was about to comment on how a Hooded One with no hood is nothing, the warrior turned towards him, and his words got caught in his throat; the laughter died on his lips.

The Hooded One was a child. No more than fifteen summers, dark face pockmarked and covered in frizzy downy fluff.

"You… You are a child."

The Hooded One's face twisted into a furious grimace.

"I am old enough to beat you if you stop acting like a coward and fight."

Cromm became aware of the crowd watching and suddenly felt the urge to run. To hide away rather than end the life of this misguided fool.

I cannot kill a child.

Yet, as he said it to himself, he knew there was no escape from this fate—no way to save this brave, blithering youth.

The Hooded One charged at him with his spear raised to strike. Bile rose in Cromm's throat as he spun quickly and lashed his harpoon across the spear to break it. He let it continue on its arc, and the butt of the shaft struck the child's face. The Hooded One fell back and landed with a whoosh of air leaving him. Their eyes met for a moment, though tears began to cloud Cromm's vision.

He stabbed the harpoon into the child's chest with such force that all three prongs buried themselves in the ground beneath him.

He left it there as he turned to the crowd, blinking back the tears.

"Do not think that I wanted this. Do not think that I have forgotten my people or left you behind. Everything I do, I do for our future—for the future of our children. Do not raise them to hate me. Raise them to help me. Not to fear me but to understand my motives. This child did not need to die. This child should have fought by my side in the coming days. I will need the strength of the sídhe. I will need all of you for us to prevail in the challenging times ahead."

He turned and wrenched his still-quivering weapon from the child.

"Take him from here and consider your future," he whispered as he walked towards the rolling hills.

MONSTER

Marbh le tae agus marbh gan é.

Killed with tea and dead without it.

Eimear knew Crea was not a threat to her. The other two hovered over the clearing, ready to swoop and attack. Combined, they would prove a worthy challenge: flying enemies. It would be an experience that Eimear could enjoy to the fullest.

The twarv was standing out of the way, spear raised. However, he would most likely hinder his allies if he became embroiled.

Let us leave the injured one until the others are gone. She will sing for us. Sword's voice was too eager.

"No," said Eimear. "She has shown me kindness. I will not show her cruelty in return."

Eimear could sense fear leaking from Crea; her desire to get to Arthmael. A part of Eimear wanted them to be together as they died.

Will I kill them? Will they attack me?

They all die. We have had enough of this.

"Please see sense, Eimear. They may have opposing views to you, but they are not your enemies. We are not your enemies," Crea said.

Eimear hesitated, giving herself a moment to consider.

Why do you wait? Why do you resist? Am I not your most faithful ally? Let me free. Release me from your inaction.

Sword rose before her, her hand powerless to stop it. It swung in lazy circles before her.

I will take control. I will make music for you. Let me free.

It was difficult to resist now. As if now making decisions, Sword directed her forward, and she could not resist.

"I do not wish this," she said aloud to Sword, but still, she moved towards them.

I do.

A buzzing sound was followed by a sharp sting in her neck.

"What is this?" Eimear asked as her hand moved up to see what had pricked her. She discovered a small thing embedded in her neck. She took it out and held it before her. It appeared to be a tiny arrow without

218

fletching. A dart? Sword and her eyes grew impossibly heavy.

"What is happening?" she asked, wondering if anyone could hear her.

Her eyes closed to darkness.

***

Her eyes opened to darkness as if waking to a night sky, where the moon was but a memory. Yet she had not seen the moon since passing from her world. She strained her eyes and could just about make out her hands before her. Nothing else. The back of her head ached. Reaching back, she felt a fine-sized lump.

"Sword. Are you there?"

I am.

"What happened?"

The twarv must have turned on us.

"He could not have stolen up on me. He was nearly frozen to the spot."

Had you let me do my work, he and the others would have been dead, and you would be there and not here.

"Where are we? Why is it so dark?"

I do not know.

The ground underneath her felt strange. Dry. The gritty sand, coarse against her fingers, confirmed her suspicion that someone moved her.

"Who are you talking to?" Cern asked.

Eimear froze and reached out for Sword.

"A little to your left," Cern said.

219

Eimear reached across and touched the familiar old scabbard.

"Where are we?" Eimear said.

"Who are you talking to?" came the reply, from where it was difficult to judge.

"Why can I not see?"

"You must answer my question first."

Eimear stood, buckled on the sword belt, and drew Sword.

A chuckle came from somewhere. Cern was flying around her; soundlessly. He could see her.

We need him to land.

"You have cast draíocht on me," Eimear accused him.

"To blind you? No. You will need to guess once again."

Eimear paused. She strained her eyes. If she waved Sword, she could make his shape out in the smothering darkness.

"My guess? My guess is Arthmael hit my head. Then you brought me somewhere … ah … I see. You brought me to the Old World."

"You must realise that what we felt returning here was nearly overwhelming. Overwhelming to bring you here, to whatever end."

"I understand it well enough, bird."

"I am not a bird, mangblood," Cern said crossly.

"I am a mangblood, bird. What do you plan to do with me? If you come near me, I will cut you up."

Cern laughed openly. "I never thought you to be such a fool. I have been flying with you for some time. I know which way I travelled and I can see for miles in any direction. You can barely see your hand. Fool."

He landed before her, leaning in so that she could sense his face almost touching hers.

"Kill me, should you wish it, mangblood fool. Cut me up. See how you enjoy this place without me."

Sword did not speak.

"I am not a fool," Eimear said.

Cern laughed in her face. "What are you then? What good are you? None. Talking to your sword like one whose mind is gone. What do you hope for, mangblood? You do not know. You do not know anything. Neither of us does. You should be silent and allow for what needs to happen. I need to bring you there." If he pointed, Eimear did not know. "I need to go to where they are calling, and you must come with me."

"Are we going to your people then?" Eimear asked.

"I do not know. I cannot remember this place. Except for the darkness." He paused. "I have missed it."

She was tired. Weary. Her sword was a barely distinguishable shape in the murk. What was she good for? Nothing. Nothing at all.

She slid the sword back into the scabbard and stood, dropping her hand to her side.

"Dry away your tears. They are not convincing. I will carry you, mangblood. But we will fly high, so high that if you do anything foolish as you oft want, you will drop like a stone to become a mess. Do you understand? You are not as important to me as you were to Crea. I bring you because I feel I must. It is my hope that I will get to leave you here so that when I return to the Fae realm, it will be richer in your absence."

Eimear nodded.

"Do you wish to eat?"

Eimear nodded again.

"I have provisions and a water skin. I will leave them at your feet. When you are done, we will go."

"I need to make water."

"Then do so. I need to fly. I wish to see what I can see."

Eimear did not know if he had left when she found her supplies. She ate and drank and then squatted.

***

Cern returned what seemed like hours later. It was difficult to know. She had moved very little since, taking the time to fly into her mind as Hógar had asked so often. Sword was quiet as if realising his inadequacy in this place.

There was nothing to herald Cern's return. He just spoke, and Eimear jumped a little from the fright.

"Tears? Again? You will need to control yourself more appropriately for whatever lies ahead."

"What does lie ahead? Did you not just go to find out?"

"No. I went East towards the sea. I have a vague memory of a great dark sea. I thought I might find some of my people there."

"Did you?"

"No. I found evidence of a settlement. There are none there now. It confuses me further. Are you ready?"

She nodded into the black.

His arms lifted her then, and his legs wrapped around her thighs as they took off. It was not long before she could not tell whether they travelled

222

forwards or backwards, up or down. She felt his muscles work as he flew.

"How long can you carry me like this?"

"I do not know. I have never carried anyone this far before. If I have to drop you, I will endeavour to warn you first."

Eimear thought he might be joking but did not respond.

More hours passed. She drank from her water skin twice more. The dusty sand had got into her throat. Over time, she realised she could make out the shape of his jaw above her. When she looked down, she was sure she could see her arms more clearly.

More time passed.

In the distance, slowly but surely, she saw the dimmest glow. A stain of the palest white against the nothing. A distant horizon, perhaps?

"Cern," she said quietly. "I think I can see something."

"You can. I must rest."

Her stomach lurched upwards as they flew downwards to land. A shriek attempted an escape from her lips, but she quashed it, unwilling to give Cern any satisfaction.

He set her down surprisingly gently. She instantly missed his embrace in the black. She shuddered in horror for a moment as the thought of her being alone here crossed her mind.

They had been flying for many hours. The ground underfoot was still the same coarse sand. It was difficult to imagine such a featureless place as this: sand and sea. She shuddered again.

"Why do you speak to your sword as you do?" Cern asked from a distance.

"Sword is my only friend."

"What of Crea and Arthmael? Are they not friends to you?"

"I do not know what they are to me. I think … I know strange forces make people do things they would not normally do. I think those forces made Crea act the way she did. Not friendship."

"Do you even know how to tell a friend when you see one?"

"Perhaps not. As I cannot see, I don't think it matters much."

There was silence for a moment, and then Cern laughed loudly.

"Perhaps you are not the fool I thought you to be, mangblood."

"I do not care what you think, bird," she said.

The expected response did not materialise. Eimear cursed her words as their taste lingered in her mouth.

"I am sorry for calling you bir—"

"Silence. Listen."

Eimear did as he directed. His tone had an urgency that left no doubt of his sincerity.

"Draw your sword, mangblood. I will fly. I will try to draw them away from you. You must lash out at anything that comes near you." He paused. "There are many of them, it seems."

"Of what?" Eimear asked, but he was gone.

She strained her ears, and this time she heard something. Strange howling moans in the distance, getting closer, coming toward her, coming for her.

She drew Sword and raised him, ready. The howling sounds became louder. Alien cries pierced Eimear's heart. They were close.

"How shall we fight what we cannot see?"

They will come to us.

Before Eimear could respond, pain exploded where the fear had been, and something knocked her onto her back. Wind whooshed out of her lungs as if answering the cries of her invisible attackers. Eimear felt panic building as something was on her. She could just almost see sharpened talons reaching for her throat.

Sword was right. She did not need to do much except let them come to her. She thrust Sword into the scrambling form, and the thing cried out.

"You have found me," Eimear hissed. She slashed again. The creature rolled away, and Eimear rolled after, driving Sword into the retreating form. Another howl lifted her heart. She sat up.

There was a beat of wings and talons raked into her shoulder and arm, trying, perhaps, to carry her away. She allowed the creature to lift her until she stood, ignoring the pain, then lashed out at where she thought a body might be. Once, twice, thrice, she struck, and the creature fell before her.

"You have found me," she screamed. "Come and sing with me."

Two came at once, then. Eimear listened for the wings and leapt backwards to avoid the razor-sharp talons. She could hear more of the creatures above her somewhere.

Now. Bring me to them.

Closing her eyes, she leapt straight up towards the sounds, allowing Sword to do his work. He swept around her as she twisted in the air. The alien howling changed. A more familiar panicked scream warmed her heart. One of the things attacked Eimear as she started to fall towards the sand, claws and teeth burrowing into her body. Shooting out a hand to hold it close, she ran Sword through the creature, twisting. A harsh scream erupted from it, and she rejoiced. She started to sing and let the beast's slow fall bring her back to the ground.

Eimear whirled into a spin as she heard more wings, feeling Sword bite. Then again. Bleeding from wounds all over, she felt light-headed. More things attacked. Sword was there to meet them.

Eimear stumbled on a fallen creature. It was still moving. Her heel smashed down on whatever part of it had tripped her. It wailed.

Something cut across her head and face. She immediately felt blood spill from her, stinging her eyes.

I could not see anyway. I have never seen.

Eimear laughed—a laugh that had been a long time coming: long before she leapt across a river; long before she pretended to learn from Hógar; long before she smiled at the red fathach; long before she even came to these strange worlds; forsaken by the gods, the sky and the sun.

I should have laughed at Seasún's stories.

The woodworker had been so kind, so patient.

I killed him.

She grimaced at Sword's admission.

Eimear swatted away oncoming claws and talons. She could hear them all—every move they made. As Sword moved among them, it was almost difficult not to kill them, swat them down like flies, nothing more than an irritation. She did not need her eyes.

None of this was my choice. None of it. Nor was it my fault.

She had never had any choice; except to do as those around her expected; demanded.

She leapt again to kill three creatures whose flight paths had aligned. This time there was hardly any screaming. She chided herself for not just wounding them. She felt light-headed again. She was still bleeding, but none of the creatures could touch her.

Perspective.

Eimear realised it. She had only ever seen the world others created for her, never trying to make a life she wanted for herself. She never understood what Hógar meant by journeying inside herself to begin to know the world around her. Only here in the dark could she truly see. The places she visited meant little. She had neglected those places inside her that she needed to visit.

Her clothes were wet.

You remember how we were working on you flying into your mind? To look down on the valleys below and know them? To visit the deep dark caves and the highest peaks in equal measure?

Hógar had shown her the way but it had taken her until now to comprehend fully. She would spread her wings and soar into herself. Here, in the dark, where she could see the clearest.

None of the things remained around her. Most were dead. There were few screams left. In the distance, she could hear Cern battling a group of them. She went to them in a single bound. Sword flitted from one to the

227

next, not biting as hard. Their shrieks were the chorus to soothe Eimear's malaise. She walked among their fallen forms, letting Sword kiss them; tickle them; motivate them.

"Why do you torment them so?" Cern asked, breathing ragged, voice weak. "They were hunting for food. There was no malice in their actions."

"Shhh. Listen," Eimear said. She hummed her sad song as they made their music. Cern would not understand. He was nothing to her. She could sense his shock in the darkness. Feel it drip from him as blood dripped from Sword.

"Let us begone. You are wounded. We need to keep moving," Cern said.

"Shhh. Do not tell me what to do. I will tell you."

The sounds of their suffering faded.

"How did you know where they were?" he asked.

"They are weak."

"What do you mean they are weak? How did you know?"

"You are weak too, Cern. Though you do not realise it."

"I have carried your deadweight, mangblood. You owe me gratitude."

Her laughter came once more. She wondered why she had not laughed before this.

She felt freedom in it.

"Do you hear me?" asked Cern. "Do you even recognise that you needed me? That you still need me? You are helpless here without me. A lost child as you have been from the beginning. You no more belong here than you belong on the Fandside. How dare you laugh, you miserable twisted wretch?"

Eimear went to him and let Sword cut him. Cern tried to defend himself, but it was hopeless. Eimear had had enough of him, so let Sword work, slicing and biting. Cern screamed, which delighted Eimear. Her laughter mixed with his cries: though not as soothing as her sad song, it pleased her immensely. Sword was focused. He protected her from further harm.

I am all you need. We will never be helpless when we are together. We are more than any of these creatures—any of these places.

Yes. I understand.

As Cern's protesting cries quietened to silence, Eimear's light-headedness made it hard for her to stand.

She sat down in the darkness.

It was cold here.

She put her arms around Sword and closed her eyes.

"We will do lessons."

A voice. From the past. Hogar.

"What are lessons?"

"Where you will lessen your ignorance."

"What must I do?"

"What are you?"

"I am a girl."

"What is a girl made of?"

"I do not understand."

"What is this?" He poked her.

"My arm."

"What is the whole?"

"My body?"

"Yes. Your body. What else are you?"

"I am only this."

"Surely there is another part of you." He tapped his temple.

"My mind."

"What is your mind?"

"I do not know."

"It is everything. It is anything. Anything you need it to be."

"How?"

"That is what we will explore. We will explore your mind, Eimear."

"How?"

"Close your eyes and breathe deep, slow breaths."

Eimear did as told: deep, slow breaths.

"Picture yourself standing in a meadow, long grass at your ankles."

"Here or in my world?"

"Neither. This is a new place. This is you."

Eimear could see the mountains and valleys within her mind. Those vast plains and churning oceans they had constructed over their years together. She launched herself towards them.

***

Eimear woke into darkness.

"Sword?"

Silence.

Her fingers felt around her. Coarse again, but soft coarse. A blanket, perhaps? She ran her hands over herself, checking for injury. Soft bandages wrapped her torso, arms, legs, and head. She sat up gingerly because even the slightest movement caused her eyes to close and her jaw to clench. She did not recall such pain when she was last awake.

"Heartiest mornings," said an ethereal voice.

Eimear jumped, and pain erupted in response.

"Is there great discomfort?" the voice asked.

"Am I the only one in this place who cannot see?" asked Eimear.

"Curses," growled the voice. "I am forget. Veil eyes."

"What?"

A flame sprang to life in front of her, and she jumped again. The pain came quicker this time; waves of wracking, intense pain. Eimear hissed as a light in her eyes echoed the sensation.

It took several moments for her to adjust to the light, though she veiled it with her hand as the voice had suggested.

"Who are you?" Eimear asked. "And where are you?"

Gazing around, she noticed a firepit at the centre of a wide, slated circle. There were carved stone benches at the edge. It was impossible to make out anything beyond the light's edge.

"Cannot you see me?" a female voice asked.

"Unless you are a fire or a bench, no."

"Fissures above."

"What?"

"Fissure? Is there no word?"

Eimear grimaced an equal mix of pain and frustration.

"I do not understand you."

"It does not oft happen for me to speak such ways. I am saddened."

Eimear gasped as what appeared to be a sparkling gust of wind flew around the fire to alight beside her and stopped, swirling gently in the air.

"Smiles," said the wind, apparently pleased.

"What are you?"

"I am draoí. I am Ériu."

Eimear's mouth dropped agape. Instinctively, she searched around for Sword.

"You will not be hurting me with these. You are not so able. Not as you end Cern."

She felt her face get hot, tears swelling in her eyes.

"What do you want of me? What is happening? I didn't want to be here. He brought me."

"I brung," said the wind named Ériu, her voice childlike.

"What do you mean?"

"No."

Eimear jumped a little as the voice was suddenly inside her mind.

- Perhaps it would be wise for me to communicate with you like this? -

Eimear closed her eyes. The voice was too loud. "How are you inside my head?"

- I am draoí. -

"That is not an answer."

- It is answer enough. Do you require food? -

"I need to know what is happening."

- I will tell you though you may find it difficult to hear. Perhaps after some rest. You are gravely injured. -

"Tell me. Please."

The voice went silent.

"Please tell me. I need to know. I beg of you."

Silence again until:

- We were born here. Many aeons ago. When we found the way, we left to explore the planes and places, and the worlds within them. Some explored the dark spaces to see where they would lead and were lost. Many stayed where their journey led them. A rare few of us returned here to ... -

"To die?"

Eimear felt a wave of humour.

- It is difficult to explain. No. Not to die. To travel to our next destination away from ... all of this. Away from life and death. Many have moved on. Most. -

"Why am I here, Ériu?"

- A thing has happened. It first happened on the day that you arrived in the Fae realm. An abomination; an abject violation. One of the Fae came to this place and consumed one of the draoí. -

"Consumed? How? Why?"

- Power, Eimear. Why does anyone consume a thing that they do not need to survive? Power. Self-importance. How wretched the creature who allows their desires to turn to greed, who succumbs to their greed, allowing it to lead their thoughts and guide their decisions. -

Eimear felt Ériu's sadness. Her frustration.

"That is not enough of a reason. That does not answer why. And how did they consume one of the draoí? How is such a thing possible? And none of that explains why I am here. Why you wanted me here."

- Ah, but it does, Eimear. As my kind near the end of their time here, we are increasingly vulnerable. We could not defend ourselves from the Fae creature except to hide. It has become apparent that as he

233

consumes us, his powers grow. He can sense us and takes one of us with each visit. -

Eimear felt her fear. Her pain.

- The draoí are among the most ancient races. For a predator to come among us at this stage in our existence was something none could have foreseen. For him to consume us for his own gain, it was ... it is unspeakable. -

Eimear felt her resolve. Her lust for revenge. Something was missing.

- You already know what is missing, Eimear. We felt fury when he came. Rage. Hatred. Though we could not act upon those feelings. In such feelings was such power, but we had no way to channel it. We needed a weapon. A living weapon that we could imbue with our rage. A very act of fury in the flesh. You, Eimear. You are our spite. Our fury. Our revenge. You. -

"How can this be. He only came here long after I was born. I was here when he came. I have been … the way I am for a lot longer." She reached out a hand but could feel nothing before her.

- It is difficult for you to fathom such things, but time does not have the same rules here as in many of the realms. Once you have power over it, it can become a valuable tool. We required a joining in your world. It would have been too obvious to the Fane and Fand had it happened here. Or in their world. We let those men know where your parents were. We let them know where you would be. We watched them kill your parents, and we made you aware of their suffering. We filled you with our hatred as you would fill a waterskin, knowing that one day you would come here. We knew the price we would pay, but those of us left have long

since resigned ourselves to the fact that not all of us can share the same path. Sacrifices were made. -

"You did all this to me? You admit it so? That is … vile. Evil. You are evil." She moaned out loud. Ériu's words became waves that threatened to drown Eimear.

- No Eimear. Not evil. We protect our own. I know what you will do. I know you will feel no guilt, so I will not say too much to you except this. Take the hand of the little one when they offer it. After you have finished with this, there is a way for you to be free from our influence, but the little one is the key. –

"What …what are you talking about?"

- I did not see his work. I did not see what the Fae beast plotted. How could I? It is unthinkable. But he did not see you until it was too late. He still might not know fully. The price of looking into futures is steep. -

Eimear's head swam, vision blurring. Her stomach turned, and a sweat formed across her brow.

"You tell me so openly of your evil deeds? You tell me you know what I will do? What do you …"

Eimear stared at the sparkling wind gently stirring before her.

"You want me to consume you."

- I do not want it. Yet I have seen it and know that it will be. You must breathe me in. -

"Consume you? Sword. Sword are you there?" she cried.

- You must destroy him. You must destroy the one who has done this. The fathach named Aébhal. He has become more powerful than any of the Fae before him. If you do not, he will become too powerful for anyone to stop. Even the Fand. He will destroy the Fae. He will

235

begin conquering the other worlds; your own will be the first to fall. -

"Have you not seen that?"

- I cannot see past my demise. It is the price I must pay. You have almost paid your price, Eimear. You must do what you were created to do. Complete the task that we have set for you. Use the draíocht we have bathed you in. Use it to capture my spirit and take it inside you. Become the power you were born to become. You must do this thing to save my kin. -

The wind wisped through her head, and she knew how to capture Ériu. To take her. To use her. Eimear gulped down frantic breaths as her anger threatened to overwhelm her.

"I must?"

- What else can you do? Once your task is completed and the remaining draoí are safe from his growing appetites, you will be free to go home. To exist without our rage fuelling you. -

"You are the monsters. Not me. It was not my fault. Never my doing."

- You will be our right hand, Eimear. Not the Fand's. We have waited for this day. You must be our vengeance incarnate. You must look in his eyes and cut the threat he represents from this plane. -

"I must? I must. It has been I must this and I must that for as long as I can remember. I must. I must."

Eimear reached out her hand to touch the sparkling wind, eliciting a slight gasp from the voice. It did not move away, however.

"You are the monsters. Not Aébhal. Not I. You must be destroyed."

She closed her eyes and drew the sparkling wind closer. Reaching out her arms and the draíocht she now felt around her to welcome it, she inhaled deeply. There was little resistance. Ériu stood by her word to stand as the sacrifice. Eimear felt the draoí enter her body. She could hear Ériu's thoughts and fears. She quashed them to almost nothing. She crushed Ériu down until there was only a kernel of her left. Pain rippled through Eimear to surge behind her eyes. Another being had become a part of her. She felt stretched. Swallowing the urge to scream, she curled her lips. The pain was indescribable. Had she no other reason, she would have begged for death then; however, her new reason to live burned as brightly as the pain she felt.

I will not kill him, Ériu. Aébhal will live. However, I can assure you that he will no longer threaten your kind.

A power grew in her as the numbing pain sought to end her. Her eyes saw as if in daylight. She could see for long miles in each direction. She stood atop a gentle mound in a featureless plain. The pitch-black sky above her was vast beyond thought. In the distance, she could see more gusts of swirling, sparkling wind, travelling around the plains as if agitated.

Are they the other draoí? The other monsters who allowed this? They are all watching me? she asked the grain of Ériu, though she did not let Ériu answer. Eimear only wanted her to see what the power allowed her to do.

She opened her arms once more. In the distance of her mind, she heard a shriek as she breathed one of the distant gusts towards her. It resisted. Its bitter thoughts stung at Eimear. It mattered not. If Aébhal could consume them, then so could she. Distance would not stop her. Pain would not stop her. His dreadful lack of ambition signalled his weakness. She was strong. She was rage. She had been constructed by those some considered gods. The hard part was over. Everything else would be easy. She inhaled the second draoí, absorbed the female spirit, and crushed it as she had Ériu. Eimear then curled into a ball as the agony of her spirit stretching made her shriek. She became a writhing, squealing creature. Unable to think straight.

I will die.

Would that be so bad? asked Sword.

Where have you been? I needed you. Pain wracked her body. Blood was dripping from somewhere on her face.

Can you not see? Are you so blind, even now?

I needed you, Sword.

I am not Sword. I am you. You know that.

I am alone.

Everyone is alone. You are better prepared for it than most.

Eimear felt a new wave of power within her prison of excruciating pain, a new level of clarity as if snorting in the icy air of the winter mountains. She could hear the draoí thinking, their despair at the perceived betrayal. They could not believe that she had been able to consume a second. Aébhal had indeed tried and almost perished at the attempt.

Eimear threw her head back and laughed. She could see everything in this realm: the portal dolmen; the ancient metal buildings; the flying creatures; the smallsky denizens; the strange scaled half-men, half-fish creatures of the black sea and loping long-necked beasts of the shadowed mountains, many thousand leagues in the distance.

I am more powerful than anyone who has come before me.

What should we do?

I will keep my promise. I will take them all.

It will kill us.

I hope it does.

She reached her hands out and heard the draoí despair as she drew them towards her. There was nothing they could do. She used the draíocht they had gifted her. A slight tinge of guilt pricked her.

Not all of them.

Be silent.

Sword went quiet. Eimear knew this was madness. Already being torn asunder, she would die. She willed herself to draw them into her, making ready to inhale them as they neared. She listened to them scream and beg for their freedom. Freedom that they had taken from her. Her head went back once again, but this time it was difficult to tell whether she was laughing or crying. There was more blood from somewhere.

"Come to me and see the monster you created," she cried.

She breathed deeply in, all of them, as they screamed—screamed like never before.

FANE

Ná hoscail doras na hiaróige.

Let sleeping dogs lie.

FERRAGH WATCHED HIS son grow as a leader, a ruler. Aébhal hardly even noticed him, busying himself with newfound duties. The Fae under his command hardly noticed the Fane riding the great horse in his finest hunting suit. It had been a struggle for the Fane to fit into the *triús*. Ferragh shook his head, feeling his jowls wobble in protest. Some skilled tailoring had allowed his legs passage into the tight green caves. How far he had fallen. Under his rule, there was peace and prosperity for an age. Was that not enough? What had he done to deserve this quiet uprising? This slow death behind a smile and a cup. His son's ambition was a mystery. He wanted for nothing. The sides were balanced, and all was right.

Ferragh shook his head. As the horde neared the crease, his discomfort was growing steadily. What did his son plan? Was peace in danger? Ferragh had tried to send word to his Fand that something unusual was happening, to let her know that the meeting at the crease was not of his doing, but he could no longer trust anyone. He had engaged in revelry for so long that emerging, he found the world changed. Those around him had changed. Long trusted advisors addressed him coolly as if he had done them a grave injustice. Where were his friends? Those who had filled his mug and sang songs with him. Those who had clapped his back and cut meat with him. There had been so many then. He could not even seem to remember who many of them were.

Aébhal carried no weapons, but it mattered little. No one had seen Ferragh's sword for as long as any could remember. He had difficulty recalling what he had named the skilfully crafted blade.

Something to do with power.

Ferragh could not challenge his son. When he was Aébhal's age, he could have cast the fathach down and danced around him to amuse all those in witness.

Ferragh's throat constricted as Aébhal checked his giant stride at the vanguard and fell into step alongside Ferragh's great horse.

"It is a fine beast," he said without looking at his father.

"It is a strong animal indeed."

"It needed to be."

Ferragh felt the blood rush to his cheeks. Cursing himself, he hoped that Aébhal would not notice the flush on his face. His son looked up for a moment. The edges of his lips curled upwards ever so slightly.

"What are we to do with you, Ferragh?" Aébhal asked.

"Am I not your liege, Aébhal? And your father? Do you forget to address me accordingly?"

Aébhal took hold of the great horse's reins and stopped them both. His black gaze bore into Ferragh, near smiling lips bared to expose his razor-sharp fangs.

"My liege? Do you see nothing? Do you no see the thing you have become? The beast of burden that you now are?"

"You will need my help, Aébhal. In any campaign you launch in the face of the Fand, you will need my help. You are not strong enough. Nor is Cromm. Neither, nor both of you. Do you not see that? And what of this Eimear? You have not managed to deal with her. You need me, my son."

"Caen is coming. I will send him to deal with the girl."

Ferragh had to squeeze his legs together to stop himself from falling from his mount.

"Caen? How? How did you find him?" His voice sounded shrill to his ears.

"I had someone find him. It was just a question of searching in the right places."

"You seek to control Caen? You think he might serve you, Aébhal? I think, perhaps, it is time for you to cease your madness and accept the wisdom I can provide you. Together, we will be stronger than apart."

"Perhaps it is time to cease our ongoing charade, Ferragh. You have sat in your piss, stinking of your shit, believing your farce for too long. This side deserved attention and direction since long before you forgot it existed. Other than to sate your ever-growing appetites. You sat in a drunken stupor believing yourself a worthy Fane. All were judging you as you sat. I did not want this. Your people came to me. I think it is important that you understand that."

Aébhal clicked the great horse forward as he started walking again.

"You will name me Fane and then begone," he said, neck stiff, staring forward. "It does not matter to me where you end up. It shall be thus. I do not wish to wet my feet with the wine that would surely pour out of you if I ran you through."

Aébhal was at the vanguard in five mighty strides. There he stared steely-eyed towards the crease.

Ferragh's first instinct was to lean over to throw up. How had this happened? A sudden headache caused him to rub his temples frantically. Betrayed by his son, his people stolen from him by an upstart. An upstart who sought to banish him: to banish Ferragh Fane, Fane, the *Fae Rí* himself. He felt his face contort into a sneer.

Aébhal does not even feel the need to kill me. Impotence. That is what he said. Impotence.

Ferragh closed his eyes and tried to slow his breathing and calm his thumping chest. He would need to teach Aébhal a lesson. A lesson that Ferragh's people would understand when freed from Aébhal's impending oppression. Freed from the tightening grip of a false king.

Ferragh nodded slowly, eyes wide. They would see the true wisdom of a Fane. The true grace of the *Fae Ri*. The deft subtlety of the long-time ruler. They would love him and rejoice. They would celebrate with him in the Great Hall. He could picture it in his mind: flagons, voices and spirits raised.

"A true Fane once more."

"Your wisdom and skilled leadership have made this side what it is," came the quiet voice of Cromm.

Ferragh leapt.

"Must you always creep up on me, Cromm?"

"It was not my intention to cause alarm, my Fane." Cromm had painted his chestnut brown skin in colourful streaks. His harpoon rested on one of his lithe shoulders as he marched.

"Where have you been through all this? Why have you not come to me? Are you so blind to it all, or are you, in fact, colluding with your brother? Speak the truth, for I shall know it if you do not."

"It has been outside of my control, my Fane. I have been to many settlements to gather your horde."

"So, you claim to be ignorant of Aébhal's intentions? His plot to supplant me?"

Cromm's smooth forehead wrinkled slightly. He brought his long harpoon, *Greim Tapaidh*, some called it, before him as if standing for inspection.

"Everything I have done, I have done for you and your glory, my Fane."

Ferragh eyed his son's famous weapon, feeling a renewed sense of hope. "Will you use that to protect me then? Will you put an end to his schemes? You are the only one who could best him bar the Fand herself."

"That is not true, my Fane. The mangblood child is a match for us two."

"Forget that whore," Ferragh spat. "I ask you plainly. Will you do as I ask?"

Cromm's head tilted to one side, and he ran his impossibly long fingers through his tight hair. When he spoke, his voice was low.

Why must he sound so bored?

"Without us two to defend this side from her skill, this side will be left nigh on defenceless. With the two hordes so close to battle, it could mean the downfall of the Faneside. Is this what you wish?"

Ferragh knew this truth, but the anger in him did not lessen.

"I want this side to be strong in the face of her advances. How can this side be strong without its Fane? He seeks to destroy me."

"If he becomes Fane, we two can defend this side. Perhaps there is a way that you can support his proposed transition, my Fane? To allow change to happen freely. To help him build this side, without distraction."

Realisation struck Ferragh like a blow.

"I should have known. I should have known that you would side with him. Loyalty means nothing to you. You forget why this side has been strong enough for your young life not to have witnessed war."

"War is due."

"War is due? We have been at peace and prospered; can you not see this?"

"I see no progress. War is due."

"Did you know he had summoned Caen from the far lands?"

A slight opening of Cromm's mouth and a head tilt told Ferragh all he needed to know.

"No, Cromm. You did not. It seems you are not fully informed of Aébhal's plans. What does that make you, then? An equal or a lackey?"

Cromm's lips pursed.

"You do not know the answer, I think. Perhaps Caen will. Until you discover which, go. Fight your war, Cromm. Help your brother." Ferragh moved close and spoke slowly. "But do not think that you have everything figured out. The Fand is also cunning beyond your combined wit. She has power beyond your limited comprehension."

Cromm smiled. "Your wisdom is always warmly received, my Fane."

His sudden mocking tone made Ferragh bristle. Cromm turned and walked away.

CROMM

*An té a bhfuil uisce agus móin
ar a fheirm féin tá an domhan a
bhealach féin.*

He who has water and peat on
his own farm has the world his own
way.

FERRAGH WAS SUITABLY addled. A tinge of guilt pricked at Cromm as he walked away from his Fane. He had long loved Ferragh before his slow descent into decay began. At the start, Cromm had tried to divert the Fane from his merry-making. Cromm urged him to rule. Yet the Fae world had become soft. The settlements of the Fane were well established, requiring little in the way of oversight and little in the way of a leader's vision. Yet, in such times the need for true leadership was most keen: the need for an eye on the future. Both of Ferragh's eyes had set firmly on mead and bosoms.

The need justifies my actions.

Heightening Ferragh's paranoia was a necessity. While he was obviously struggling to contain his madness, he was still the Fane and the horde, though gathered under Aébhal. would not quickly betray him.

Cromm needed to expedite Ferragh's downward spiral into madness.

The Hooded One's face flashed in his mind, and he shook his head to rid himself of the thought.

What have I become?

He checked once again to make sure that the blood of the boy had been cleaned from the tips of his weapon; a weapon that felt less and less familiar to him. The lifeless eyes of the boy appeared in his mind's eye, and he stopped walking, raising a hand to his head.

Think of something else.

Walking faster, he tried to picture Caen's arrival and what it would mean for Cromm's plans.

However, the boy's dead stare would not leave his thoughts.

"Eimear," he said aloud.

As he said her name, he immediately pictured her solemn face and some of the tension left his shoulders.

Eimear, he thought.

Her beauty was exquisite, even if she was not Fae. The young woman had grown into her body, stirring something deep inside him.

Eimear.

It was time to go and see her. To watch her once more.

Time to stand before her?

Thoughts of meeting her, speaking to her, being with her, were intoxicating.

For now, I will watch once again, but it is nearly time.

To make the leap with so many eyes upon the crease was increasingly difficult, yet he was determined. It was time to make the final leap to the Fandside.

The last one with the world as it now stood. The next time he set foot on the Faneside would be as the Fane. One last leap after he had changed the world.

CREATURE

*Ní thagann an crúiscín slán ón
tobar i gcónaí.*

The jug doesn't always come
safely from the well.

PAIN.

The thing jolted into consciousness and pain. Was this the underworld? There was no fire, though it burned. No demons slashing, though it bled. No screaming voices but its own. The thing could not open its eyes. Perhaps they no longer worked. Its skin was too tight. Its bones too stiff. The pain was indescribable. It could only scream.

Black reclaimed it.

It woke again and wished to its tumultuous core that it had not. The waking world was pain. Nothing else. It was aware of another being in close proximity. The being spoke; said something, but the thing did not wish to hear.

Pain.

The thing woke into a storm. There was no wind, nor sound around it, yet its body was being ravaged by a similar force. It tried to scream but no sound emerged. Its throat was red-raw. Another noise came from within. A tune the thing had heard. A sad tune with no words. Battered, curled into itself, it gasped it's tune through wracking sobs.

Pain.

It woke. It sensed the being close by once again. Words escaped its cracked lips but were not audible with the first attempt. The thing tried to wet its lips. As if in answer, a trickle of tepid liquid met the thing's working tongue. Swallowing caused its whole body to burn.

"Kill me," the thing croaked.

"After watching you for this long? That would make me nearly as big a fool as you. Although, that said, no. It wouldn't. I daresay too many will ever match you for being a fool."

The thing tried to repeat its request, tried to beg for mercy, for death. The pain halted its efforts. It moaned.

"Well, if that's how you're going to be about it," said the voice, "perhaps you should go back to sleep a while longer."

Another dribble of the tepid liquid rushed down its throat. It could neither resist nor complain enough to match the pain. The thing closed its eyes.

Pain.

"Do you know what you did?" came the voice.

The thing must have been awake to hear it.

"No," said the thing.

"You destroyed the draoí. You took them into you. It is a remarkable thing indeed that you yet live. What is your name?"

"I … I have many names."

"No. No you do not. You have a name. You, the one who stole the draoí."

A thousand thoughts passed through the thing. Memories, feelings, views. Many were not her own. Her. The thing was a girl. She was a girl. The many other voices were noisy. The pain was distracting.

"Who are you?" she asked the voice. She strained to open her eyes, but she could not see anything. "Are we in darkness once again?"

"I am Alma. Yes, we are actually. I had forgotten to make you a fire so you should see. I will do so in time."

"Where am I?"

"You are among my people," she said, busy with some task or other.

"Who are your people?"

"You would call us the smallsky denizens, yet that is not our name. Our sky here is vast beyond reason. You are safe. You are in no danger. You have saved us. From the draoí who have used us as slaves. You must tell me your name."

"Hógar."

"Your name is Hógar?" asked Alma.

"No. Hógar. He was good to me. Afraid of me. He loved me. I never thanked him."

"Well. Perhaps you can thank him in time."

"No," she whispered, her mouth dry. "Mirdhí. Seasún."

"I think you are not making sense," Alma said, voice hushed.

"Nothing makes sense," she said. Tears streamed from her. She tried to move her hands. They felt strange, as if unfamiliar. The pain receded to the back of her mind, with the older pain that had always been a part of her. "Nothing makes sense, Alma."

"You are wrong. You're fixed in melancholic thinking. Kindness makes sense child, does it not? Empathy?"

"I am tired."

"Sleep then. Tomorrow you should probably try to eat something."

Pain.

She was not sure if she was asleep or awake when Ériu's voice whispered to her; distant, forlorn.

- You have ended our line here. -

"You created me. You have paid the price."

- We will torment you forever. You will never have peace from us. Aébhal knows this and he only took one of us. We will drive you to madness. -

"I would never have had peace. You ensured that, did you not?"

- I told you Eimear. Once you had completed your task, we could have helped you be rid of our hatred. -

"Eimear. That is my name. I had forgotten. I was near to death. I suppose you were too. All of you. Again." Eimear felt like laughing, though her lips remained downturned.

- You will rage forever. This will be our curse. You will be Síor Feargach. We will see to it. -

"You will see. You will see how I allow Aébhal to live a long life. You will see how I walk past the Fae realm and go home. You will see me forget about you. As I become nothing, you will too. And when I die, you will fade to nothing. That is what you will see. Nothing, Ériu. I have ensured that no one will ever suffer your vile scheming again."

She heard Alma's voice.

"Sleep."

***

The Gruagach children had teased her incessantly before they became afraid of her.

Eimear had run to her hut. Hógar had come to the door. Perhaps to console her?

"Why do they tease you?"

"I am different."

"I am different to you. Do you tease me?"

"I do not wish to answer your questions today, Hógar. Leave me alone."

"They tease you because they do not know you. They do not know that you share many feelings with them."

"I do not wish to share anything with them. They are mean. Like all of the children I have met."

"Let them get to know you. Open up to them."

"What is there to know? I am nothing."

"That is not true."

"You did not wish me to be here. You were compelled to take me because the Fand ordered it."

"That… is true." Hógar had tutted. "But things change."

"What do you mean?"

254

"I mean that I did not want you here, Eimear. I did not know that I would grow to care for you."

"You do not show me that you care. You give me lessons and you make me work."

"I do not know how else to show you. How about this? Let's both try a thing. Let's try to show each other that we care about each other. It will mean opening up a little. To everyone. The other children will come around."

"Who says I care about you, Hógar?"

Eimear moaned, wishing she had never said it.

He had blushed. Even in the darkened hut.

"I am sorry, Eimear. I have no experience in this kind of talking."

"Leave me alone."

Why? Why had she sent him away? She hated herself for her words. Perhaps she could change them here in her memory.

"You are not nothing, Eimear," he had said quietly. "Believe that."

Eimear had watched him leave.

***

Pain. Each time she woke into the searing pain, she wished more and more that she would not.

There were so many questions. Why had she been brought before the Fand? Why had she been trained for war? Who had been behind it? The Fane? Surely not, based on the rumours and reports that she had heard of a gluttonous fop, a toothless tomcat.

The Fand. That pompous witch was capable of the most splendid declarations, and ever more splendid self-importance, but she was directionless. Headless.

There was someone else between her plans and those of the draoí.

A wracking jolt of agony caused her to scream. She felt her own piss warm her buttocks and thighs as she lay.

The watcher. That constant yet distant feeling in her periphery. She could never have been sure, yet the watcher had never seemed an enemy. Nor a friend.

All these years later, she still did not know.

"The watcher," she said.

She heard Alma's voice.

"Sleep."

Time passed. The pain became less, and then tolerable, easing each time she woke. Eimear learned how to eat and drink.

When her body started to discover itself anew, she learned how to reach, move, walk. Healing slowly. It became obvious to her very quickly that changes had occurred. Her senses were heightened in a manner she found almost comical. She could see quite clearly in this darkened world. She could see for many miles all around her. She even spotted Sword lying many leagues away, waiting patiently for her. She could finally see and hear the creatures of this world: snuffling rodents, clicking insects and many forms of flying creatures—many with distinctive sounds cast out before them like feelers.

This vast, dark place was home to countless inhabitants. Eimear found the presence of these alien creatures ignited her curiosity and drew her away from the constant threat of morbid thinking. Such thinking became a constant here, spiralling in and out of focus.

She could watch the strange multilegged insects go about their business from a world away; witness their little triumphs or failures, their survival or demise; each one entirely sure that their struggle was meaningful.

Eimear had travelled to three separate realms. She had learned of many more that the draoí had gone to colonise. There were countless portals to countless worlds here. Inhabitants of each were all entirely sure that each of their struggles were meaningful. Eimear suspected that they were equal in meaning to the clicking insects of the endless plains around her.

Why are they here then? she asked herself. A stab of something echoed through her chest. *Why am I here? I am the same as those insects. I am nothing.*

Finding another creature to watch, each time the dark thoughts grew, was the only way to keep the dread temporarily at bay.

Alma came regularly enough; curt at times, with near-warmth shining through at others.

Alma would ask her questions, and Eimear would answer. Eimear knew her answers were sometimes frustratingly short, but she hoped they would keep Alma asking more.

Eimear had been slow to ask Alma questions in return, but as her health improved, she found that her curiosity in all things was a tonic to combat the dread.

"Why have I not met others?" she asked Alma, who was delivering food.

"They are terrified of you."

Eimear nodded. She had come to be used to the reaction. The gruagach children were too. It was understandable.

"Will you tell them that they are safe from me?"

"Are they?"

"Yes."

"I will tell them you said it. They will not easily believe it. Some were watching when you killed Cern. Some are very angry with you. Others see you as a saviour. The draoí way has been hard for us here. Now that they are no more, it means we will not be subject to the decrees of the contract."

"The contract?"

"Between the Fae and the draoí," said Alma. She was clearly intrigued at Eimear's sudden interest in her world. "It is a complex set of arrangements, but largely boils down to the Fae staying on their side of the portal and the draoí staying here. In the past, when there was mixing of the two sides, the results tended to be unpleasant. The draoí offered three of my people … slaves as an incentive. Emissaries, they were called. The contract has been in place for ages. The Fae had no knowledge of how the draoí were leaving and how those few that remained were increasingly weakened. Until the giant came."

"Aébhal."

"Yes. His desire for power outweighed his sense of tolerance for old laws. The draoí tried to make us slay him. But their threat ended for us when he consumed the first of them. We have been waiting. Waiting for them to be gone. Waiting for a chance to govern this place ourselves. You have given us this chance."

"So, do you think I will meet the others in time?"

"In time Eimear, it is our hope that you leave. You have done something inconceivable. Though it aided our objectives, what you did was beyond wicked. There was considerable debate among my people about killing you while you slept. Many considered it wise."

"Did you?" Eimear searched Alma's huge eyes.

"I did."

"And why did you decide against it?"

Alma paused to consider her words. "Destroying the draoí was evil beyond words. You are evil beyond words. They named you to us as they were dying. Síor Feargach. They screamed your name in fear. Yet to kill you while you were writhing in screaming agony for so many months would have made us evil too."

"Months?"

"Eimear, you destroyed the draoí more than two years ago in our time. It is nearing a time when you should leave."

"Two years? How?"

"The draoí were not easily subdued. They tried to tear you apart from inside. They resisted you with every fibre of their collective being. Yet you overcame them. You have taken their essence. I suspect you would be able to destroy this whole realm, should you decide to do so."

"I will not. I am not evil, Alma. They created me. They made me. They were the evil ones."

"Perhaps. You will need to leave this place, Eimear, for us to feel secure. Until that time, you will need to rest and finish recovering your strength."

WOMAN

*An ní a tháinig leis an ghaoth
rachaidh sé leis an bháisteach.*

What comes with the wind will
go with the rain.

TIME PASSED. EIMEAR felt stronger with each day. She felt draíocht coursing through her veins. She felt sure that if she wished she could leap and land beside where Sword lay. Further. She could leap to half a world away, where the strange darksea creatures that Alma named as merúchs. On occasion, she thought she could hear the voices of those draoí that she had consumed, but she studiously avoided paying them any attention.

Alma visited her less, intentions clear enough. The less welcome Eimear felt, the quicker she might leave. On the occasions that she did visit, they would sit across the firepit from each other, where the flickering flames would colour the dark world around them.

"Tell me about time, Alma. You told me that I might be able to control it as I pass back through the portal."

"That is so. There is no sun here. No moon. We can only tell the difference between day and night because we can feel it. Our time passes as a constant, however, our time is not matched with the Fae realm. One's journey through a portal can cause dizzying discrepancies. The draoí could control the time that they arrived in the world of the Fae. That is what made them dangerous, even when their numbers waned dramatically. Had they wished, they could have travelled through time to anywhere in the history of the Fae and done as they pleased. The Fae realised the danger. The contract suited both parties."

"Why did the draoí not just destroy Aébhal at the time of his birth?"

"They had become too weak here, and the draíocht that they created and left behind them has grown strong in the Fae realm. Aébhal was the first to realise this. Others would have in time I would imagine."

"What about the draíocht in me? Will it diminish when I go back?"

"To an extent, certainly. You will never be as strong as you are here. You have the draíocht from two worlds and the essence of the draoí themselves within. If you wished, you could call the sea across this land. You could break the plains apart with your fists. You could rend the sky open and drag a sun here from another realm. You are a God here, Eimear. And I ask that you leave tomorrow. You will be weakened the further you go from this realm. You will never hold the same power

261

again. That said, there are none who will match you for draíocht, wherever you may go. You have become a bottomless well of draíocht."

"If I do go back, could I not just go back to meet myself coming through the portal dolmen with Barragh? I could go home and avoid all of this?"

"Meeting yourself would not be wise. Travelling backwards through time is never wise. How can it be? If you tell yourself not to come here, everything that has happened will cease to be. It could cause this world and ours to shake apart while you get to go home without much more than a passing thought. There would be two of you where there was one. What if one of those decided to go through the portal towards a different time?" The denizen rubbed her face with long fingers. "You can see, I'm sure, how quickly the world might come undone."

Dancing shadows shifted across her face in the colour from the fire. It was unsettling to behold.

"You must come to this place–though you have done those terrible deeds. It has already happened. If you do not, it could end the world in which you stand. There are other forces than draíocht and the passage of time."

"But there are so many wrongs I could right. I could save Barragh, Hógar … Cern." The firepit spat sparks at her. Eimear knew that there was little sense in her words.

"For a short time only. As I have told you. What is done is done. If you undo it while its mark has been made, there will be friction that could destroy everything we know. Perhaps while you spend your last hours with us, you can consider the time you need to arrive back at. Perhaps it might be wise to allow the two years to have passed?"

"No. Crea and Arthmael might yet be saved. They will need my help I think."

"Consider then. How can you save them? When do you need to go back to? And can you do so without creating friction?"

Eimear closed her eyes. She thought she could hear Ériu laughing. A question that had niggled with her had been answered.

"I know when I need to go back."

Alma's face became troubled. "In that case, I hope that you recall the evil you have already done. I hope that you do things for good."

"I hope so too."

"I will not see you before you go, Eimear. I wish you well and hope that you can find what you need to help you."

"I need a little one to invite me somewhere."

Alma's face registered her confusion.

"Thank you for healing me, Alma," Eimear said.

"I have not been healing you. I was the one chosen to watch if you would live or die. I gave you water to lessen the shrieking. I would have tried to kill you, but my courage failed me. We will try to close the portal forever once you leave, in the hope that you can never return here."

She stood and turned without waiting for a response.

"Wait," Eimear said. "You cannot leave."

The creature's shoulders hunched. "Why is that?"

"You must teach me how to control time as I go back through. I do not know how."

Alma turned back towards her, hands raised on either side. "I cannot teach you that. You must think it and do it. That is all. You must leave."

Eimear noticed a trickle of sweat down Alma's forehead.

She is not speaking the full truth, Sword said from far away.

Perhaps it is fear that drives her. Let me take the truth from her. Come and fetch me.

"Alma, it will be easier if you help me. It is something I need, and I would not like you to deny me this."

"You threaten me after I refuse. Is this your way now?" Alma's rage mixed with the fire's shadows.

Eimear considered for a moment and then shrugged. "Did you not say that I am a God?"

Alma walked to her, lowering her face so it came within a whisper of Eimear's.

"And this is the kind of the God you wish to be? Do you wish me to prostrate myself before you? To worship you and do your bidding?" Alma's lip quivered. "I have told you I cannot help you."

"The problem is this. Sword feels that you intend treachery. Perhaps if I try to pass through the portal without caution, it might destroy me. You told me yourself; you wish me dead."

"Please," the word burst from her lips in a sob. "Please, leave us alone. We fear that you will destroy us as you did the draoí. Please, just go."

Eimear cast a gaze to find Alma's village in the far distance; her people living their shaded lives among the funnel-like peaks as they busied themselves with their changed lives. In her mind she had named them as darksky denizens, as the sky in this place had no end. They were seemingly invigorated by the end of the draoí. They feasted and celebrated and sent hunting parties farther than ever before, using long pipes to blow poisoned darts at prey. They were cunning and silent, watching the prey from a distance before swooping in to dart them and fly them back to their home. Their newfound boldness intrigued Eimear and she wished to be among them more and more often; to experience their vigour in up close.

She noticed a group of smallsky denizen children, playing a game on the wing. "We. They fear me even though they have not met me. Even though they do not know me; know my motivations. I am the one who has been ruined. I am the one who became a game piece for the draoí to move around. I am the victim, Alma."

"We have seen your deeds. Your words will not change our view, Eimear."

"Come," Eimear stood.

"Where?" Alma's eyes opened wide.

"I wish to meet your people. I wish to meet them and show them that I am not what they fear."

Alma moved to her, placing her shaking hands on Eimear's chest. "I watched over you. Please. Do not go to them."

Eimear could not help but smirk. "Watched over me. So, you did. Do not fret. I will leave Sword where he lies. Follow me at your leisure, Alma."

She leapt, trusting the draíocht to lift her, and she landed outside Alma's village. The setting was otherworldly indeed. Large fingers of stone jabbed out from the rocky terrain into the endless black sky. Each one darkened again by a thick covering of moss like flora. The towers of stone were pockmarked by cave entrances, many of which had smallsky denizens fleeing inside. Many other of the creatures took to the dark sky and flew away.

The group of children she had seen landed before her, seemingly immune to the terror she was causing the adults. One by one, the young were removed from her presence by frantic parents snatching them from the ground and flying back to their caves.

Only one remained. He was very young and stood looking around him, not fully grasping the situation. His gaze came to focus on Eimear and his head tilted in a way that reminded her of Crea.

"Who are you?"

"I am Eimear. Who are you?"

"I am Garren. But everyone calls me Gunch," he said with a shrug.

"I prefer Garren. Where is your mother? Your father?"

"I perfer Gunch. My mother is minding the new baby. I do not have any father at all. Where are your wings?"

"What is the new baby's name?"

His face scrunched into a comical mask of concentration. After a moment, he shrugged. "I don't member."

"Is it a boy or a girl, Gunch?"

His nose wrinkled. "Girl. Eemar. Where are your wings?"

"I don't have wings. Can you take me to see the new baby?" Eimear cast out her senses. She could hear the wail of a new-born and her heart fluttered.

You should have brought me.

I will not need you.

Gunch shrugged again. "You can't go without wings. I can't carry you."

"I'm very good at jumping."

"What's djumping?" he asked, his own wings flapping a little.

Eimear showed him and he cackled laughing.

"Gunch. Gunch, come here," said a voice from above. The child's mother, leaning out of a cave. Behind her, the baby wailed. "Gunch," she said as she took flight, descending slowly towards them. "Come on now. Garren. Come to me." The strain in her voice was apparent.

Gunch turned back to Eimear, head tilted once more. "She's 'fraid of you?"

"She is, Gunch."

"Why? Are you draoí? You don't look like one."

"Because I did a bad thing."

"Oh." The child looked up toward his mother, who was still calling. Gunch's wing's unfurled and flapped a little.

"Did you mean to do it?"

Eimear considered it, under the watchful gaze of the child with enormous eyes. "I think so."

Gunch's mother landed beside them, with her wailing infant in her arms.

"Gunch. Get up home. Now."

The child shrugged and flew away.

"Why did you come here? Do you mean to destroy us now too?" said the mother, face trembling.

"No. I came to… I don't know. I just came to see." Eimear wasn't sure her answer was heard over the wailing baby.

The denizen moved towards her, and Eimear's breath caught as the mother held out the child. "Will you destroy her as you did the draoí? Will you kill Gunch as you killed them all?"

Eimear reached out and took the child in her arms. Something passed through her body. A powerful wave and she choked back a sob. "I did not kill them," she murmured.

The child stopped wailing and its eyes opened as if suddenly aware of the change.

Eimear felt her heart thumping. "What is her name?"

The denizen watched; hands pressed to her chest. "Telia."

Eimear shifted her arms so she could bring the baby closer to her swelling chest. "Why does she not have wings?"

"She is too young."

"I mean you no harm," Eimear said, bowing her head towards the mother. "She is beautiful. Telia."

The baby wriggled for a moment and closed her eyes.

"I did not want any of this," Eimear told her. Told her mother. "I was taken when I was Telia's age and have been passed around to many; none of whom cared for me as you care for her. I had no mother."

The denizen frowned. "So, you destroy to quell your pain? You feel that because you were a victim of misfortune, you should deal worse to those you encounter?"

268

Eimear listened to Telia's breathing. The baby had fallen asleep. "I want her to grow up in a world where such terrible things are less likely to befall her."

The denizen extended her arms to take back the child and Eimear felt another wave of something. She wanted to keep the child longer. She wanted to protect her from the horrors of life. The denizen stiffened and took a step closer.

"Please. I want to take her home."

Eimear saw a tear land on the child's face. Her tear. She gently handed the child back to its mother.

"Thank you. Now. Please go from here. Please leave us alone. Maybe, one day, you can have a child of your own and you will understand."

"A child?" Eimear could not hide her shock at the thought and the baby left her grasp, leaving a space as immense as the crease itself.

She turned away.

A child.

Perhaps her own life had been ruined in a way she could not mend. *Would I not ruin a child's life too?*

Hair standing on her neck alerted her to the increasing number of darksky denizens that now hovered, what they thought, was outside of her view, blowpipes ready with poisoned darts.

Raising her hands, palms open, Eimear walked from the rocky place into the desert. She found Alma waiting for her.

"What will you do?" the denizen asked, ashen-faced.

"I will go back through the portal and never return."

"It fills my heart with joy to know this," Alma's wings stretched wide and rippled from a shiver.

"I have one request before I go. I ask for your assistance," Eimear's hands remained open, to show Alma that her intentions would cause her no harm.

"If it means you leave, I will do my best to aid you, Eimear." Alma's voice shook.

"Good," nodded Eimear. "Good. Do you have a child, Alma?"

The denizen took to the air and hovered above her. "I did. They took her from me to give to the Fae." She flew away towards her village.

"Sword," Eimear said aloud. "It is time."

Yes. I have been waiting. It is our time.

"It is my time, Sword. Mine."

Draoí

Is iomaí cor sa tsaol.

There is many a twist in life.

Eimear walked through the portal dolmen. She thought of the time she wished to arrive back to, wondering if it would be so. She looked around her at the strange curving world circling around her. It was pleasing to be able to see colours and detail from close to the centre of the world. The realm of the Fae was uniquely beautiful. Though she was leagues away, she could see details from this height that were incredible. She could see the leaves on the colourful trees, the ripples on the babbling streams, the scree spilling down the mountainsides.

She could see the Fane's armies massing on his side. A vast horde, weapons sharpened. On the Fandside, a small group had broken away to continue the hunt, while the Fand's horde changed direction to march to the longshore. She saw hoodoons creeping through the endless forests. She nodded slowly and started searching for the clearing.

She followed on from the direction the hunting party was heading and sure enough, her keen sight saw what she was searching for.

Cern and Dalla hovering above the clearing where stood Crea, Arthmael, and herself.

Eimear watched herself talking to them. Watched Crea plead. Watched herself drawing Sword with a flourish.

She drew the blow pipe given to her by Alma and a smile surprised her. In the history of all the worlds and the future of all the worlds to come, this would surely be the only time that a person shot themselves with a poisoned dart. She knew that it would not kill her. The fact that she stood contemplating it was a testament to that.

Judging the distance, Eimear knew that hitting herself with a dart from here was surely impossible for anyone to achieve. Yet she knew in her heart that she could do it. She had the power of the Gods within her.

She raised it to her lips and pictured where she had felt the sting. Eimear took a huge breath and forcefully blew through the tube.

Even from this distance, their confusion was plain on their faces, as the other Eimear fell into a stupor and then into unconsciousness.

"How…?" said Cern in disbelief. His huge eyes searched around him, but Eimear knew it would not be possible for him to process the vast distance the dart had travelled. She did not even need to hide herself.

Using Ériu's voice, Eimear spoke to Cern in his mind. - *Bring her through the portal to me. I wish to see her.* -

Cern's hands came to his head and his mouth opened wide.

"There is a voice in my mind," he said to the others. "A draoí voice."

Eimear watched their faces change. None of them could mask the shock.

- *You must bring her, Cern. Do not speak of any of this to her. She must not know of my part in this.* -

Cern spoke aloud. "I do not understand."

- *It is not important that you understand. It is critical that she is brought to me. It is the only way. Bring her to me Cern. Carry her.* -

"The draoí." He said to the others. "She commands me to bring her through the midportal. To her.

"If it is in keeping with the will of the draoí, must we not comply?" Dalla asked.

"Not we," Cern said. "This task has been given to me."

"We three must see this done, Cern," Dalla insisted.

"I must rest," Crea said. "I cannot go."

"You will help me bring her to the midportal, Dalla. Then you will go back to your work. This task has been given to me and me alone. I will see it done."

He moved to the unconscious Eimear and poked her body with his foot.

"I will be glad to get help to bring her as far as the portal," he shrugged.

Eimear tired of the scene. There was much to be done.

273

- Hurry - she whispered to him. - Before all is lost, - she added.

She surveyed the land below her for a moment from her vantage point. It was time to move. She smiled as she spotted what she was looking for and leapt down into a creaking forest.

"Come Dalla. It is time," Cern said. He turned to Crea. "Rest sister and recover. I will return when I can."

With that, the two smallsky denizens took the unconscious other-Eimear and flew towards midportal.

Eimear listened to Arthmael and Crea as she waited for the others to be gone.

"There is nowhere for us, I think," Arthmael said.

"There was never a place for us Arthmael. What will we do?"

"Perhaps we should go to Éire? We can hide there in the Forests. We can find a quiet corner. Perhaps we will be left alone?"

Eimear thought she heard the draoí laughing somewhere inside of her. She leapt from the forest to land near the two.

Both recoiled as she alighted.

"Eimear?" Crea said. "But you just… Wait. You seem different. You look different too, Eimear. What is happening?"

The twarv moved between them, eyes narrowed, lips drawn tight.

"You are changed," he said. "You are not Eimear."

"I am Eimear, Arthmael. There is no need to fear. I had not thought of how I would explain what has happened to you. I have had a lot on my mind," she shrugged. She stifled a laugh. It would surely be harder to convince them that she was herself if she burst into laughter.

"We deserve whatever explanation might best describe what is happening, Eimear." Crea's voice was flat. Her eyes narrowed too.

"I went to them. To the draoí."

"What of Cern?"

"I was there for many years, Crea. I was in the old world for many years. They have been... had been using me."

Eimear shrugged. There was little to be gained from games.

"I killed him in my madness."

Crea put her hands to her face and wept.

"What have you done, girl?" Arthmael growled. "You are changed."

"The draoí. I know now that they did this to me. Made me what I am. It was their plan for me."

"What are you talking about?" Arthmael asked as he moved to comfort Crea. "You have done the things you have done. Not because of anyone else. Because you are you."

"No," Eimear's voice sounded strange in her own ears. "No. They made me their weapon of vengeance against Aébhal. Crea," she said. "Look at me."

Crea dropped her hands to her sides. Tears shone in her eyes.

"I was their tool. They have been sending me their draíocht since I was born. Ériu told me this herself. I swear to you both that it is the truth. They made me Síor Feargach so that I could destroy Aébhal."

"Why would they do this?" Crea asked, sobbing.

"He consumed one of them. He took one into himself. Took their power and made himself strong."

"He consumed a draoí?" Arthmael's face showed his shock; his lips trembled, and he began to turn pale.

Eimear knelt before them.

"They have made me what I am. I didn't have a chance to be me."

"How did you get away from them?" Crea asked, breathing heavily.

"I did something that ensures they cannot do what they did ever again. I finished what Aébhal started." She realised she was breathing heavily.

Arthmael knelt too. "Speak," he hissed. "Curse you, child. Tell us what you did."

"I took them all."

Both Crea and Arthmael gasped.

Eimear felt her cheeks get hot. Hearing her own words left her head spinning.

I destroyed the Gods.

"My only regret," she continued, "was that I never got a chance at a real life. I never got to know my parents and their love. It was all taken away from me by those things. The fruit of their labour became their poison.'

"All of them? How?" Crea's voice was barely recognisable.

"Does it matter?" Eimear sat back and reached for a nearby waterskin. "My throat is dry," she said.

"What does it mean?" Arthmael whispered, though it was hard to know who he was speaking to.

"None here have seen nor heard of them for an age. It is the same in my world. It will matter little." Eimear recognised the lie as surely as they did. She took a drink and was pleased by how cool the water felt in her mouth.

"It will matter little?" Crea put her two hands on a rock in front of her. "They are the source of all draíocht."

Arthmael put his hands to his head as Crea had.

"No," Eimear corrected. "They *were* the source of all draíocht. Now I am." She did not feel as sure as she sounded.

"That is to say that I may now be the source of all draíocht. Though I do not feel it leaving me so perhaps I am the end of all draíocht." She shrugged. "It is done, and the truth remains to be seen I think."

She stood.

"It is my intention to travel back to my old home once I am finished here. I will accompany you both. I will ensure you find somewhere quiet. Perhaps Mirdhí and my … friends there will be able to help you."

The two were silent as they watched her.

"It is more likely that you will kill us than any of the men there, Eimear," said Crea. "It is more likely that you will destroy both worlds.

"No. No, I will leave you in peace once we get there. I will leave before you find your place so that I can never find you again. It is also worth noting that you do not have many choices left. The Fand is closer than you think."

As if in answer, her keen hearing alerted her to the approaching horde. They were close.

Arthmael looked at Crea. She had wilted from the news and her wound. It must have been harrowing for him to see. Kneeling beside her, his huge arms encased her delicate wings.

"We are caught in the current, my love," he said. "This is the way the river is flowing. Let it take us where it takes us. You haven't had a chance to recover. And I haven't had a chance to mind you as I should. Perhaps Eimear's world is not the horrible place that it's reputed to be."

"If you are there, I don't see how it could be, Arthmael," said Crea, eyes closed, voice weary sounding. "I need to sleep," she whispered.

"Are we safe from you?" Arthmael asked, suddenly glaring at Eimear.

"Can you not see what I am? Though I have grown in power, I have grown the same amount in wisdom. I am your friend, Arthmael."

He released Crea and stood, walking to face Eimear.

"Answer me plainly. Yes or no. Are we safe from you? Can you promise it? Yes or no."

Arthmael waited tight-lipped, and when Eimear nodded, she heard him release the breath he had been holding.

"We should all get some sleep, Crea," said Eimear. "You most of all. Let us find somewhere that can provide us with shelter and shadow."

No further words were spoken until camp was set. Arthmael tended to Crea and the two whispered away from Eimear's ears. She could hear them. She could hear the hurried steps of the insects in the trees above them. Terror mixed with disbelief coloured their words. They would grow accustomed to the new way of things, just as the insects would after the camp was struck and the place belonged to them once more.

They sat together around a small fire and shared a meal. Few words were spoken, but Eimear did not feel awkward, rather enjoying the unlikely peace.

Suddenly, in the distance, she heard something and felt something. A strange presence had arrived on the Fandside. She reached out her senses as she heard Sword whisper, Danger comes.

Yes. I feel it.

Eimear stood and stretched. It was a power that was different from what she had felt previously. Different than that of the draoí or the Fand. Raw. Pure. Intoxicating.

"I need to leave you, but I would have you wait here until I return. Rest as best you can, Crea. There will be trials ahead for you both. Do you understand?"

Neither spoke as they exchanged a glance. Curt nods signalled yes. She paused before moving away.

"This is a new thing. Is there some warrior of the Fane that I have not yet met? A foe of great strength? Perhaps even stronger than Aébhal?"

"There are none stronger than Aébhal, bar the Fand. Perhaps Cromm is an equal in some ways."

"No, this is none of them. There is something old that has come from Faneside that is… different; strong, furious."

Crea shook her head slowly, then she licked her lips before speaking. "There is Caen."

Arthmael turned a frowning gaze on Crea.

"No one has heard tell of Caen since the old world. It cannot be him."

"Tell me of Caen, Crea," Eimear said.

"I do not know what to tell," her voice cool, gaze fixed on Eimear. "A beast of a bygone era. A monster.

A Faneson from a sire long-passed. You have heard tales as a child, I'm sure, of the Unspeakable Beast?"

Eimear nodded quickly. "With his fearsome roar and sharpened claws," she recounted.

"Indeed. Those stories came from his stories. Those in which he would destroy settlements on a whim; battle the mightiest warriors and best them with ease."

She looked at Arthmael and then back at Eimear.

"I do not know that he exists. If he does, I do not know what it may mean. If he is doing the Fane's bidding, the Fand is in terrible danger."

Eimear closed her eyes. "He is not here for the Fand. Not yet at least. He is here for me."

Crea shifted; a grimace creased her smooth features.

"And you would go to him?"

"He will find me. I think it would be best if I lead him away from you both. You would not be safe."

"You will not be safe, Eimear. If it is the creature of lore, even if he only has a modicum of his legendary strength, his power is immense. Though you are cloaked in draíocht, you are young and lack experience. He is older than your world. The Fand must face him."

"Perhaps you are right, Crea. I am sorry for the harm that I have caused to you and to those here that I came to think of as friends. I meant, nor wanted, any of this, this life. If we do not meet again, it means that he has killed me, and in doing so, I hope that you find a way free of the trouble I have made for you. For both of you."

She turned and walked towards the fury.

***

They came to face each other on the top of a broad hill. A conspiratorial mist blanketed the meadows around them, making sure that whatever was to pass, would not be witnessed.

The beast was terrifying. Its head, that of a horned hound. Its body, that of an impossibly muscled giant. Its legs, that of a bull. Her nostrils twitched when a familiar scent of wet fur reached her. She thought back to Donkey and the thought stung her heart. Opening her hand, she tried to recall the feel and sounds of his wet nose snuffling it.

The creature's harsh breathing was the only sound here, unless it could hear her heart pounding, and it knocked her out of her wistfulness. Her own breathing sounded shallow.

"Can you speak to me?" she said.

Only in thought, came his voice in her mind. It was not unlike the draoí, but it was heavy. Laden with barely suppressed rage. Goose pimples rose on her arms.

"You seek to kill me?"

What are you?

"I am Eimear. I am from the other side of the portal dolmen; from Éire."

The creature's sneer turned to a snarl.

You lie. You are draoí. What trickery is this?

"I am Eimear. I am Síor Feargach. I took the draoí."

Its pitch-black eyes narrowed into slits.

Took them?

"I do not need to explain it further. You can feel them in me?" She felt her face harden. Caen did not know yet, but he would.

281

The creature threw its head back and roared. Eimear found that she had taken a step backwards. Tutting, she took a long breath and stepped forward once more, this time with her hand on Sword. She would take no more backwards steps.

How did you do this? His near-feral voice in her mind was insistent.

"Because they were arrogant. Because they were evil, wilful. And because they could not stop me."

What do you seek?

Eimear paused. It was a question for which there were many answers.

"To make music."

You speak in riddles. You speak of taking the draoí, though it is not possible.

"I could not speak more plainly to you. I took them because I wanted them. I wonder is there a way that I can take you too, Caen?"

She drew Sword, who remained silent; tentative.

This time it was the creature who shifted backwards.

Do you not know me? I will tear your limbs from your frail form. I am the dark itself; the frost; the howling gale. I am older than time. I am death.

Eimear started to hum as she walked towards the thing. The song sounded cold in the mist.

"Show me."

It attacked; a blur of curved talons and razor-sharp fangs, moving at such speed that sections of the mist around the hill furrowed, long into the distance.

Eimear watched the creature from where it had launched its attack. She raised her arms.

"My limbs are still attached, it would appear. You will need to be quicker, howling gale. Show me."

The thing shot towards her with such a leap, that great plumes of mist were dragged behind it like a cloak. It stopped, head lolling, openly confused.

Eimear could not help but smile as she walked from the hillock of gathered mist behind him. Disbelief twisted his nightmarish face.

How do you do this? his voice snarled.

"You know so little, Caen."

It was Eimear's turn. She moved to the beast and cut off a tuft of his fur, then stood an arm's length from him to display it. Its maw opened signalling shock at her sudden appearance, so close to him.

"This could have been your head, Caen."

He launched a savage attack of claw and fang, and this time she did not retreat. With the flat side of Sword, she blocked and dodged his barrage. Eimear watched his movements and took note of his faults. He continued to attack, tirelessly, for a year, or a day, or a moment. Had there been anyone to watch it, none could have perceived the battle, for the two became the mist around them.

She felt the draoí within her bask in the violent beauty of their oldest living work and their newest living work; knowing that there would never be an equal to the deadly skills of this pair.

He cut her skin and left her bloodied, but he could not land a blow to injure her gravely.

When Caen stood back, panting loudly, shoulders sagging, Sword spoke to her:

It is time for me to make music. Now.

Eimear lowered the blade and gazed into the creature's eyes. "You will scream for me, Caen, but I will not rejoice in the sound as I should. I do not wish this to be your end."

Her stomach churned. Under his rage she could feel his sadness. She knew it and felt sick at the thought of killing him. His terrible maw twisted. A smile?

You will not kill me.

"Why do you say that?"

Because I have seen the moment of my death. It is a death I have come to know and long for. I am old; spent.

For a moment something passed across the black of his eyes; something that was familiar to her. A humanity?

I had hoped that I could set free those that you have captured inside you and would be allowed to go with them when I die.

"I do not understand. You are so certain I will not kill you?"

As much as I wish for it, you only have one sword.

It turned and started to walk away.

Sword screamed now. He screamed at her to cut the thing; to make the music. A whining, grating sound. His scream made her lip curl, and she silenced him with a sharp thrust back into his scabbard.

"Will you go to the Fand?" she asked the creature.

I will wait until it is time to cross over. It will end there as the way closes.

The fury emanating from him eased for a moment and Eimear felt a wave of something… of hope.

The creature turned its terrible gaze on her one last time.

I was as you were once. We are the same now. I do not know what kind of beast you will become but I know

*that you should have let me kill you. You will long for
death as I did; as I do; as I will.*

Caen disappeared into the mist, that opened its arms
to welcome him.

***

Eimear returned to Crea and Arthmael. She refused to
answer their questions. Though Crea seemed somewhat
improved, there was no doubt that she was suffering.
Her face was drawn, the usual sharp features, dulled.

"Are you ready?" she asked Crea.

"I am," Crea said, voice quiet.

"Arthmael, we will need some supplies before we
go. I will need you to go and find some. Most
importantly, water. Fill our waterskins to brimming.
Crea will not be able to fly to get some more. She needs
to do as little as possible. Find us something to eat along
the way. Be quick."

Arthmael nodded, took the skins and his spear, and
made ready to leave.

"Not that way," Eimear said. She pointed in the
direction furthest away from the approaching hunt. "I
spotted a fast-moving stream a league in that direction.
With luck, you will find all that we need on your way."

He looked first at Crea, then at Eimear. Nodding
curtly, he disappeared into the forest.

"He has always been too trusting," Crea said.

"Perhaps he, from all of us, might be able to escape."

"You intend to bring me before the Fand?"

"I am sorry, Crea. I need to be brought before both
of them. The two of us together will ensure that."

"It is true. You are evil."

"No, Crea. There is neither good nor evil. There are only needs and the will to see them met. I am Síor Feargach. I have recently decided that I am going to change things."

"Change what things, Eimear?"

"Everything, Crea. Everything, everywhere. I will try to protect you. But first I must use you."

"To what end?"

"I am going to kill them."

"Them? Who is them, Eimear? What are you talking about?"

"The Fane and the Fand," Eimear said, unable to stop her lip from twitching. "I am going to give the Fae world a change of vision. As I did the Old World. As I will in my own world. I will get you back to Arthmael. Trust in me."

Crea shook her head slowly. "What have you become?"

"Welcome," said Eimear.

Warriors of different settlements arrived to surround them. Their weapons were drawn, and several arrows were trained on the two females. Eimear could hear the bowstrings humming, bows creaking.

"What have you become, Eimear?"

Eimear's face softened and she started to hum.

WATCHER

*Breithnigh an abhainn sara
dtéir ina cuilithe.*

Observe the river before you
venture into its currents.

CROMM SAW HER return. He watched her as she spat the dart that knocked her old self down. He saw the power that came from her. Draíocht was a curious thing. It came to those who drew it, yet he as he watched her, he knew what she had done. He saw what she was. She had become a source of draíocht.

Has she taken one of the Draoí as Aébhal did?

He wondered if she knew she was landing in the same forest from where he observed. She had not looked towards him, yet she landed within a short distance from the branch where he was sitting.

When he worked with Aébhal to consume the draoí, he had only considered the difficulty in capturing a second one without killing his brother. And the difficulty in killing Aébhal after it was done.

He had believed that Caen would be the one to help him achieve his goals, but now that she had bested Caen, those plans were squashed. How had he not seen it before? Eimear was the answer. As he had watched her over the years, though he had become intrigued by her, he had seen a threat, a pawn, a tool, but never seeing her for what she was.

Eimear was the answer. The strength to obliterate the weakness and banish it forever. With her as his new Fand, he could become the greatest Fane in history. Together, they could reshape the very foundations of the world.

Cromm shook his head, but he could not forget how beautiful she had grown. Her grace and her loveliness radiated brighter than the incredible draíocht around her. For all the power she now possessed, her beauty was still more powerful by far.

Desire made his lungs heave. Urgent, driving desire.

For all his schemes, the hand of fate had drawn them together across time and space. There were none who could now match her for power. Not here or anywhere.

But Cromm knew that he could challenge her mind. He could guide her through what would be a difficult time. Dealing with her new-found power could destroy her. She needed him as much as he needed her.

Eimear must have known he was there when she landed.

Together, they would ensure the Fae world would be a precious stone compared to the desolate rocks of any other.

Together, those other worlds would fall into line and become greater under their protection.

He stretched his arms out wide and laughed loudly.

"I am close. The time is nigh," he whispered to his harpoon.

Fae Rí

Fear na bó faoina heireaball.

The cow's owner must go under
her tail.

THE HORDE OF the Fand stood at the longshore of the crease.

Before them stood the Fingers of the Crease. Every time Ferragh laid eyes upon them, that same sense of awe accompanied. The largest buildings ever constructed anywhere in the Fae realm. All four of the incredible towers, larger by far than the palace of the Fand. Larger than the abandoned mountain fortress of the warlord Domhnall. Larger than the fabled dizzying structures of the dragans. Built by many tribes over three hundred years, they told the story of the true potential of the Fae people working alongside each other. Striving towards a common goal.

No one had seen such vast numbers gathered for many ages. Ferragh stole a glance at Aébhal and wondered what he had planned, what he had promised. Aébhal was not a leader who leaned towards fist thumping speeches to fire the belly. No. He was more akin to the trickling mountain stream that flowed out to the fearsome waves of the angry sea.

Aébhal's army knew what to do. The Fane, it seemed, was the only pathetic soul left in the dark.

Ferragh clutched the ornate dagger under his cloak. The fear of being cast into the shadows led to dark deeds. Ferragh could already hear himself delivering the fist-thumping speech over the body of his son. He understood his subjects in ways that Aébhal could not dream.

The greatest revenge is the one most witnessed, Aébhal, he thought to himself. He checked across the crease. There was still no sign of the Fand and her horde. Ferragh would bide his time.

He heard someone behind him and wheeled quickly to defend himself. A quick scan revealed no-one. He had imagined it. Still, it was good that he was prepared for treachery. He would need his wits about him.

Ferragh looked at the parallel longshores. Both perched impossibly at the edge of the crease. For all the times he had laid eyes upon the place, he still had the knot in the centre of his stomach when he thought about what would happen if he fell in. To fall forever. Alone in the darkness. Madness would not come quickly enough.

He shook his head.

Aébhal's voice rang out.

"Lower the bridge."

Ferragh gasped. The bridge being lowered was a wonder that he had never witnessed in his long life. He had no doubt that the gruagach proprietors would have the mechanisms in working order.

The sound of the enormous wooden bridge descending was hypnotic. Impossibly slow, it seemed that it might take days for the task to be finished. The repetitive whine created a song that reached inside Ferragh. Even the bridge complained to him. It begged him to restore order so that they could once again rest silently.

He went to confront his son who was striding towards the longshore.

"What is your intention, Aébhal?"

"Stand out of my way."

"Speak to me. Do I not deserve at least some respect as the Fane?"

Aébhal paused.

"I am going to make the leap. Then I am going to lower their side. We will meet the Fand's horde on their side. It will make what I must suggest more urgent, I suspect."

"What if you are the cause of a war? We have held the peace since I became the Fane. Do you detest peace so, Aébhal?"

Aébhal's clawed hand wrapped tightly around Ferragh's throat, quickly cutting the air off.

"I detest your fat, gluttonous ways. I detest the Fand's preening hubris. Here, where the draíocht is strong enough to allow us to create a mighty world; a world of conquerors; a world of plenty and of superiority. I wish to change it and do those things. I have become strong, Father. I have taken a draoí. Consumed it. Taking its power unto me. Making it my own. All this, I have done for this world. It is time for us to spill out into the other worlds. To take what our power allows us. To spread ourselves into the stew of worlds that draíocht links us to. Peace can be ours, here. That does not mean that we need to be sheep to have it."

"That is not our way, Aébhal," said Ferragh, disgusted at how cloying his voice sounded. "This is not the path the Fae have ever chosen."

"Paths change, Ferragh. Over time, they disappear into the forests and new ones are beaten to become great roads. I am finally her equal. Cromm will assist me if she bests me, but between us, she cannot win. Be warned. If you stand in my path again, I will cast you aside. You are nothing only a title. Soon, I will take that title and make it mean something once again. My sons will know conquest, not the shame I grew into."

Shame. Ferragh understood what Aébhal had felt, for he felt it in waves. Aébhal had not been looking at his father with hate in his eyes all this time. It was shame.

"I ... am sorry, Aébhal. I did not see. I should have attended more to you as you grew."

"It is late for such thoughts, Father," said Aébhal. "Too late."

He brushed roughly past his father. His chest bumping off the concealed dagger. Ferragh's heart almost stopped as his son slowed for a moment, head turning to address him.

"Is that for me ... or yourself?" he asked softly before continuing to the longshore. As Ferragh's hands slumped to his sides in grim resignation, Aébhal leapt suddenly, crossing the great length of the Crease in a bound to land on the longshore on the other side.

Ferragh watched him make his way towards the bridge tower there.

Ferragh watched in amazement as the enormously wide bridge lowered slowly. The whine of the two sides now moving created a bitter fugue. Tears made every effort to stop him from watching clearly.

The Fane's horde made towards the slowly lowering span. Some, eager to see their kind on the other side. Others, eager for war and conquest. All, destined to cross once the two sides of the bridge joined. Two sides joined. What did it mean?

Ferragh searched the far shore. There was no sign of any of the Fand's horde. No defenders. Even the gruagachs from the bridge-keep must have retreated upon the arrival of the Fane's horde. Aébhal's army.

Ferragh searched the crowd for Cromm. His absence at this point was a mystery. An occasion such as this would shake any Fae to the core. The potential for a descent into chaos was significant. Perhaps he would reconsider his position since things stood so close to the brink. His gaze landed on the far Longshore. Where, for that matter, was the Fand?

As if to answer his question, a horn blew in the distance.

CROMM

*Chíonn beirt rud nach
bhfeiceann duine amháin.*

Two people see a thing that one
cannot.

DALLA FLEW AWAY as the Fand arrived at the meadow where Cromm stood. He could never understand why he was drawn to long grasses. Yet here he felt most at ease, where the tall strands of many greens, nodded the direction of the wind; constantly bowing, but all the time growing. Spreading. Covering vast plains and always ready for more.

Dalla's word rang in his ears as he watched the Fand approach, surrounded by a retinue of duillechán warriors. "You are counting on too many things that are out of your control. There are too many ways for this to fail. My heart is filled with fear, for I think now that all is lost."

His mother's words shook him from his thoughts.

"My son," said Doireann. "How are you here? How did you know that we would find them here?"

"Luck perhaps?" he shrugged.

The Fand was youthful in form, wearing loose fitting transparent robes. She kicked off her sandals and her toes wriggled in the grass. When she faced him, she wore a smile that was all teeth.

"Luck. I see. Long may it last for you, Cromm."

"Long indeed, my Fand."

"Our time is close."

"I believe so." He bowed his head slightly.

"Do you know your part in what is to come?" her voice was airy.

"Do you know what is to come?" he countered.

"Death."

"Yes. And my part, Doireann? In your mind?"

"At my side, no matter who must now fall."

He searched her face for some sign of emotion, but it was a mask of serenity.

She bent low to run her hands through the long grass. Pulling a tuft, she drew it to her nose and inhaled deeply.

"Aébhal will tear you limb from limb, once he discovers you have been betraying him, my son."

"Of that, we can be sure, my Fand."

"You are resolute then?" She offered him the tuft of grass, studying his face as he accepted.

Cromm took a moment to reflect on the question while pressing the grass to his face.

"I think that it would be difficult to find a better description of how I am currently feeling."

"What was it that Dalla said to you?"

Dropping the tuft of grass, he met her gaze.

"You see many things, my Fand."

"What did she say to you."

"She has been helping me. Firstly, to watch Aébhal. Secondly, and more recently, to find Crea and the mangblood." He wondered about his face as he spoke. The slightest trace of a lie would surely cost him his life. Aébhal tearing him limb from limb might even be a blessing in comparison to incurring Doireann's wrath.

"You did not think to tell me that she was your agent?" Doireann moved to stand closer to him. Her face began to change. A flash of sharpened fangs in her mouth made his stomach turn to ice.

Resolute. I am resolute, he chided himself.

"What would you have me tell you, Doireann? You wish to know everything I know? See everything I see? Have I not earned your trust enough to allow me to work my way?"

He turned to walk from her, offering his back.

"Why does it concern you that Dalla and I have become allies? Has it not long been such with you and Crea?"

"I suppose it has, my son." Her admission was softer in tone.

He spun to meet her gaze once more.

"You are the Fand. Of that, there is no doubt. But do not forget that I am Cromm. I have my ways, as well I must. For I am the second Faneson and my world is treacherous. I have no palace nor feasting halls. I have only my wits and my resolve."

He cursed himself for raising his voice. It was uncouth.

Doireann smiled and this time it reached her eyes.

"Oh, I do enjoy when you show me that fire, Cromm. You will need it for us to succeed in killing Aébhal. And Ferragh after. You will make a most glorious Fane, my son."

When her finger came to rest on his chest, it had a vicious talon perched on the end.

"We might have to work on your decorum while addressing your Fand, but that can come with time."

He felt his face redden.

We will see about that, bitch, he hissed in his mind.

Something flashed in her eyes and her brow furrowed for a moment. Did she know?

He kept his face a mask of stone. Reddened or not.

"My Fand. Only together have we arrived at this place. If I am tense in my delivery, believe that it is the severity of the situation itself. We stand, together, teetering on the end of an age. We cannot underestimate the Fane or his first son."

"As they have underestimated us," she nodded.

Me. Me Doireann. As you have always underestimated me. As they all have.

His thoughts drifted to Eimear for a moment. Her power overshadowed them all, and he was the only one who knew her. Probably better than she knew herself after so many years of watching her grow.

"Let me go and bring Crea and the mangblood before you. Let us begin the end."

Nodding again, she took her finger from his chest and put her hands behind her back.

"I can see how you have come to love the meadowlands, Cromm."

"You see many things, my Fand."

SMALLSKY DENIZEN

An áit a mbíonn toit bíonn tine.

There is no smoke without fire.

CREA WATCHED THE warriors of the Fandside surround them. A great weariness settled over her. It had all been for naught. She could not easily recall the series of decisions she had made to bring her to this point, yet here she was.

Eimear was the cause. The galling thing was that she had clearly intended none of this to happen.

She frowned as Cromm appear from amidst the encircling warriors; his famous harpoon, *Greim Tapaidh*, held loosely in his hand.

A flicker in the smallsky above, marked Dalla's return from midportal. Crea's weariness deepened, not allowing her to feel the terrible shock that she should, as she watched the two join each other standing before Crea and those around her.

"I do not understand," she said, shaking her head at her sister.

"I know, Crea," said Dalla.

"It was never for you to know, Crea," said Cromm. "You were … distracted."

He glanced over at Arthmael.

"As was I," said the Fae prince as he turned his attention on Eimear. Crea noted the clear admiration in his gaze.

"I have watched you, since the day you arrived here."

"You were in the trees while Aébhal spoke to me?"

Cromm nodded slowly.

"And you would come to watch me in the practice paddock, and often over the years?"

"You saw me?"

"Sensed you."

"As you did when you landed in the forest?"

Eimear smiled and Crea saw that it was the smile of a young woman.

"I thought it fitting," Eimear said.

Cromm and Eimear walked to stand before each other. Eimear had the sword in her hand; Cromm, the harpoon in his.

"I have often wondered about my watcher. I had often hoped that you would come to talk with me."

Cromm nodded. "As I have spent many hours wanting to do so."

301

"Why did you come now?" she asked him.

"It is not so easy a thing to answer," he shrugged.

Crea noticed a bead of sweat on his brow as he spoke to Eimear.

"As I say," he said. "I have long wished to approach you, but I could not risk it until I was sure about you. About your role here and your future in this place."

"I do not understand," Eimear said.

"Speak plainly to us, Cromm," Crea said, words harsh as they left her.

"I watch many things," Cromm said. "I became aware of the draoí and their plan for you, Eimear. I have been going to them for many years. Whispering to them. Listening to them. At first, I found your existence curious. As I watched, I found your growing skills both unique and hypnotic. Now I see you as a woman. I see what you are. Your strength; incomprehensible. Your speed; dizzying. More, however, Eimear. The sound of your voice; calming. Your form; exhilarating. I have not had the chance to look closely upon you, but now that I can, I find your eyes intoxicating. Your face; mesmerising. Your lips; tantalising."

He moved closer again and their weapons made brief contact.

"I adore you, though you have never spoken a word to me. It is a thing that I should have been able to control in myself, but you removed that power from me with every one of your actions. Though I thought I was only watching you, I know now that I was falling deeper and deeper in love with you. And now I am here. And while I feel nearly overcome from my feelings for you, I also feel sheer terror. I feel powerless before you. I beseech you to choose your words carefully, so you

302

do not rend my heart from my chest. Let me love you, Eimear."

If Eimear had any strong feeling on the revelation, her face did not show it.

"You love me, but you have come to kill me?"

"No. I love you. Aébhal sent Caen to kill you, but it seems that he was not up to the task."

"What did you come to do?"

"I came to bring you before the Fand."

Crea reeled in shock. She looked from Cromm to Dalla. "The two of you? The two of you have been in league with the Fand?"

Dalla shrugged. "The Fane has effectively been dethroned. Aébhal's ambition will destroy the Fae; our way of life; our prosperity. The Fand will help Cromm to become the new ruler of Faneside. We will need her help to defeat him now that he has consumed a draoí and taken their spirit?"

"Yes. I know," Crea whispered. The beating of her heart slowed and then quickened as she recalled what Eimear had done.

"What you don't know is that he plans on taking more of them. More of their essence and their draíocht. It will soon come to the stage where none of us will be able to balance his power. We need to kill him before he consumes more of them."

"That is not something you should worry about," said Eimear, turning away from Cromm, seemingly only half listening. The girl stood, taking in the world around her.

"What do you mean, mangblood?" asked Dalla.

"He cannot consume any more of them. They have gone to a place where he cannot reach them."

303

All gathered were silent. Crea waited for her to elaborate, but she did not continue. The memory of Eimear's words filled Crea with the dread once more.

Eimear tutted and shrugged.

"Why should I help the Fand?"

"Because if you do, you will become my consort, my *Rúnsearc*. You can help me rule the Faneside as my second. Though it is rare for a female to do so, it has happened in the past and can again, in the future. If you have bested Caen, it will help Fanesiders know that you should help rule."

"Why would I want to be your consort?"

"Do you not feel an attraction to me? Do I not please you as an equal? I am one of the two brothers. I am a force on both sides. I have made the leap to watch you many times. I would be yours."

"You are not my equal, Cromm. You do not know it, so I forgive you for your comment. I have never taken a lover. Perhaps you could be my first. However, I would never consider becoming your consort."

"Why not? It would be a life of pleasure; of joy; of challenge. Once I become strong as the Fane, I can install you as the Fand and we can rule as one. We will not need Doireann for long. There is nothing that we cannot achieve together."

"Because both sides will fear to speak my name," Eimear hissed, spinning to face him.

"I do not understand."

"You will." Eimear sheathed her sinister blade. Crea noticed that there was blood on it and wondered from where it had spilled. From whom.

"You can watch as always, Cromm. Watch where my path has brought me. Take me to the Fand," Eimear said opening her hands either side of her. "I wish to speak to her."

"Will you not consider my proposal further? I fear my heart will break if you ignore my advances so." His spear dropped to the ground; hands coming up to his head.

"There are worse things than your heart breaking, Cromm."

"So, you say it will not be?" Cromm's voice shook. Crea felt empathy towards him. Love was not a small thing.

"Perhaps we will share a story. Your affection is flattering. However, it will not happen the way you have planned. No one's plans here are sacred. The Fand wanted me to come. I am here. If you wish to love me, obey me. If I am to be your *Rúnsearc*, bring me to the Fand."

The Fae prince nodded once, his mouth a straight line. He picked up his spear and turned.

"Bring them all," he said to his band.

***

Crea fell in beside Dalla as the band moved through the woodland.

"We are all lost, it seems," said Crea.

"Not lost, I fear, Crea. We have become a part of the change. The day that Eimear arrived here, I sensed it coming. We whisper of those who have crossed over here from her world. We whisper about how it spoils them; destroys them over time. We never considered that her presence became like a rot. To spoil and destroy our realm just as markedly. At first, I resisted." Dalla's gaze focused on nothing, her voice soft.

Crea looked over to Arthmael, who was watching her. "I'm not sure I resisted at all."

"I knew how wrong it was when Cromm came to me on behalf of the Fand. To think him capable of betraying the Faneside, while Aébhal himself betrayed the Fane. Once I knew, I could not report it without causing the destruction of what we know. I had no choice… draíocht or draoí. Fand or Fane. This realm or others," said Dalla. "I wondered where the origin of the change lay for a long time. Now I know. It is clear. It is her. She is chaos and her presence alone will bring chaos to us. It is upon us."

Crea felt the pain subsiding somewhat.

"What is left for us, Dalla?"

"Death."

"They have not taken our weapons. Perhaps the Fand will only punish some of us."

"Perhaps."

As they moved from the woodlands onto the plains close to the longshore and the crease beyond, they saw a sight that filled Crea with dread. In the distance the Faneside horde had crossed over and had spread out across the longshore. The horde of the Fand were moving to intercept.

The Fand's voice came from behind them causing them all to turn. Her wrinkled old face appeared kindly.

"What a band. What an unusual collection. Two of the denizens; long held in my opinion as the two fairest creatures in the land. The Faneside prince, the twarv and the visitor, Eimear. A strange sign of these times. It seems Cromm thought better than to try and disarm you, Eimear. I think he was correct. This is what I wanted. You, here with me as we come to the end of

306

this age. Yet… you are different, girl. Something has happened to you?"

Crea watched as Eimear walked before the Fand, seemingly without fear.

"I destroyed the draoí, Doireann. I destroyed them all and took them into me. I am Síor Feargach and I am going to make you pay as I did them. I do not need to take your essence. It would be worth very little to me. As for you taking control, I think your vision stopped here, for another reason entirely."

She drew her sword. A trickle of blood from the blade fell onto the long grass. Weapons hissed into hands, as the warriors of the Fand leapt to protect her.

Cromm's harpoon came to rest on Eimear's shoulder.

"This is not the anointed time for the Fand to die. This is the time for us to become one, you and I."

The Fand stood watching, still an old woman, but her kindly face had changed. A ripple of panic twitched across her features.

"The draoí? You destroyed them? What do you say? Why do you say this?"

"So that you know what you did. You brought me here, seeking to use me. They brought me there, seeking to use me. They are all dead. As are you. I will leave then so that Aébhal may do with this place as he pleases. But not before I leave my mark among your armies. A lesson can be a costly thing to learn. The arrogance of your race has been galling. When I leave here, I will leave a chastened realm. I will leave a stain in the memory of your people."

Crea saw that the Fand had become the beast, though she had not seen the change. A lolling tongue fell from between jagged fangs. Her resemblance to Caen was unmistakable.

Cromm moved to stand between the two females, his harpoon still resting on Eimear's shoulder.

"You discovered what Aébhal has been doing?"

"I did," said Eimear, without taking her eyes off the Fand. "Though I know now that little of this has been his doing, Cromm."

"And you did the same in turn," he said, lips pursed.

"I did. But where he took one or two, I took them all."

Cromm's face became a show. His harpoon dropped to his side.

"What does this mean?" he asked, seemingly to himself.

A line of clear spittle, dribbled from the beast's maw.

"What does it mean, Eimear?" asked the beast.

"I am no longer Eimear to you. To you, I am Síor Feargach..." Her arm flicked around Cromm's lithe form in the blink of an eye. "...and it means your death."

A tear trickled down Cromm's cheek. As it did, the Fand's head started to fall from her body. There was a slow parallel as both tear and head fell to the long grass.

Crea, slack-jawed, watched Eimear lean in to kiss Cromm. Most present wailed their anguish before raising their weapons to avenge the death off their Fand.

Raising her sword high, Eimear started to hum a tune and moved amongst them. Screams of anguish became screams of pain. Horror distorted their faces as her sword stung and cut them, their weapons useless against her.

Crea's hand snaked out to stop Dalla, who moved towards the slaughter. "We may live if we do not move. But make a move against her, and it means the end."

Dalla's noisy weeping made Crea realise that she was also weeping. Arthmael came to stand beside her, and he took her hand in his. The sounds of Eimear's butchery made Crea nauseous.

Cromm stepped forward, watching, mouth agape.

As the sounds diminished except for the increasingly familiar tune that Eimear hummed, Eimear put her bloody sword into its scabbard. Her face had changed.

She turned to Dalla, her eyes egg white. "Crea was correct. You would have died. You may yet, for my needs remain, yet I gave my word to Crea and Arthmael and I suspect they would be more upset with me."

Crea felt light-headed. She could not clearly hear the words that she found herself speaking.

"You have murdered the Fand. You have killed her. You have destroyed the Fandside as surely as you have destroyed the draoí. I do not have the words to describe the ramifications."

"Do none of you see?" Eimear cried. "This has all been according to his plan." Her finger pointed to Cromm, whose harpoon remained at his side. "I chose none of this. I asked to be left alone, yet all of you plot and scheme against one another, thinking to use me for your own ends."

"The Fand pursued her own misguided vision for the future. I showed her the ramifications of her decisions. The Fane is next. Do any of you wish to challenge me?"

She turned to regard them one by one. "You Arthmael? You Dalla? You Crea?"

She squared up to Cromm. "You? What are your plans for me now? Do you wish to challenge me?"

None spoke.

"I do, little bitch," said a voice that bolted Crea where she stood.

Aébhal marched up the longshore towards them.

Crea turned to see Eimear's reaction, but the girl was bent over with her head in her hands, face frozen in agony. She screamed a piercing scream that brought silence over the Fandside.

THE LONGSHORE

*Caithfidh gach éinne deachú na
sláinte a dhíol.*

Everyone must pay the tithes of
health.

Eimear

PAIN EXPLODED BEHIND Eimear's eyes as the draoí
inside her revolted. They roared at her in unison. A
choir of rage. Over the many voices came Ériu's:

*Will we help him to kill you after all? Did you think
us so defeated? We will destroy you for your treachery.
Little bitch, he named you. Little whore.*

Eimear could not answer. The pain of the dark realm
repeated inside her. The draoí were trying to tear her
open.

She became aware of the giant speaking to her from somewhere. Then a flash of earthly pain jarred her, and she felt herself falling hard.

She had been struck. A shockwave passed through her body. A kick, perhaps. Though the pain was new, it was insignificant.

You will kill him. Then you will fall on your sword or we will torment you until you succumb. You are a child. We possess the wisdom of ages.

Another streak of pain wracked her. She could not tell from which source it came. She could not cry out. She could only exist in the suffering.

End this. Amend your heinous act.

Each part of her burned in agony. She dug her fingernails into her face so that she might feel a lesser pain for a moment.

You can make the pain disappear. All you need do, is comply. End your own misery. The misery that is your entire existence. Do you agree to our terms?

She flew into her own mind. The valleys and mountains, grasslands and forests below her burned. Flames ripped across them, turning them black. In the distance, Eimear saw the sun was starting to set. She had never considered it. Her mind was dying as her body was broken. She turned to face reddening sunset; an end to her pain – all of her pain. Eimear flew towards the dusk and the darkest places of her mind.

Arthmael

Tears made it difficult to see. Eimear's body was being buffeted by Aébhal in a rage that was stomach-churning to witness. Aébhal's primal roars silenced the length of the longshore. Both hordes were drawn to the commotion, keeping a distance from each other.

Arthmael knew that one or two more of the Fathach's violent blows would kill Eimear, regardless of her draíocht. He held her up by the hair, her arms hung limp by her sides.

Aébhal raised her up for the gathering crowds to behold.

"This beast sought to ruin our world. I have not allowed her to do so. It is not change we need to fear. It is creatures like this one. It is those otherworlders who would so happily take everything we have and everything we hold dear. Change is upon us. This beast has murdered the Fand."

A ragged cry arose from both hordes. Many Fae knelt or fell, others ran away screaming. Some ran to the edge of the longshore and leapt into the crease.

"She has brought change," roared Aébhal. "It is time to take revenge. It is time to go to her world and drive their peoples into their seas."

A roar rose from the masses.

"The Fand is no more. The Fane has asked me to rule. Until we rid ourselves of the curse of men, I will do just that. There is no Faneside; no Fandside either. There is the Fae world and any who reject this will be cast into the crease."

Another quieter roar. Aébhal stood to his full height and raised his arm.

"So, I say to you all, you will join me. You will accept me as the Fane of all. Any who do not, will pay the price this very day; and that price is death. Look inside yourselves and look at those who would stand beside you. Do you wish for war, or do you wish for power? For Glory?"

Arthmael found himself amidst the Fae of the two hordes. Many were clearly dismayed at the death of their Fand.

"Those who wish to join me, join with the Faneside horde and see yourself welcomed. But be quick, for my patience is thin."

Arthmael reached out towards Crea. She went to him then, and he wrapped his arms around her.

"It is the end, Crea."

"If it is the end, in your arms is where I wish to be."

They both spun when they heard Aébhal roar, "Choose your fate."

Eimear

"The crease is unfathomable. Do you know what that means?" Eimear recalled Hogar's voice from the past.

"It is forever."

"Yes. Your mind is more."

"How?"

"It is a forever that is yours. A crease inside you where you can travel anywhere in an instant. Not just to your memories, or experiences. To unseen worlds; through vast distances. Do you see? To be able to visit any part of eternity itself."

"I cannot."

"Not yet. But you must know. You must realise what you are. You are forever, Eimear."

Where are you, little bitch? Do you think to try to escape us?

"I cannot bear the pain. I am flying to the edge."

The edge? What are you speaking of?

Eimear flew towards the darkness as the sun set; the shrieking draoí somewhere behind her.

Where are you? You cannot run.

"I do not want to run anymore. I want for this to be over."

Do as we command.

"You face oblivion."

Better oblivion than captivity.

"So be it." Eimear flew faster.

Ferragh

Ferragh's fists were balled tight, his shoulders hunched. *He has named himself Fane. Even as I stand here among the men gathered under my banner.*

He closed his eyes, scarcely able to believe what was happening. *Doireann. She has murdered my love. My Fand.*

There were cries coming from both hordes. The death of the Fand left everyone numb; stunned; empty. Some were standing, looking at Ferragh still atop his mount. *For leadership? Do you remain loyal to me?*

Many were clearly considering Aébhal's command. Others had already started to move from the Fand's horde to the Fanes. A foul stench of desperation surrounded them all.

"I will not give you another chance. Save yourself from execution," continued Aébhal. My son. My wretched, treacherous son.

Ferragh slid from his horse and found himself walking toward Aébhal. *He has ruined the Fae world. He has betrayed me.*

He reached inside his cloak; his fingers found the hilt of his blade and he drew it without removing his gaze from the Fathach.

Sensing an air of panic around him, he took the confusion as an opportunity, using his duillechán draíocht to disappear from the sight of those around him. He started to move faster. His quickening pace matching his pounding heartbeat. He sucked in his protruding gut and marched at his tallest.

Aébhal stood tall before the swelling numbers of the Faneside horde.

"We cannot have resistance. We can only move forward through unity. Unity is power. Order where there is disorder. Prepare to attack those who do not join us."

Eimear

You mean to let us die? asked Sword.

I mean to escape the pain. All of the pain.

It is the same.

So it is.

What if he casts us into the crease? What if we cannot die? We will fall in this pain forever.

I do not know what else to do.

There must be another way.

"There's a way over every stream, Eimear," said Hógar's voice from the past. "Across every river. Across the widest ocean. That's here, in our world of limits and flesh."

316

He pointed into the crease. "There are even limits down there. Though we cannot comprehend them. There is only one place where there are no limits."

His finger tapped his temple. She could not see his face. "Here, there are no limits. Believe this. Know this. Will this. Within you are all the answers you will ever need.

"Your Father knew it in many ways, but love changed him. He filled up his mind with your mother, with you; even though he never met you. Someday, I hope you will too. But before that, fly free. Without limits."

Eimear flew. Free.

Little bitch. Where are you gone?

"I have told you. I go to our end."

How do you mean to end your life in your mind? Or is it your mind you have lost?

"I can feel that this would give you pleasure, yet you only exist in my mind now. If I do lose it, what becomes of you? What if he casts me into the crease and you are trapped here in my madness?"

Eimear saw the truth. The pain they inflicted was born from their fear, anger, hatred. Their rage.

"I feel your rage, Ériu. As you fed mine. I feel your fear also. You should hope that the darkness ahead is the end, for both of us."

You are twisted beyond words.

"I am your creation."

Cromm

His plans were in ruin. His goals becoming distant. After all he had given for this place, his brother, who

317

Cromm had empowered, now stood ready to reap the fruits of his toil.

I cannot let him end her now, or there will be none left to stop him.

His mind reeled. Eimear had taken the draoí for herself. All of them. The death of the Fand had been sooner than he had wished, yet now it was done, Cromm needed to finish it. He needed to kill his brother and save her.

My love. Is that what she is?

He searched his heart to see if he had spoken the truth to her.

What is the truth?

It did not matter.

There was only one truth left. Aébhal needed to die.

He gripped the shaft of his harpoon tightly.

Gréim Tapaidh they named it.

It suddenly felt like a piece of wood with an elaborate decoration topping it off.

He went to stand before his brother, but fear rooted his legs to the ground below him. His own sudden inaction galled him.

I have hidden in the shadow long enough. I am Leafdancer.

Swallowing down his bile and his fear, he willed himself forward. One step. Then a second. In the back of his mind, he heard the tune that Eimear would hum to herself. A sad song with no words.

No words are needed. Only deeds.

Crea

Eimear groaned loudly and Aébhal was reminded. He marched to her, and Crea felt Arthmael move instinctively towards her. *To protect her?*

He grabbed her by the throat, lifted her and threw her towards the longshore; the crease looming wide before them. "Come close and watch her fall, my Fae brethren," he said as he marched towards her. "Come to me and watch the first act of vengeance."

Crea's breath caught. Cromm went to stand before Aébhal, his harpoon at the ready.

"My brother," he said quietly. "I cannot let you destroy her. I have worked too hard, for too long. You must put her down."

"You do not understand, Cromm. I have changed too. I have done a thing to make the realm powerful beyond our derisible past. I have long known of your plans to betray me, brother." The last word hissed through his snarling lips.

"You speak of betrayal? Everything you are is what I helped you to become. Without me, you would have sat, waiting for change that would never have come. You would never have beaten the Fand. Even with the draoí I gave up to you. You are a coward now, as you always have been."

Aébhal's gaze darted around as if judging who could hear them.

"It does not matter now," he hissed. "It does not matter what you planned or what you think, Cromm. It matters only, what you can do about it."

Aébhal's backhanded swipe met nothing. Cromm had moved back out of range in an instant.

"You have outlived your usefulness, Aébhal. You were a weapon in my scabbard, but now you are in my way. You are dead to me."

"To us," Arthmael shouted, causing Crea to hold him back.

The Fathach's black gaze alighted upon on them and she despaired.

"I am surrounded by enemies, it would seem," growled Aébhal, crouching down, talons curled.

Crea released Arthmael and took up her bow, while he raised his spear in defiance.

Beside them, Dalla brandished her long-whip and dirk.

"Go back to your own side, Aébhal," Crea found herself saying. "Go back with your horde before the madness becomes chaos."

"I want chaos," said Aébhal. "I am chaos. Faneside warriors," he roared, "Do your duty," and he leapt forward.

Eimear

Eimear flew away from the mountains and valleys of her mind; past the point that she could make out anything except strange looking land masses, blackening behind her.

The pain was not as severe. As if she was flying far away to forget. Going back, meant going back to the pain, and that, she would not do.

She blinked as she searched for the sunset, yet there was no light ahead. She flew on.

"…you can travel anywhere in an instant…," echoed Hógar's voice.

Eimear stopped. To the end, she willed. Nothing happened. She closed her eyes to consider. She did not know her mind well enough.

"Within you are all of the answers you will ever need," came the echo.

I do need an answer. I do not know the question.

She opened her eyes to survey her surroundings, and something caught her eye in the distance. A tiny speck of light, flickering faintly.

A star. A star in the dark reaches of her mind.

Eimear had not seen a star since she had arrived in the Fae realm.

She looked again and there were others. All around her. The longer she looked, the more she saw.

A thought came to her.

Arthmael

The longshore erupted into violence. While many of the Fae were too shocked to fight, many obeyed Aébhal and the assault on those who had not joined his ranks began.

Thousands of Fae died without raising a weapon to defend themselves. Others stood bravely before the wave of Aébhal's warriors. Arthmael wondered about Serissa and his people. They would not have joined Aébhal and were surely fighting in the battle.

A trickle of sweat dripped into his eyes. He longed to be there with them; to defend them as he had always done.

A snarl from Aébhal signalled his frustrated attempts to lay a hand on Cromm. Cromm darted away from each attack, but was unable to counter, such was the speed of his brother.

Crea's first arrow flew and lanced into Aébhal's shoulder. Dalla's long whip wrapped around his wrist and she attempted to fly around behind him to cause him to spin.

Aébhal dragged his arm down, bringing her almost back down to the ground.

Warriors from his horde arrived among them. Arthmael sprang forward to protect Crea, flicking his spear out before him, cutting deep into the increasing mass of bodies. Dalla realised the danger and flicked her whip to release if from Aébhal's wrist. She flew over the Fae warriors, snaring, dragging and cutting. Crea's arrows whooshed past him as warriors began to pile around the three of them.

"Crea," screamed Arthmael. "Flee, Crea. You must retreat. I'll keep them at bay. Go."

He looked to see if she was going and realised that they had been surrounded. If she tried to fly now, she would surely be speared. Gritting his teeth, he turned to attack.

Eimear

"Come to me. All of you."

Where? asked Ériu.

"I will show you." Eimear reached inside herself and drew the collective draoí presence to her. They surrounded her. She could feel their rage, yet they were awed by the place she had brought them.

"I will show you," she said.

What is this place?

"It is where you wished to travel. It is eternity."

We wished to ascend to a higher plane. To follow those gone before us. You took that from us.

"You cannot follow. This, however, is a higher plane beyond any others. It is everything you wished for. You will need to leave me; to fly out amongst the stars and to create your own future."

How can this be?

"Because there are no limits here. Neither for you, nor me. You can surely sense that, even from here. You are with me in my thoughts. Yet here, you can help me explore. Here, you can be anything or anywhere you desire."

You have wronged us so. Now you want us to scatter into your darkest recesses. Into you?

Eimear did not respond. There was silence. Eimear could feel nothing from the host of draoí spirits gathered around her.

We hate you. We curse you, Síor Feargach.

"Do so if you wish, but your hatred is wasted. And I have been cursed since the day I was born. Just remember; you can be all you wanted to be. You can have all you wished for. I can create it for you."

What of our revenge?

"Revenge, it seems, might be your undoing. It is also there for you if you wish. I will not go back to the pain you inflicted upon me."

What would you have us do?

"Go in there. Deeper into my mind. I will ensure you have what you want as long as I am alive. If you do not, you can finish what you started here. Examine your work."

The smouldering, blackened landscape in the distance darkened as she watched. She was watching herself dying from inside.

"Go in there and find what you seek. Whatever that might be. All that I ask is that you help me to keep my body strong. Leave me the draíocht you bestowed upon me. Just make your decision. A beginning or the end?"

They whispered to each other. Harsh, fevered whispering. Eimear waited.

So be it, came Ériu's voice. *Let us see.*

One by one the draoí flew away towards the distant stars, some together, others alone.

Eimear turned back to where she had come from. The landscape was no longer black, though it was too far away to recognise those parts of her that she had come to know. The terrible pain had faded to what she felt in her flesh and bones, and perhaps her heart.

"I am used to that pain."

What now? Sword asked.

"I don't know. Back, if it is not too late."

Will you come with me first?

"Where?"

Somewhere I went to when the pain was at its worst.

"But I am you, you are me."

Yes. Follow me.

Cromm

Cromm remained patient, watching for an opening that did not offer itself. His harpoon remained poised,

324

feeling light in his grip. Aébhal showed signs of being wounded, yet Cromm knew well enough that only a killing blow was worth the risk of exposing himself to the terrible danger before him.

Circling, dodging, weaving, and leaping had kept him clear of the danger until now, yet he knew his time was running out.

As a wave of Faneside warriors surrounded them, Arthmael, Dalla, and Crea were caught up in the fighting. His brother's terrible gaze rested on him.

"The draoí inside me told me what you have been doing. Did you not think I would discover your aims?"

"Then you know that what I do, I do for the Fae."

"You are not strong enough to rule as I can. You have never been strong enough, Cromm."

Aébhal moved to attack with terrifying speed, talons and teeth flashing within a hairsbreadth of Cromm.

He managed to evade the attack once again, still biding his time for a clear strike. He feigned an attack to read his brothers response. Aébhal moved, twitched, and stood there, a smile appearing on his lips that did not reach his eyes.

"Still, you cower. You tremble before me. You wait for a gap, but that is only because you are too afraid to fight. There is nowhere to hide. I will not tire. I will not fade. Come, brother. Let us see what you are truly made of."

He leapt forward, raking claws swooping towards Cromm.

And there. There it was. As his arms raised, Cromm finally saw the exposed side that his weapon could pierce. He lashed out with all his speed, all his might. The blow should have landed, but this time it was

Aébhal who sidestepped, and the harpoon only managed to land a slicing cut across his brother's ribs.

Cromm's eyes bulged as Aébhal grabbed the back of his neck with one hand and the harpoon with the other.

Greim Tapaidh, thought Cromm for a moment, as he watched the weapon break in two.

Aébhal turned the prongs towards him and rammed them into Cromm's body. A whoosh of air left him, leaving him unable to scream his frustration, his pain. Aébhal drew him close, as Cromm tasted blood that burst from his mouth.

"Thank you, brother," growled Aébhal, "for helping me win."

Cromm felt no pain, as his own harpoon twisted inside of him, dragging his insides into the gentle light of the midsun.

Ferragh

Ferragh moved through the blurred landscape, teeth bared.

Treacherous Aébhal. Wretched, vile Aébhal. I will show them all what it means to be the Fane. They will know it. I will avenge Doireann, and they will love me for it. It is what I was always bound to do. It is my destiny.

Ferragh slowed as he got nearer to Aébhal and the girl. The girl was near death; her face a mess of blood and bruises; her body limp. He could not help but smile.

Little bitch.

Lying in the long grasses approaching the crease, her damaged form would hardly be visible to the writhing warbands. No one would witness his deed.

He turned towards the hulking back of his son Aébhal. *He is the one who is trying to usurp me. He thinks me bloated; spent; feebleminded.*

Ferragh watched Aébhal kill Cromm. A feral snarl escaped his lips. His jagged breathing caught. Cromm.

"Cromm," he cried to no one. It did not matter now. There were none who could hear him, for his sound was at one with the battle. None who could see him, for his stealth was legendary. He was the Fane. The true Fane: Ferragh duillechán.

His course was fixed. His mind made up. Two of his children must die instead of one. He thought of beautiful Doireann and her intoxicating smile. Aébhal had caused her to die.

Ferragh raised his dagger and made ready to strike. Aébhal was enormous, but if he were to be punctured by many holes, he would leak like a bucket. The cloaked snake was known to kill many an unwary hoodoon. Size. His son would now learn, was not as important as the potency of a strike. Aébhal was unaware of Ferragh; of Ferragh's blade arm, coiled like a snake.

A roar escaped the fathach as he held Cromm up for all to witness. Many turned to look. Ferragh knew it was time, as sure as a hidden snake would, coiled and cunning. He leapt tall and the draíocht took him to Aébhal's bare and unprotected back. He grabbed Aébhal's long black mane and gripped his son's back tight with his legs.

He heard himself laughing as he plunged the blade into the red skin; once, twice, thrice, and more.

"Now, leaking bucket. No Fane. A leaky bucket."

Cromm's body fell as Aébhal's clawing hands reached around to pull Ferragh from him. Ferragh made himself small and stabbed one of the wrists.

"No Fane! None here!"

He dug the blade downward into his son's shoulder, over and over, and Aébhal screamed in pain.

The fathach twisted quickly and managed to grab Ferragh's leg. Ferragh was wrenched from his mount and dragged to hang before Aébhal. A mistake from the would-be usurper. Not so cunning as his father. Ferragh lashed out with his blade again, cutting into Aébhal's arms, causing his son to drop him.

Ferragh cackled with glee as he made to escape. He disappeared into the duillechán haze and ran a few feet from Aébhal to survey the damage.

Aébhal seemed to be looking straight at him, mouth agape, bleeding from many wounds. He was never so red before, as he was now.

Slack-jawed child now learns.

"No Fane, I say. Traitor!" Ferragh cackled. "Leaking bucket. Punctured wineskin! Dying, dying, red blood flying!"

Aébhal took two giant steps and brought a cloven hoof down on Ferragh. Ferragh felt disgusted that his stealth had let him down. He tried to laugh once more, but his breath was gone.

His eyes closed.

He tried to speak to his son. A strange twitch made him jump. Something was wet.

He drifted off.

Eimear

They moved in the space between the land and the sky for moments or days, or years. Sword led her to a place she did not know, though it seemed, at times, familiar. They passed hazy fields and meadows, by a jagged woodland that loomed dark as Eimear drew near and then to another place—a small, bright and comfortable place.

A hut. Sitting in a place that was not unlike Crúach. Large flowering plants surrounded the place, swaying, making it vivid to behold. The life from this place was nourishing. She wished to enter, but she knew she could not.

Listen.

Eimear couldn't make it out initially. The sound was very faint, as if she was listening under water. It was masked by the sound of a beating heart. It came from inside though. She focused on it. Someone was singing a song.

Then, she knew.

The sad song.

She gulped back a sob and strained to hear the words of the song, being sung to her by her father, Bégha.

Though off I go, fo fo

I will return

For just to be with you

Is what I yearn

I must away, ay, ay

To work the day,

But as the evening comes

I will be home to say

That I love you, ooh, ooh

So, rest my dear

Perhaps you'll join me

*when you've grown another
year*

Eimear felt a wash of emotions to which she was unfamiliar. Warm, tingly feelings that filled her up and made her happier than she thought possible. Powerful yet comforting. Everywhere yet nowhere.

"I want to stay here. I want to go inside the hut."

You can.

"How?"

Leave me here.

"Will it change me?"

Do you want to change?

"Yes."

Go and change then.

"What does it mean if you stay here?"

Perhaps you can bring the love you feel now with you. And leave some of the anger here with me.

Love. "Love? Is that what I feel here?"

Yes. You have the capacity for love, like anyone around you. It is just unfamiliar. You need to find someone, or something, to feel out there as you feel it in here.

"There is no one left for me to love. No one left who loves me. No love."

Find it then. Hunt it as you hunted your music in the past. Find the one to help you.

Eimear nodded.

Crea

She could not believe what was happening. As they turned to face Aébhal once more, anger welled in her, Arthmael came to stand at her side, his breathing heavy.

Crea released an arrow at Aébhal who was bleeding heavily. Her arrow thumped into his barrel chest but did little to slow his progress. Arthmael leapt high as his spear snaked out before him. Aébhal's red arm swung out and knocked him from the air, spear spinning harmlessly away.

A cry escaped Crea's lips and another arrow was loosed to lodge in the same arm that had struck her love.

Aébhal loomed over her when Dalla's whip suddenly snared his neck, dragging him backwards.

There were other bodies all around them. The battle was spreading across the land like a plague of insects.

Crea could not get a clear shot at Aébhal. Dalla was using the whip to drag the Fathach off balance and dart in to strike with her dirk. He grabbed for her, near mindless in his urgency, barely missing her each time.

She went to kneel beside Arthmael.

"Are you hurt?"

"Barely," he grunted.

"What do we do, Arthmael?"

"Can we run away?"

Crea drew in a deep breath. Pain shot across her body. The fighting was everywhere. It was spreading across the land like a plague.

"I do not think we can."

Arthmael gritted his teeth and slowly rose.

"Then we must win."

"I do not know who is fighting who," said Crea. "It has all fallen asunder."

"We can rebuild. We must rebuild. There is one thing that must happen first." He looked at a fallen spear and bent to pick it up. Crea saw his movements were slow and guarded.

Arthmael nodded towards Aébhal. "Come, Crea. Let us help Dalla to kill the new Fane."

Eimear

Eimear tried to open her eyes. One, though the vision was blurred was just about working. She raised a hand to touch the swelling keeping the other one shut. As she tried to move, she felt her body was broken. She could not feel her legs. Her breathing was shallow, agony.

She willed the draíocht to lift her. She knew the power that resided within her. Her own, and the collective power of the draoí. They were one.

The pain of her bones knitting back together made her back arch. The jagged cuts in her flesh mending together made her scream silently. Her missing teeth growing anew made her fingers curl. The pain, though excruciating, was mild in comparison to that which she had just escaped.

By the time Eimear stood, she was strong. More than strong. She was all the gods in one body.

She stood at the crease, surrounded by battle; by screams; but her heart did not rejoice as once it would have. Not now. Searching around her, she spotted her old sword in the long grass nearby. Eimear walked to it. She dodged a thrusting blade, a passing arrow, a falling body. Moving through the battle as if it was not there, smiling fondly as she thought of a duillechán haze. She went to the sword and picked it up. It was bloody.

What do I do now?

The sword did not answer. It was not the same.

A familiar roar from the longshore made her head turn. A triumphant roar.

Aébhal stood with his arms wrapped around Crea; a crushing vice; her wings crumpled and twisted. He hefted her towards the crease and threw her into the abyss.

Eimear screamed as she saw Crea; her friend, attempt to fly. Her broken wings kept her aloft for a moment, before starting to come apart. The smallsky denizen started to fall into the crease.

Eimear leapt to the edge of the longshore, but Crea fell faster. Eimear looked for a way to reach her, but there was none. She tried to reach out with her draíocht, but the crease had her.

"Crea," she whispered.

From the edge of the longshore to her left, a shape launched itself towards Crea. Arthmael. He had cast himself into the crease. To save her? Crea's mangled wings flapped furiously, until the two bodies came together.

To be with her.

They wrapped their arms around each other and plunged downwards. Eimear reached out a hand and watched. She could feel their love from where she stood. It made the draíocht around her fade for a moment.

She watched them pass out of sight, to fall, in love, forever.

Síor Feargach

*Is mairg a bhaineann sólás as
dólás duine eile.*

Woe to he who gets pleasure
from another's trouble.

Eimear stood, and her head swam.

How can I find love? All there is for me is rage.

"Is this what you wanted?" she whispered to Aébhal.

The battle seemed to slow, then it stopped. All present turned to her. They had all heard.

"You all wish for battle?" she asked them all. "You must not realise the cost."

The old sword swung, and a score of warriors died. Eimear looked at Aébhal. "You wish to rule? To take power with violence? You must not have known the path ahead."

Another swing and bodies flew. The screams should have made Eimear exultant. Not this time. Her draíocht pulsed through and around her. The long grasses bent away from her. The midsun burned brighter than ever before.

Eimear saw that Aébhal was wounded from many cuts, and she smiled.

"You can have this place, Aébhal. However, not until I show you what you wished to see. I would have you know what will happen should you grow bold in the future."

She stuck her blade into the ground between her and the longshore. A crevice opened and the chunk of land, toppled and fell into the crease. Hundreds of Fae warriors fell with it. Thousands. Their screams should have drowned out Eimear's voice, but when Eimear continued, all the warriors gathered on the longshore watched her and heard her words, their eyes open wide.

She caught the eye of a nearby sídhe warrior, who soiled himself noisily.

"You have led yourself to this," she said to him. To all of them. "All of those who I have cared for, are gone from here. Leaving you with a version of me that you should have tried harder to avoid."

She leapt high into the air and came crashing down onto where the battle had raged the fiercest. A swathe of earth exploded upwards around her, sending bodies and debris flying higher than she had leapt. As it alighted, a thousand more died. The fields became a darkened red of blood and shit and piss.

Eimear looked at Aébhal. His eyes were wide open. She walked towards him, rending bodies and earth.

Warriors scrambled to get away from her, but most could not. Mounds of bodies appeared in her wake.

The music was deafening, but she no longer listened.

"Though I will not kill you," she said to Aébhal. "I wonder if I should not cripple you. The Fane could become a living breathing reminder of my work."

"What is it you wish? To end this. What do you want?" His voice sounded hollow.

"I want to ensure an end that satisfies me, Aébhal."

"I am wounded. I will be no sport for you," Aébhal said.

"Wounded or not, you would not be sport for me. You took to shattering my body when I offered you no resistance. And yet here I walk towards you and the only way you might injure me now is if I slip in the piss that streams from you, along with your fear."

"Tell me what you want? My screams?"

"Your screams, when they rip from you, will make no difference to me."

"Please," Aébhal howled. "Please, Síor Feargach. Leave us in peace. I repent."

"Your repentance is hollow." Eimear walked on, her sword a scythe. Many of those warriors before her took to begging for their lives.

"There will be a Fand. You will be the Fane. You will go back to the old ways. Or I will be the new."

"Yes, a Fand," Aébhal gasped. "Whatever you wish. Please. No more."

"I'm afraid there must be more. I cannot leave here until I make sure this realm is bridled. I'm afraid I must show you a terrible thing. A thing that you will never forget. Never."

The warriors of both sides fled all vying to get as far away from her as they could. Even Aébhal was knocked over in the stampede.

"You cannot run from me," said Eimear. She raised her sword high and focused her rage for the blow that would change their world. Ruin their world as it had ruined her; leaving him with little to rule over, except burning the dead. Droplets of blood fell from the blade, landing on her head.

"Eimear," came a familiar voice behind her. "Eimear, my love."

Eimear turned, hardly believing her eyes. "Mirdhí?"

The old duillechán smiled.

"Hello, young lady. You have grown into a beauty, no doubt about it."

"Why are you here? You are in danger."

"Not if you come with me."

"But... you do not understand. I must... I must... show them the way."

"Eimear, you've shown what you need to show. Come with me. Come home."

Eimear's mind reeled. Home. *What does that mean?*

"Mirdhí, what are you doing here?"

"The Fand is dead, Eimear. She had bid us not to interfere, but she is gone now. Cromm came to us. The damnedest thing. We all nearly shat ourselves when he appeared. He said you would need us if he could not convince you to join him. Commanded us to care for you if you lived through it all."

She could feel Mirdhí's fear, though she concealed it well. Eimear felt a terrible shame. "Have you seen? Were you watching... what I did?" Her hands covered her wet face and she fell to her knees sobbing.

338

"Eimear, you have not had a chance. Never. But enough is enough here. Come home. Let's start afresh."

Mirdhí's hand extended towards her. "I can sneak us both back to the portal. Though, I daresay, none will stand in our way. Forget this place. You've had enough screams to last you for a day or two anyway."

Eimear looked at the small, gnarled hand inviting her back through the portal, and a great longing filled her. *Home.*

"But I must do this one last thing. I have said it and must show them."

"Eimear," whispered Mirdhí. "Look around you." Her eyes were brimming with tears.

Eimear looked and saw. The long grasses were red. Corpses and limbs were strewn as far as the eye could see. Cries and wails of the injured became a chorus, that should have filled Eimear with joy.

Why? Why do I want the screams? What is wrong with me?

She thought of Caen's words, and they stung at her. What had she become? What would she grow into?

"Eimear," urged her old friend. "My darling, you've done enough. The draíocht here changed your mind, as we feared it might. But I'll tell you this now. Love and care will set you right. Love and care. You won't want any of this anymore, when we fix up your hair and have you milk goats and make cheese. When you sit with us and tell us your adventures. Come home."

Standing, Eimear put her bloody sword into the battered scabbard and took Mirdhí's hand.

"I am a monster, Mirdhí. How will I face the others after what I have done? I don't know how to do anything except destroy."

"I will tell you this once. We have loved you since the day you were born. We will love you until the day you die. Come. You will be safe with us. You can stay forever."

She eyed the old sword. "Why don't you leave that here. You won't need it anymore."

Eimear closed her eyes for a moment. "Sword is gone already."

Mirdhí shrugged a little, turned and the two disappeared into a duillechán haze.

DUILLECHÁN

*Is í an chiall cheannaigh an
chiall is fearr.*

Sense bought dearly is the best
kind.

THE OTHERS WERE out to meet them when they arrived. Mirdhí knew they would struggle with the near overwhelming draíocht radiating from the child, but to their credit, they masked it well.

They fussed over her and had her kneel, so they could each hold her close—even Tildhe. Hot tears streamed from her, and she could not find words for a long time. They all spoke too much to make up for her silence. They sat with her and gave her too much food and too much drink. All of them tried, in their way, to give her the one thing she could not have too much of— love. The common thinking must have been, to try and make up for her life of hardship in as few short days as they could manage.

Mirdhí watched the hard edge soften on the girl over weeks. When she slept, Mirdhí took the sword and buried it in the forest, hoping that it would be forgotten. Despite their best efforts, Eimear spoke little and slept for increasingly long spells.

When it was time, they brought her out into the world and showed her the beauty that she might have forgotten. Little displays of wonder, to guide her to good places. The pristine spider webs in forest glades. The hypnotic dances of the starlings above. The local badgers snuffling through the rich soil with their cubs.

Eimear was always appreciative. She appeared to enjoy each experience as it happened but would quickly descend into increasing bouts of melancholy. The duillecháns would speak long into the night about different ways to drag her free from her disconsolate prison, yet they could not find the way.

It was the arrival of Bláthnaid, the druidess with which they sometimes traded, that things changed. She held a baby in her arms.

"The child is born of two worlds. His mother was a gruagach. She hid the boys true form from those around her. His father, Cumhall, has been murdered." Bláthnaid's gaze rested on Eimear. "His name is Deibhin. They will hunt him if they discover his real identity. I need someone who will foster him and help him as he grows. I have long since sensed the draíocht here. Now I see you, I know you are the one who can help me... who can help the child. Perhaps you can bring him to the Fae realm for his safety, and to learn about his heritage?"

Eimear stepped forward; hands curled into fists at her side.

"No. He must not be brought to the Fae realm. They will ruin him as they did me."

"What do you suggest we do with him so, Eimear?" Mirdhí said, eyes sparkling.

"We should… Perhaps I can…"

The child's hand extended towards her and Mirdhí heard Eimear's breath catch in her throat. His blue eyes peeped out at her from under a mop of white hair.

"Take him, Eimear," said Mirdhí. "He wants to go to you.

Eimear stood, eyebrows raised, mouth agape.

"Me? Take him?" Eimear gasped.

Bláithnaid offered the child to her, a gentle smile creeping across her face.

Eimear looked from Bláithnaid to the child. Carefully, she wrapped her arms around the bundle and accepted him. The wave of feeling she had experienced with the denizen child washed through her once again. Stronger this time; keener.

"You will not be alone, Eimear. We can help you."

Eimear had closed her eyes.

EIMEAR

Is buaine port ná glór na n-éan,
is buaine focal ná toice an tsaoil.

A tune is more lasting than the
song of the birds, and a word more
lasting than the wealth of the world.

IT IS HE. He is the one who can save you. Ériu's voice
whispered from deep inside her. *It had only become
clear to me now. All of this was forewritten by destiny
it seems. We have found our way. He can show you
yours.*

Who is he? How can he do this? He is but a child,
Eimear asked.

*He is the one who can save you. I do not know more.
There is no prophecy. There is only what I can sense.*

Can you guide me? she asked the draoí.

344

No. For us to rest, we must go to parts of your mind where you cannot know us. Where you cannot hear us. Our strength is your strength, but we do not wish to share your thoughts like this. Farewell, Eimear. You have brought about our end and a new beginning. Farewell.

Though she had only known them a short time, Eimear felt strange as they left her thoughts. They drifted from her awareness, fading into nothing. She sighed a deep sigh. As often before she wondered how her life had come to be this way. Yet, she also felt a sense of freedom. Perhaps for the first time.

I can choose my own way. I can do what I please.

The child shifting in her arms caused her to hold on a little tighter.

Or can I? Perhaps my life was never mine to control. Perhaps it never will be.

Eimear looked into the child's eyes. The child needed her. She felt more alive looking at him than she had since she had arrived back from the Fae realm; perhaps since she had ever felt.

Could she protect this tiny creature? After the terrible slaughter she had wrought in the Fae realm and the old world alike. She had ended a civilisation and surely crippled another. She was a monster of rage and of hate. The child in her arms was pure. What could she offer? Love? Care?

Lessons?

Have I not learned enough lessons for both of us?

Have I learned wisdom?

None here truly know of the depth of my evil acts. Can I now pretend to be good?

She thought of the place that she had heard the song and left Sword's voice. The warm memory that was as bathed in love as the child was bathed in draíocht. What would she have become had her parents lived and passed that love onto her?

"Fionn," Eimear found herself saying aloud. "We will call him Fionn, after his beautiful hair." A tear trickled down her cheek. Eimear kissed his, and sang to him, keeping her voice low.

Though off I go, fo fo

I will return

For just to be with you

Is what I yearn

I must away, ay, ay

To work the day,

But as the evening comes

I will be home to say

That I love you, ooh, ooh

So, rest my dear

Perhaps you'll join me

when you've grown another year

Eimear felt her heart swell. She felt things that she found hard to process. The strongest; an urge to safeguard this child from the horrors she had endured; the horrors she had wrought. To bathe the child in love and affection so that he would not turn out like her. A new love for this person, whose draíocht was so evident to her. Her heart thumped in her chest and a wave of purpose passed through her.

He is the way.

An anger swept through her, at the thought of the cruel world that the child would face.

"I will protect you from any who would harm you, Fionn Mac Cumhall. In this world or any other. You will a part of no one's scheme but your own. You will be free. I swear this now."

We swear it, came a voice from the forest.

JOHN DÉ BURCA

John lives on the mysterious and rugged shores of the West of Ireland in Galway. From a young age, John was immersed in the rich traditions of Irish oral language storytelling, amassing a vast collection of mythology and folklore. He joined a storytelling group when he could find one and started to hone his skills.

HIS WORKS

John's debut novel, *The Last Five Swords*, is an epic fantasy adventure set in a dark and beautiful ancient Ireland.

Blurb

When Eoghan and Rúadhan find a girl up a tree, it heralds an epic journey.

Rhíona is a Fae princess on a quest to find a hero. She is hunted by her father and his agents, ambassadors and assassins, all set on thwarting her plan.

They soon fall in with Donnacha, an archer with a secret.

Together, the four enlist the help of the last of the fénnid. A world-weary group, far removed from the legends described in fireside stories.

In the dying days of magic in Ireland, the motley band sets out to find the greatest champion ever known: a man long thought dead. There is no other choice because only Fionn Mac Cumhal can save Ireland one last time.

Praise

"Wonderful Irish fantasy storytelling by debut author, John de Burca"

Conor Kostick, international bestselling author of Epic.

Amazon Links

For the UK: www.amazon.co.uk/dp/B0BKTL5NBS
For the US: www.amazon.com/dp/B0BKTL5NBS

PERCHEDCROWPRESS

Dear reader, thank you for choosing to read *The Music of Swords*. We hope you enjoyed the ride. We are a small Indie publisher who pride ourselves in giving a voice to the underrepresented writers of Ireland.

PerchedCrowPress is an imprint of Philip Hughes Publishing

To find more information about us, you can visit our website at:

www.philhughespublishing.com

Contact us at: info@philhughespublishing.com

OUR HISTORICAL BOOKS

Milesian Son of Light

I am dying tied to a rock! Connacht's finest are watching, waiting for my end. Too afraid of me to kill me, and too afraid of her to leave!

The hero is tied to a rock. He is dying, but slowly. The warriors of Connacht are sitting around their campfires, swords across their knees, watching, waiting. All can hear the flapping of The Raven of Death's wings. It is only a question of time. The hero will not stand against his rock and wait in silence. He knows it is his fearsome reputation holding back the warriors. He tells his tale. The true tale and they must listen, because to leave would be to invite the wrath of their warrior queen. And so it is that they hear the true story of the Milesian Son of Light!

Available: https://www.amazon.co.uk/dp/B07QH1JY48

I enjoy Irish myths and legends and what I liked about this was it was the familiar story of Cú Chulainn but told in a completely original way. All the politics and the action is very realistic, not at all magical. It's the grim and dirty version, as if Cú Chulainn was an historical person. Thoroughly enjoyable.

Conor Kostick, bestselling author of Epic.

Milesian Daughter of War

Warrior Queen or Witch? Enemy of Ériu or Saviour?

The Five Kingdoms are about to discover!

Medb has been unsuccessful in her attempts to punish King Conor for raping her beside the banks of the River Bóand. Burdened by a weak husband and a weaker army, she pressures the kings of Leinster and Munster to bring war to Ulster; her professed target, Don Cuailnge, The Brown Bull of Cooley; her actual target, the head of Conor Mac Nessa, king of the Ulster.

In sight of her goal, Medb encounters the greatest hero Ireland has ever known. The hero's successes in holding her armies at bay, force the queen to ever more desperate measures until the boundaries between the Good she professes to represent and the Evil she is attempting to thwart are blurred to the point of nonexistence.

Available: https://www.amazon.co.uk/dp/B08GM7YGP8

After Gairech

Imagine a world where the Romans are in ascendancy; a world where Christ is soon to be born. A world where the Battle of Gáirech has ripped the heart out of Ireland.

Medb's armies have been destroyed! Survivors are ravaging the Five Kingdoms in search of the riches they were promised!

While working to repair the damage, Cathbadh is murdered and dies beside his son. Genonn vows to avenge his father. But, with the culprits locked away in their fastnesses, to break them out, he needs Elder Council approval, and they will not provide it without proof.

Genonn needs Conall to help get the proof, but Conall is gone, searching for the head of Cú Chulainn. So Genonn sets out to find him, aided by the beautiful Fedelm, the capricious Lee Flaith, and the stalwart Bradán.

Bernard Cornwell meets Ellis Peters in this historical murder mystery.

"I thought this novel was amazing!" – I Got Lost in a Book – Internet Book Blogger

Available: https://www.amazon.co.uk/dp/B093TF86Z4

A Prelude to War

Five Kingdoms. One Invader. One Hero.

Conaire is made high king because the Elder Council want a peaceful kingdom. They fear invasion by the horde from the south, the Romans. Inadvertently, their manipulations weaken the Five Kingdoms and war does come to Ireland, but from an unexpected place.

After a bloodletting at the hands of a British pirate, The Kingdoms are eventually saved by the Red Branch warriors of Ulster, but not before The Peaceful King is killed by the invaders.

When Conaire is killed, the Kingdoms are in turmoil. The council still want a strong king. **Conor Mac Nessa**, king of The Ulaid, tries everything in his repertoire of evil skills to gain the high kingship but he is opposed by **Queen Medb**, the Warrior Queen of Connacht.

Their rivalry gives birth to Ireland's greatest hero, **The Hound of Ulster**.

Available at: https://www.amazon.co.uk/dp/B08428DHLS

HISTORICAL SHORT STORIES

Genonn Rising

Taught by the druid, Cathbadh, Genonn goes to Ráth Droma as adviser to the chieftain. Young and idealistic, his moral compass is put to the test when the chieftain falls for the daughter of one of his land workers.

The girl is betrothed to a young woodsman. They are in love. The chieftain, Mathaman, wants her for himself but she refuses.

To get his way, Mathaman accuses the woodsman of stealing a sheep. He will be strangled with the knotted hide if Genonn cannot prevent a miscarriage of justice.

Available: https://www.amazon.co.uk/dp/B08BDML5WK

Genonn in Shadow

Genonn has seen the injustice of his father's world, the world of the Elder Council. He has decided he does not want to belong in it. Overhearing some warriors talking of their exploits in a hostel just north of Átha Clíath, he heads for the Smithy of Cullen to have a sword made and go to The Shadowy Isle to learn how to use it. Despite ten years training to become a druid, Genonn's naiveté is no preparation for the brutality of his chosen path.

Available: https://www.amazon.co.uk/dp/B08GZGP814

OUR CRIME NOIRE

Archie's Problem

Bald Archie Moses has been the butt of peer jokes all his short life. Abandoned by his mother when only a few days old, maltreated in the orphanage where he grew up and discharged by the army he loved as family, Archie takes pride in a role as a bodyguard to celebrities. While defending his client, Archie is arrested and then sent by his lawyer in search of a wayward son. What should have been a simple job turned into an Odyssey. An Odyssey during which Archie falls in with his antithesis, and together they pit their combined wits and muscle to the detriment of a vicious Camorra clan.

Archie's Problem is a fantastic book. It's well written, well thought out, and if you like twists and mysteries, this is the book for you. [...] The characters are well rounded, the settings come to life in Hughes['s] capable hands, and I certainly wasn't expecting the ending. I believe this is part of a series of books and though this one stands alone in its own right, I wouldn't mind reading the other two as well.

Gloria (Amazon Customer)

Available: https://www.amazon.co.uk/dp/B06WRV5BH3

Gigi's Cause

Released from prison after sixteen years, Gigi felt that he had something worth fighting for. It was not something that would have the masses scrambling to donate money they did not have to celebrities they did not like, but it was his, and he was proud to have it. Better a worthless something than nothing at all, that was Gigi's mantra. He was not to know that it would lead to love and ultimately to death, but it was Gigi's Cause!

Excellent read. Love the slightly dark comedy which [brings] the characters to life. Great descriptions of life in southern Italy. I have enjoyed all of the writer's novels to date. Looking forward to the next one!!

Amazon Customer

Available: https://www.amazon.co.uk/dp/B07451NJKX

Izzo's Solution

Pietro Izzo has been returned to his position as Senior Investigator for the Pozzuoli region of Italy's Antimafia squad, the DIA. High Command has finally realised that Sub-Lieutenant Cipolle was out of his depth and have busted him back to the role of Investigating Sergeant under Izzo.

Shortly after the inspector's reinstatement an American sailor is executed in the middle of the day outside the village bar in Lucrino, and Cipolle is killed by a sniper later that same day. Izzo must work with a Senior Field Agent of the NCIS to discover the killer. This becomes a major problem for the Italian, because not only is the investigator a foreigner, she is also a feminist.

A chauvinist and a feminist are a bad combination, but to be successful, they must learn to work together.

Eventually that comes to pass and together they achieve Izzo's Solution!

I loved this book. It took me into the heart of Neapolitan life, as well as through a story of burgeoning romance. It has all the elements of a great read: love, intrigue, crime and blood. I highly recommend!

Amazon Customer

Available: https://www.amazon.co.uk/dp/B07B2YRPQH

The Hidden Syndicate

The Hidden Syndicate is the omnibus edition, which combines the trilogy Problem, Cause and Solution. As well as combining the three, it includes changes to the original stories to make them more enjoyable.

Available: https://www.amazon.co.uk/dp/B0862GX8W6

The Reticent Detective

'We are all outside the law, just some of us are further out than others.'

The words uttered by Laconto's stepfather, echo through the detective's mind as he tries to come to terms with his reality as a police inspector with a past, he does not want to discuss. He'd graduated the academy with ideals buoyed by innocence, only to have them crushed by policing a quasi-dystopian state, ruled by Mafiosi. 'Just some are further out than others,' bouncing about his cranium, a bat trapped in his one-room apartment.

Following his dream of crushing organized crime, Laconto encounters a transvestite mugger and his lover being hunted by two bent cops, all being manipulated by an unscrupulous Secret Service Agent.

His success or failure in the balance, he resorts to some questionable methods to achieve his goal.

Available: https://www.amazon.co.uk/dp/B07YGPGCBG

The Alcoholic Mercenary

They said, "See Naples and then die!"

Rachel had thought it was to do with the place's natural beauty. A misconception she soon lost after climbing down from the C130 troop carrier. Her predecessor's suspicious death, the murder of a sailor, and an enforced liaison with a chauvinistic and probably corrupt cop saw to that.

"See Naples and then die!"

Some said the saying was anonymous. Some attributed it to Goethe. Still, others said it was Lord Byron or maybe Keats. When the young brother of a mercenary hitman became her main suspect, Rachel leant toward Keats. Didn't the poet die here? Somewhere near, for sure. He probably coined the phrase on his deathbed.

And then, the cherry on the top of her ice cream soda, she could smell grappa on the breath of the mercenary when she interviewed him—the only thing worse than a violent man: a violent man who drinks.

The only thing worse than a violent man who drinks is a violent man who drinks and considers himself Rachel's enemy.

Printed in Great Britain
by Amazon

27251199R00205